ONE WAY IN, NO WAY OUT

A Mann Walker Adventure

Written by

Malcolm Boyd

Published by

Three-Legged Elephant Publishing

ISBN 978-0-9986164-0-7

DEDICATION

I would like to thank all of my family and friends –
Paul, Dave and his wife Sue – for all their belief and
support – but mostly for their collective *'It's about
time!'*
I also have to thank Ms. Jones who, without her tireless
work, dedication and support, this book would not be
in print.
Thank you, sis.

Chapter 1

.

I should have recognized from the start that today wasn't going to be your normal day, but then, what's normal? I'm pretty sure that most people's idea of a normal day is miles apart from mine.

It's kinda hard to know where to start this story. What you need to know is that my name is Mann, and for years I've had a running battle going with my addictive personality — and that includes controlled substances as well as the lifestyle that comes along with it.

I know what you're thinking: Here comes one of those "I was lost and now I'm found" stories.

I wish.

Been there, done that—and it didn't work. So after years of ups and downs, ins and outs, and back and forth with this thing, I've come to the conclusion that some of us just ain't gonna get clean, at least not in the AA sense.

As important as that realization was, it still meant I was stuck with the problem of living this life. To be honest, it seems to have all the trappings of a good life. I figured what I really needed to find was a way to *take control* of it.

You may think that sounds crazy—and maybe it is. But here's the situation as I see it.

I went from small-time drug dealing in the 80's to full-time drug dealing in the 90's—and by the dawn of the new millennium in 2000, I was also a big-time drug *user.*

By that time, I'd finally figured out that if I kept it up, it wouldn't be too much longer before they — my family or "business associates" — would be planting me in the ground.

So, I developed Mann's new and improved *System for Life in the Fast Lane.*

After letting the cokehead lifestyle run its course, I started focusing on my skills as a salesman. And I became fairly successful again—meaning that I managed to sell more than I ingested. I figured that I'd worked myself up from a rank "user" to something more like a connoisseur.

Once I finally stopped fighting myself, accepted who I was, and tried to find a way to work with it, life began to take on a bit of normality. I saw it as "business as usual."

Well, like I said earlier, your idea of normal and mine may be a little bit different.
So, my life became a conundrum and I'm not really sure

if I sell to support my habit, or if I have a habit as a result of dealing with the lunatics I call customers. Either way, life has led me down some interesting paths, but none crazier than this last one.

My customer base is, shall we say, "colorful." They run the full range—everything from strippers to doctors— you name a profession and I sell to one of its members. Cocaine doesn't discriminate: it loves everybody, and of course, everybody *loves* coke. Some love it too much, others *way* too much.

But I'm hardly in a position to point fingers. I'm just doing the best to deal with the hand I've been dealt, and wish the next guy "good luck" finding a way to deal with his.

Some people are destined to fall from grace but I do try to stay away from the corner crack-head, or some poor bum who does so much coke he doesn't have a place to lay his head.

It also seems to me that the older people get, the better they handle it. Of course, that's assuming they live that long.

One of my customers is this old guy; I found out that he's a middle school principal. He spends a lot of money—and I mean, a *lot*. I don't know if he's dealing himself or what, but I did a little digging and found out his school is tops in student performance, and it is said to have the best, most energetic team of teachers. I sometimes wonder if maybe he's putting it in the kids' hot lunches or the coffee machine in the teachers' lounge.

Then there's Benny, the car salesman. I'm a little worried about him. Benny is a complete train wreck but he can sell an 18-wheel semi-trailer truck to blind lady during childbirth. You see, his sales are his commission; his commission is his cop money. The bigger the sale, the bigger the commission. The bigger the commission—well, you get the idea.

Not too long ago, Benny calls me near the end of his workday. He says he has a customer who's ready to pay cash for a $60,000 truck, and says to come over right away, that by the time I get there he'll be done with the paperwork, and *"Benny is spending big tonight!"*

This isn't the first time Benny has gotten his hands on a large commission, and it's also not the first time he's blown it all on cocaine. So everything sounded as normal as it ever is in Benny's world.

I stopped what I was doing, jumped in my car and headed straight to the car lot. By the time I arrived, it seemed something had gone wrong with the deal. I hear the truck guy tell Benny, "Better luck next time," and walk out the office.

Well, Benny ain't having it.

He jumps up from behind his desk, screaming, "Two hours of kissing your fat, fucking ass, then another hour test-driving all over this goddamn city — not to mention the time I spent in the manager's office getting you one hell of a great deal! And after all that, you fat farmer fuck, you got the nerve to tell me you're not going to buy that truck because *you need to check with the lot down the street, the one that has the commercial with the American flag in it*?

"Well I hope you're a veteran, because if you don't buy something from me today, they're going to need that American flag to put over your coffin!"

I figured I'd be wise to stay in my car. Good call, because next thing I know, Benny's chasing the guy around the lot with the same truck the guy was supposed to buy. I just put my car in reverse and slowly backed out the same way I came in.

So this is the kind of craziness I'm used to, which is why I have a serious concerns about my tomorrows.

I have a customer-slash-friend who's a local radio DJ. His name is Max. He's pretty well known, and he likes his coke. The more coke Max does, the crazier he gets on the air. And the crazier Max gets, the more people love him. He's done everything from calling up the mayor and cursing him out— live on the air—to recently getting on the roof of the radio station's building and calling the police. The cops get there, look up and see Max standing on the roof with his pants down, ass pointed at them, which just happens to have a picture of the city's police chief stuck on it. And there also happened to be what looked like a turd coming out the chief's mouth, like a cigar.

After I bonded him out of jail, I asked him what the hell that was all about. Seems that when the mayor of Denver was running for reelection, he called up Max and asked him to come to his office downtown. Said he wanted to give Max an exclusive interview. Just the two of them, and no-holds-barred. Max can ask him anything.

The Mayor gets great PR because Max is the hottest DJ in the city. Everyone listens to him. And it's great for Max, 'cause it proves how important and powerful he is.

So Max arrives for his live interview. He interviews the mayor of Denver, Colorado. They have lunch together, complete with all the VIP shit. Or as Max puts it, a lot of back-patting and Good Ol'Boy-ing, closer than two balls in a nut sack.

After the interview the mayor tells Max that they're friends for life. The mayor says to him, "If you need anything, just call me: I got you." And there's Max, sucking it down big time.

So when Max walks out of the building and finds that the cops have attached the Denver Boot to his car's front tire, he figures, "No problem! I'll just call my new-found best friend at City Hall and show these traffic cops they'd better not mess with Max's car."

So Max called his best buddy, the Mayor. And sure enough, the Mayor says 'no worries'; he'll just call his pal the Chief of Police and fix it.

The Chief of Police, a well-known closet cross-dressing homophobe, not only tells Max, "No deal: pay up or take the bus," and somewhere along the way, the Chief also manages to get his hands on the money Max was *supposed to* get paid for doing the interview. Then he tells Max that the City of Denver thinks it would be best if that money - what Max was to be paid — is used to pay his outstanding bill with the City of Denver. Turns out that still only put a small dent in what he owed the city for parking tickets, which totaled a mere *four thousand dollars*. Four thousand dollars in parking tickets! That had to be some kind of a record.

Still, Max is a good dude, so bailing him out wasn't a hard decision. Especially considering the fact that, as long as I have Max as a customer, there's not a concert that will come through Denver that I can't get backstage passes for.

Oh, brother! The things that happen backstage at rock and rap concerts— especially with a pocket full of coke. But I have found myself in church the next morning after a couple of those back stage adventures—looking over my shoulder, and knowing for sure that the Devil, with God's permission, was coming through the church doors and dragging my ass away!

Max and I sit and talk about everything either one of us can possibly think of before I pop the magic question: "So when do you think you can pay me back for springing you?"

He thinks long and hard as he does a few more lines, which, Max informs me, are also at my expense, and slowly the situation at hand begins to become clear.

Not only has the police chief screwed him on the money he is supposed to get for the interview, the radio station (Max's fourth in two years) suspended him indefinitely. But not to worry, he says, because he has, as he puts it, *A Brilliant Idea* about how he's going to square the circle. "How would you like a free, all-expenses-paid, three-day trip to Las Vegas?"

He'd better be joking.

"Look, Max, you have — ok, maybe you *did* have — the #1 radio show in Denver, everybody in town listens to you. And this condo — you're overlooking downtown Denver. Hell, you had Rodney Rawlins living across the hall from you until he split for New York — and don't tell me the NBA's MVP was pinching pennies. What's this costing you? Two million dollars? You drive — or did drive — a brand-new Ferrari Italia, so I know you're not trying to convince me that you're broke!"

The look on Max's face is starting to make my stomach churn. "You *are* broke," I finally say.

"Well…not exactly. But you gotta understand that the FCC fined me so much that the station would only agree to keep me on the air if I agreed to pay the fines myself. We worked out a payment plan and they're taking over seventy percent of my pay. I'm still paying for the time I put the pit bull puppies in the lion's cage at the zoo!"

My mouth flies open. "You are? But that wasn't even at this radio station!"

"That's right—it was the *last* station. And then there's the rent at this roach-infested so-called luxury condo. I think the roaches here snort more of your coke than I do!" Max sheepishly shakes his head a little. "Oh yeah—then there's you, my friend. I've spent more money with you than Obama did with the government bailout! By the way, I don't see you hurting for anything. Why don't you take this roach motel off my hands? I'm sure you can afford it." Max takes a quick snort.

"No thanks," I reply. "I'm saving my money for a rainy day."

"Well, brotha, monsoon season has just arrived!" Max takes another snort. "Take the Vegas trip or take a number. Afraid that's the…" he takes two more snorts for emphasis, "best I can do, buddy."

Max reaches in his pocket for something to wipe the powder off his nose, but instead pulls out two tickets. "What the…?"

He looks at them for a moment and brightens a little. "Hey— you want these tickets to the Heidi Barker *Comeback* tour? Comes with backstage passes!"

I shake my head. "No thanks, Max. If I show up back stage with this high-grade blow, it'll be the end of that comeback!" I change the subject before Max's brain forgets what he's just asked. "So, tell me—what's the deal with this Vegas trip?"

"Well, the radio station is having a contest, and the prize is a three-day/two night, all-expense paid trip to Vegas. Comes with the hotel and rent-a-car."

"Any cash?"

"Yeah," says Max, wipes his nose again, "five hundred dollars."

"You got to be joking with me! What kind of money is that for Vegas?"

I can almost see myself, along with the old folks getting off the typical church tour bus, with our very own personal roll of quarters for the slot machines.

"Hey! Times are hard," replies Max as he continues

snorting, "even the contest sponsors are feeling the budget cuts."

I think about it and I'm really not interested in Las Vegas right now. Still, I have to ask. "So if it's a contest, I can't wait to hear how I end up winning it."

"Don't worry about that," grins Max, between snorts. "The promotions manager at the station owes me, and I mean he owes me, Big Time. It's your fault, by the way."

This just keeps getting more ridiculous. "My fault?"

"Yeah," Max replies, snorting, "he got some of your stuff from me—that really good shit about a month ago, remember?"

I point to the straw and mirror currently fixed to Max's nose. "Looks to me like it's always really good!"

Max continues his snort-a-thon. "You can say that again," he says, with two snorts, a quick choke and a cough.

I look at him. "I'm still waiting to hear how some event - *that I know nothing about* - is my fault."

Max stops mid-snort. "Oh, yeah. Well, like I said, he got

some of your stuff from me. I was on the air at the time so when I handed him the baggie, I didn't get a chance to tell him that all of it wasn't his. He was supposed to get a couple of lines out of it, and wait for me to get off the air. But by the time I get to a break, Bill is gone."

"Bill…Bill?" I'm trying to find the face in my mind. "That tight pants, pop-bottle glasses-wearing Republican nerd guy that's always running around the radio station at a hundred miles an hour?"

"Yep, the same."

"I never would have guessed that he gets high. Especially on coke! I guess that explains why he's always moving so fast."

"He doesn't do lines. Or at least, he didn't *used to*. Because he's the station's promotions guy, he's required to be at the concerts we promote. He's a good dude, and a hell of a promotions manager. He's just not cut out for the music industry, especially not the kind of shit that we play." Max looks a bit thoughtful for a moment—then snorts up again.

Between Max's nose-to-mirror fixation and his rambling explanations, I'm losing patience. "Enough with the hype on Bill! Will you just cut to the chase? Why is it my fault?" Max is pre-occupied, getting his nose in position for the next hit. "Just—give me that damn mirror!"

I snatch the mirror from Max's hands in mid-snort. He looks slightly panicked.

"Ok, ok," Max says, eyes on the lines of coke on the mirror in my hands. "You remember the Rock and Rap Fest we promoted a few months back?"

"Yeah, I heard it was a total madhouse."

"Yep, out of control: not enough security, too many people for the venue, and I think everybody was totally fucked up — including the performers."

"Was our Young Republican hopeful there?"

"Yeah. And the poor guy hasn't been the same since."

"I heard Satan himself was there, probably looking for me," I said, with a smirk on my face.

Max laughs. "Oh, yeah, Satan was definitely there! I heard some of the kids jacked him for his pitch fork and beat him up!" Max is laughing, but his eyes are still trained on the coke that I'm holding.

"So what happened to Bill?"

"Up until that show, Bill was always about his business," said Max. "He stayed in the sky boxes, hung with the other promotion guys and record label people — never with the artists or groupies."

"Guy's smarter than I thought."

"Yeah, well, he *was* smart. I ran into him as he headed out the door that night. He said his job was done and that it was all in my hands from then on. I told him to hang out a while. You know: stay and enjoy the music for a change. Skillet Blacque is up next, you gotta hear the band coming on after him, and the guitar player is from another planet, blah-blah…"

"Let me guess which band you're talking about: *Bad Itch*!" I'm tired of holding the mirror, so I casually set it down on the table, but Max pounces on it the moment I do.

"Yep, Bad Itch," says Max, with another loud, long snort.

"Max! You let that Square Pants dude stay for a live Bad Itch show? You hear about the time the bass player bashed somebody over the head with his bass, then kept on playing?"

"Yeah, I did," Max squeezes out, coughing. "Now that I look back on it, I don't think it was my best idea."

"And — what happened?"

"Well, first off, I told the guy to lose the tie and his Men's Wearhouse sport jacket. I told him to pull his shirt out of the top of his tight-ass pants, and for God's sake, to take off those night-vision spaceman goggles. Under it all, he's actually not a bad-looking dude, you know. And after a couple of lines, he was good to go!"

I give Max a long, hard stare. "Tell me those couple of lines weren't the first time he's ever been high?"

Max smirked. "Well, I did kind of trick him, but I had to do something! Mann, the guy was shaking like a kid at the dentist's office," he said, averting his eyes from my face. "Stop looking at me like I kill baby seal pups. Bill said he was having a hard time breathing because of all the smoke in the air. That's why he always leaves the shows early."

My reply to Max's stupid logic comes with a sarcastic bite in it. "Oh, well—so now it all makes perfect sense to me! The guy can't breathe so you figure you'll just help the poor jerk out with his first hit of cocaine? Hell, ten out of ten doctors recommend it!"

Max does his best to ignore my sharp answer. "Well, he said he couldn't breathe, so I take his handkerchief out his sport coat…"

"Wait — he had a *handkerchief*?"

"Yeah, I know. Anyway, I take it and pour some blow in the middle of it, hold it up to his nose like a little kid, and tell him to sniff real hard. Mann, he damn near pulled the whole thing up into his nose! His eyes bug out, his face turns beet-red, and he starts snorting like a bull. Then it hits him: he gets this big smile on his face and he asks me '*what was that?*' I told him it was sinus medicine."

Max tries to look contrite, but I ain't buying it and he knows it; he continues his story.

"We walk around the concourse, and he said he's not ready to go down on the floor yet. So I tell him, this is *his* concert! All these people here having the time of their lives because of *his* hard work. Some of the industry's biggest acts are here because of you! Bill, the Mormon from Salt Lake City, Utah."

"Max! He's a Mormon? From Utah?"

"I believe that to be true."

"One question."

"What's that, Mann?"

"Did you?" I look Max straight in the eyes.

"Did I what?"

I hold up my hand and start naming off Max's transgressions on each finger. "You gave him his first hit of coke. We can forgive that: he's a big boy, and hopefully he'll get over that. Then you got him to stay for a Bad Itch show — he's a concert promoter, so he was overdue. But did you take him backstage?"

"Yeah." Max is fiddling with the straw. I know he's trying to get around the truth.

"How far back, Max?"

"Uhh…all the way."

"Into the dressing rooms?"

With a sheepish look on his face, Max replies, "Well, no.

Actually, the tour bus. But it was *his* idea!"

I stop for a moment, staring at the small pile of coke on the mirror in front of me. Max knows that I'm reminiscing about my own backstage experiences.

"Max, you know I've been back there. I've hung out with those assholes, getting higher than I thought humanly possible, and doing shit with groupie chicks that I still hate to admit I had anything to do with. How bad did it get?"

"Shit, Mann, the guy's an animal! The backup singer in Skillet Blacque's band has on a G-string. Bill takes one look at her and—"

I quickly throw up my hands to halt Max's explanation. "Ok — never mind! Been there, done that. I'm already starting to shake. What happened with him and the baggie of dope you gave him at the radio station?"

Max's eyes are glazing over. "Oh — almost forgot. Well, I get off the air and go looking for the guy. But he's nowhere to be found, no phone call, no message. Nothing."

"And *then* you start to get nervous, Max?"

"No, not really. I mean, it's coke: that's what you're *supposed* to do. Get all shit-faced, disappear or do God knows what. I was kind of pissed that he took off with my half of the stash, but I knew he'd turn up sooner or later, and I was sure he couldn't do all of that baggie by himself. At least, that's what I thought.

"Then, about three o'clock in the morning, I get a phone call. It's Bill — well, no, some chick on Bill's phone. I hear crying in the background, and I can't tell what the fuck this broad is talking about."

I'm looking at Max, and see he's caught up in this story. His face has an odd look on it. He takes a deep breath.

"I finally got her to slow down long enough to half-ass communicate with me. She says that she's locked herself in a closet because Bill's in the other room, trying to have sex with a dead girl!"

"How did she get your num— *what did you just say?!*"

Max is nodding in agreement. "I asked her the same thing. She told me Bill kept yelling my name. So she got her hands on his phone and looked it up. She sounds scared. Tells me Bill's a complete nut job, and that I'd better get over there before she calls the police."

"Max, just how much blow was in that bag?"

"Oh, about two or three ounces, give or take a gram. You should know — you sold it to me."

I can't believe anyone could be so stupid and still be alive. "And how much do you think they did?"

"I don't know, Mann, but when I got there, powder was everywhere. On the table, on the TV, all over the bathroom counter — everywhere!"

"Where did you have to go? I mean where did they call you from?"

Max looks excited. "Get this: they were in the Montville Hotel!"

"The Montville? Oh, shit! That's a pretty high-dollar joint! They're lucky that hotel security didn't come in the room, with that chick screaming. I'm not sure I want to hear the rest of this!"

Max's face has gotten sweaty, and I'm sure half of it is because of the coke he's still snorting — but the other half is this mess with Bill.

"I just walk in the room. It wasn't even locked. Bill's sitting on the floor next to some girl, crying his eyes out, coke all over his face. He sees me but doesn't recognize me because he almost jumps through the roof. When he realizes it's me, he runs over, damn near knocks me down. The room is a total wreck — I mean *total* wreck. 'Max, Max,' he says, 'what did I do? Please help me! I'm in so much trouble!'

"Mann, right then some crazy-looking chick comes running out the closet, with a butcher knife in one hand, and a bag of blow and a cell phone in the other, howling 'keep that crazy motherfucker away from me!'

"The place smells like a locker room, and the closet chick screams, 'Look what he did!' and points to some naked chick on the floor. Bill looks at me and says, 'I think she may be dead.'"

In my gut, I know that I need to stop listening, but can't. Max is on another planet, talking a mile a minute. I couldn't stop him if I wanted to.

"I'm like, 'what do you mean, you think she may be *dead!*' Mann, the guy's a total train wreck, shaking in his boots. He's so high he doesn't know whether he's coming or going, can hardly form a word, let alone a sentence. He finally says he was having sex with the chick on the floor, she took a hit of crack and passed out. That's when this

Nicky chick came out the bedroom, saw him, and thought he was screwing her dead body.

"I ask Bill why does he thinks she just passed out and that she isn't really dead. Bill says that he was trying to get to his phone to call me — but Nicky was in the closet with my phone. I asked him why the hell he needed to call *me*."

Max was already sweaty and jittery from the coke, but now he's off the charts.
"Bill tells me," Max croaks, "that I gave him too much 'nose medicine'! Mann, I didn't give him anything — he *took* the shit and ran with it!"

"Max? *Max!*" Max briefly re-focuses on my face, and shakes his head like a boxer on the ropes.

"Sorry, Mann — I had a flashback! That was a stressful night. Anyway, Bill tells me while he was banging on the closet door, he looks around and the almost-dead girl sits up, picks up the pipe and smokes another piece of crack. Then she looks at him with a big smile, points at him, and then points between her legs, and passes out again. He thinks that this is her thing — he thinks that when she gets high, she likes to get laid at the same time."

I sigh. "Yeah, I know…getting her freak on. Where did

he find those two crazy broads at?"

"He said the one passed out on the floor is some groupie chick from one of our concerts. The other one? Now get this: she's the groupie chick's *chaperone*."

"Oh, shit — she's under-age?"

"*Way* under. And it gets worse. The chaperone/closet chick is also the wife of some notorious Denver vice cop."

"Hold on, Max —that sounds like a bunch of bullshit to me."

"I thought so, too, but she showed me a picture of them together. She used to be a hooker. The cop used to bust her, but he fell in love and wound up marrying her."
Something doesn't add up in my head. "Wait — if the dead girl isn't dead, and the closet chick is cool, what's the problem?"

"First off, the closet chick *isn't* cool! Bill turned into a monster. He tricked them to get them up to his hotel room with some 'radio station-after-party' bullshit. After they get to his room, the closet chick —that's Nicky — sees Bill messing with his nose, and figures he's doing blow. Her old habits come back. She asks him if she can do just a little bit."

I'm still a little confused. "Then why is she pissed at Bill? *She* fucked up, not Bill!"

Max's eyes are wild.

"This is where it gets real crazy…well, real *crazier*. Bill and Nicky go in the bedroom and leave the kid in the front room. Nicky hasn't done any coke in a while, so it's not long before she's really out of control. She really starts trippin' and wants to smoke some crack. She and Bill talk the night bellhop into going to the store to get whatever she needs to cook the coke to smoke it. When it comes time to pay the bellhop for his services, guess what he wants?"

"Oh, I don't know, Max…this sure is a tough one! Gee, let me see: the bellhop wants…some dope!"

Rapidly nodding, Max continues. "But not only does he want some coke, he wants the cooked-up stuff! Bill's never been around this kind of shit, so he has no idea what he's getting into. All he knows is the coke is good and the females are all over him."

It's clear that this is not going to end good. I rub my

forehead, trying to hold off a headache that's rapidly moving in.

"Don't tell me, Max, you're finally worried! With people like you looking out for Bill, he didn't stand a chance."

"Come on, Mann! What was I supposed to do?" Max is agitated. "Hold the guy's hand? He never said anything about getting hotel rooms, or girls, or any of that crazy shit!"

"Alright, alright - I guess I can't blame you for that much. It's not all your fault. So, anyway?"

Max is placated, for now. "Yeah…anyway, all this time, the teenage groupie chick is sitting in the front room, watching everybody run back and forth. The whole time she hasn't said a word – nothing. Bill said he thought she was asleep."

I scoffed at that. "Thought or hoped? If she was so asleep, how did she wind up high, screwed, and knocked out?"

"Mann, don't give me that look! I swear, I didn't have a thing to do with this. I'm just repeating what Bill and that Nicky chick told me! So, Bill gives the bellhop some crack rocks, and he *thinks* he let the bellhop out. I figured that he probably did, but while Bill was in the room with the cop's wife, cooking up the crack, the bellhop was waiting in the front room with the girl. It's my guess they talked about what was going on in the bedroom. And when Bill gave him his stuff, the girl told the bellboy to wait by the door; when Bill went back in the bedroom, she let him back in."

"Let *who* back in? The bellboy?"

"Yeah! Bill says when he and Nicky were in the bedroom doing their thing, he kept hearing somebody moaning. He comes out of the room, and sees the bellboy's got her upside down on the couch. She's got a crack pipe in her mouth. The bellboy is ass-naked with his face buried between her legs. Right then, the phone rings. It's the front desk, and they're asking Bill if anybody up there has seen the bellhop? To make things worse, there's a knock at the door: it's hotel security. They're looking for the bellhop; seems that the last time anyone saw him, he was headed up to their room to answer a service call and no one's seen him since."

Reliving all the details is beginning to take its toll on Max. He's looking seriously stressed and stops for a moment, then carries on.

"Somehow, Bill manages to get rid of hotel security, but he said that when he had a chance to look up, the bellboy was nowhere to be found. Bill's best guess was that he walked out on the balcony. So he went to look, but — no bellboy."

My headache has just moved into second gear. "*Please* don't tell me he jumped."
Max frowns. "Mann, they were 10 stories up!"

"He won't be the first high-as-a-kite asshole to jump from a balcony. Just tell me —did he jump?"

"I told you: Bill said he doesn't know what happened to the guy," replies Max. "But now little Miss Wild Thing is licking her lips and looking hard at Bill. They're both high, so Bill falls in right where the bellboy left off. Being the turnout that he is, Bill spends the rest of the night running in between both rooms with these two chicks, having the time of his life!"

"Until?" I coax Max, "Until what?"

"Well, until Nicky comes out the room and catches Bill with Miss Wild Thing, who's now doing her 'Hit-the-Dope-Screw-Me-and-Pass-Out' routine. Nicky, her handler, being real high and half out of her mind, takes one look at Bill humping the passed-out youngster and freaks the hell out. She gets real paranoid, thinks her friend is dead and Bill is screwing her body — so she locks herself in the closet."

"And that's when you got the call, right?"

"Yep. But I said to everybody just calm down. You know, *'why don't we let bygones be bygones: Nobody got hurt or anything like that…we all go on our own ways, no harm done, blah, blah.'* But the Nicky chick isn't trying to hear it. She says Bill tricked them to get them up to his room, forced them to get high and then raped them."

"What!" My headache has just been shoved into Overdrive.

"That's what I said, but I knew better—and Nicky knew I did. So I asked her straight up, 'If Bill raped you, why didn't you call the police instead of climbing into the closet and calling me?'

"She says something about not wanting to get the police involved because she's been clean for a few years now, and her husband trusted her to keep an eye on the D.A.'s daughter at the concert."

I snap my head up to stare at Max. "What the hell did you just say? Are you kidding me? That girl in the hotel room doing coke and getting done by everybody in the hotel was the *D.A.'s daughter?*"

My head is so tight now, I don't expect it to stop hurting anytime this century. "Max, how well did you clean this shit up? Before you answer, let me tell you something: I don't know if you realize the kind of shit you've gotten yourself into with this Nicky chick. Listen to me: I *know* this bitch. She used to spend money with me, and she's a fucking rat bitch!"

I back away from Max because I'm afraid if I get any closer, I'm going to grab him by the throat with both hands and start twisting.

"Mann, you gotta calm down."

"Don't tell me to calm down! About four years ago, I just missed getting indicted because of that bitch. I also know the vice cop that she's married to. He's a real live piece of shit. Officer Spriggs — Me and him go a long way back. If he even hears my name, I guarantee he'll start to sweat!" I move in close to Max. "Please tell me that you haven't mentioned my name around Nicky?"

"No, Mann — of course not! What do you think, I'm

stupid?"

I give Max a long look that says exactly what I was thinking. "Not sure you want me to answer that question right now. But you better watch your step with this one. That cop is more crooked than a jigsaw puzzle with the border pieces missing."

"Damn, Mann — this *is* bad. Seriously bad."

"You know it. He's the main reason why Nicky doesn't want to tell anybody about their little adventure. This isn't the first time she's relapsed since she's been with Spriggs. A few years ago — after she married that crazy son of a bitch — she calls me to meet her at a motel on Colfax. I meet her in the parking lot and she hands me a couple hundred dollars, so I give her what she wants. She's in the hotel room with some trick, so I don't even go in. She's been missing in action for a few days, so Spriggs has been out looking for her. Well, he finally gets wind of where she's at. Spriggs and his partner creep up on them. They kick in the door, and get an eyeful. His wife with a pipe hanging out her mouth and the trick hanging out the other end, if you know what I mean."

My head is throbbing but if I rub it any harder, I'm afraid the skin will start coming off. But there's still more to this tale. "Spriggs and his partner beat down the trick, and they just left him face down on the motel room floor. Spriggs then starts in on his wife and busted her up real bad—so bad they had to take her to the hospital. When they ask her what happened, she tells the doctors that two black guys jumped her on the bus stop, kidnapped her, raped her, and made her smoke crack!"

Max busts out laughing.

"What's so goddamn funny? What the hell is there to laugh about?"

Max tries — and fails — to stop. "The old, trusty 'Black Guy' excuse!" he gets out between howls. "Can always count on it when our ass is in the fire and we need a reliable fall guy. I remember this — it was all over the news! I even think I reported it on the radio. They said the cop went out and saved her from the bad guys. How did the story go? Something like this…" Max puts on his deep, smooth on-air announcer voice.

> "'Cop tracks down his own kidnapped wife,
> saves her life. Be sure to tune in at six o'clock for
> all the details of this breaking story.'"

"Made him out to be some kind of hero, a real big-shit live action hero!"

"Real big *bullshit* is what it was, Max. Only a handful of

people know the real truth, and Spriggs is damn sure going to do whatever it takes to keep it that way. He finds out she was at it again, I'm sure he'll kill her."

Max gets up and starts walking in circles in front of me. "Damn, Mann! So what's his problem with you?"

"After she gets out the hospital, he's still pissed — real pissed," I reply. "Wifey was a hooker, right? You can imagine the talk around the cop shop. His buddies in blue are having a little trouble swallowing the story Spriggs is selling. Every time he walks in, they're laughing behind his back or cracking jokes.

"One of her girlfriends calls me up and says he's lost it, tells me Spriggs is gonna throw Nicky out on her ass as soon as she's healthy enough."

"So, to save her own scrawny ass the bitch tells Spriggs the only reason she started using again is because she just happened to run into an old dealer she used to cop from, and he was feeling so generous that he just gave her a big bag of dope — and the dealer just happens to be *me!*"

"Why you?"

"Hell, I'm her free pass, Max! She knows that he's so mad-dog insane, he won't even question her bullshit. He'll be coming to get me, foaming at the mouth like a

dog with rabies — and twice as insane. She threw me under the bus. She don't give a shit what happens to me."
"She should have been a lawyer because she can come up with some good ones," said Max. "I would hire her in a heartbeat."

"If you ask me, she should have been stillborn!" It feels like steam is starting to come out of my eyeballs and ears. Both of us are pacing the room like caged animals.

Max stops suddenly, turns to me and says calmly, "Mann, what did Spriggs end up doing? Did he come for you?"

"Hell, yeah he came for me! He hit the streets like he was invading Afghanistan — and I don't even know my name has been thrown in the shit pile! Even worse, the other cops aren't looking for me, so it's their own private hunting party—just Spriggs and his partner. He's all over town, busting heads and trying to find out what he can about me."

Max backs away a bit and puts his hands up in front of his chest, "Hey, Mann? Maybe it would be better if we keep it down a bit — given the circumstances?"

My instinct is to put my fist to his face, but then it sinks in a bit. "Yeah, ok. Remember I told you that I had no idea anybody was looking for me, so it wasn't hard for Spriggs and his partner to find me? I was coming out of the liquor store on Fairfax St. when this guy I've known for years runs up on me with a handful of money.

"I find out later that Spriggs had busted the guy. Spriggs told the guy that, if he did this favor, he'd let him go.

"Anyway, we step around the back of the building so I can count the dough and give him his stuff. Just then, Spriggs and his partner come running around the side of the building yelling, 'Drop everything, hands up! You're under arrest!'

"I start to run, but Spriggs hits me in the ribs with those nunchuck things that the police carry. Hits me so hard it spins me around. I don't know what the hell is going on, I'm just trying to get out of there and, on pure reflex I cold cock him right in the mouth. He just ran right into it— it happened so fast, everybody came to a dead standstill. Spriggs goes down, out like a light. I look at his partner, and he looks at Spriggs. Somebody over by the liquor store yells 'run Mann, they're gonna kill you!'

"Right about then, I know I'm fucked. It's broad daylight, nowhere to run, and his partner is bringing his gun up. I'm sure I'm about to meet my Maker, when —POW! I catch one right across the jaw, and I go down, second light out, right next to Spriggs."

Max is on the edge of his seat, sweating. "What the fuck

are you saying? He shot you in the face? I don't see any scar!"

"No, Max — Spriggs and his partner were off-duty, outside their district, and in plain clothes."

Max is silent for a moment, then asks quietly, "Mann, they were gonna kill you, weren't they?"

I stop to look at Max. "No doubt about it —but they blew it because they were in street clothes, in a different district. Nobody knew they were cops, including the patrol officer that happened to be making his rounds.

"The officer stated in his report that he was passing the corner store to see who was hanging out. When he turned the corner he saw two white males in street clothes, one with a gun, and the other with a stick in his hand, slowly making their way toward the alley behind the liquor store. "He said that he thought they might be police by the way they moved, but he couldn't be sure and there hadn't been any alerts over his radio. So he decided to jump out of his car and run around to the opposite side of the building. "By the time he got there, the cop heard a lot of yelling. He took a quick peek around the corner and he saw an unidentified black male standing over another male lying in the alley, and a third unidentified male yelling what this cop thought was a police command. The black male — that was me — turned to run.

"I swear I never saw the regular cop. When I tried to run, he stepped out from around the corner and caught me with a straight left to the jaw."

"Wow. Mann, that was way too close."

I'm breathing hard just remembering it. "I know! I've never been so happy to get knocked out! If that cop — a patrolman named Jackson — hadn't stepped around that corner and dropped me just then, I would have been a dead man for sure. Then they could've made up any bullshit story they wanted to. Hell, I'd just knocked out a cop, I had drugs on me, and by the time the investigation was over, I'm sure they would have found a pistol on me as well."

Max takes a deep breath, exhales loudly as he sits down next to me. "Mann, what I don't get is, why aren't you doing at least ten years?"

"This is where it gets real ugly. My lawyer finds out about Spriggs being off-duty and out of his district, doing what they call 'a controlled buy.' That's where they send somebody in to set you up with marked money. Nothing they'd done was right as far as the law goes. Spriggs and his partner were supposed to be running a drug sting, right? So, isn't it a little strange that no one else on the force knew anything about it? Second of all, Spriggs and his partner are *Vice*, not Narcotics — drug stings aren't their line of work.

"By the time I get to court, everybody with half a brain knows something's seriously messed up—but since nobody's talking, *hey*."

I take a swipe at my sweaty aching forehead. "My lawyer puts on the pressure to dismiss, because nothing Spriggs did was by the book, or even close to legal. The attorney also discovered that the police department had Spriggs and his partner listed as being on vacation when all this shit went down.

"So, after a lot of police department mumbo-jumbo double-talk, all charges were dropped due to lack of evidence. And I walked — free and clear."

Max's mouth flies open. "Come on, Mann: lack of evidence? They had everything! A punched out cop, his partner's word, plus the other cop that hit you—not to mention the drugs and their snitch!"

"Yeah," I agreed, "well, as it turns out, they had a little *too* much. Why were they on the other side of town, running an unauthorized drug sting? Why weren't they on vacation? And the big question is — why did they target *me*? I'm more than positive that Spriggs and his pal never planned to take me in. No way. They were going to take me somewhere I'd never be found, and put a bullet in my head. End of story.

"Taking me to jail was the worst thing that could have happened to them. Because if I go to court, I tell it all. His wife buying cocaine, tricking in a motel room, and Spriggs beating her and the trick to the point of hospitalization.

"Plus there's that big fat lie Spriggs came up with about saving his wife from the bad guys. Get this: Spriggs was the police department's big Hero of the Year, so they couldn't have him go bad on them. The police are always trying to make themselves look good, and this story would have been a major embarrassment.

"They knew something had gone terribly wrong — and they also knew Spriggs was a loose cannon. They told my lawyer that if I was willing to drop the whole thing, so were they."

Max jumps in. "That is the craziest shit I've heard in a long time. So, Mann, it's you who's the hot boy, not me! The crap I do on the radio ain't got shit on you. You're on some *Serpico-Rodney King-Mark Furman*-type shit, all rolled up into one! You make me look like a Boy Scout."

"Well, Max, don't go running to get yourself a Happy

Meal just yet. If the word gets out about the shit you and Bill got into - you're not going to be feeling good or bad—you're gonna be *dead!*

"Pay attention, Max, 'cause we have to make damn sure we've got this under control. If it's money or whatever you need to keep this quiet, then let me know now. Spriggs is a real, live nut bucket—he'll kill you, Nicky and me with a smile on his face."

By now, I'm on my feet, staring into Max's beady black eyes with a look that would burn through tungsten steel. "You understand exactly what I'm saying here?"

"Yeah, yeah, Mann—I got this all under control. I have this friend downtown, and he works at the same hotel—"

I see that familiar look on Max's face and cut him off.

"Wait a minute, Max, I don't want to hear it, and I don't want to know about it. Keep me as far away from this as possible, and try to keep your distance, too."

I take a deep breath, and change the subject. "Now how long do I have to wait for those Vegas tickets?"

"I can have them for you on Friday."

"When is the contest drawing?"

"Not until late *next* month," grins Max.

"Wait. I get the tickets *Friday* but the drawing is…" Then I remember who I'm talking to. "Never mind." I don't even want to ask.

I've heard all I can handle about Max and the mess he's in—I've already got enough for my brain to sort out. I'm picking up my jacket and getting ready to leave when Max says, "Hey, Mann?"

"What now?"

"Just one last thing."

I steel myself and turn to face him.

"I need a little more coke."

"Aww, you've gotta be—"

Max has his hands out, palms down, trying to tell me to calm down. "Hey! It's not for *me* —it's for the Las Vegas tickets. I know I said Bill owes me, but just in case he tries to give me a hard time, this will make sure he can't say no. By the way, you taking your girl with you?"

Hadn't thought of that. It's probably a good idea. "Yeah."

"How's she doing?"

"Same as usual," I said, smiling. "Pretty beyond compare, lazy beyond comprehension, and can nag the sun out of rising in the East."

After telling Max the rules of what he's gotten himself involved in, I look at the baggie of coke in my hand. I take a real big scoop, straight up the nose, but I'm not even sure why I bothered. I've got the best stuff in Denver — and this isn't giving me a buzz.

I throw the rest on the table to Max, at least a thousand dollars' worth on the streets. Turning to walk out, I tell Max: "I need a vacation!"

Chapter 2

Touching down in Las Vegas was like busting a good one: suddenly all the pressure disappeared. Temporarily, anyway. I've been on this earth long enough to know that when a person has as many loose ends and different people messed up in a situation as Max, somebody is bound to get screwed.

My mind sees it like this: there are six people and three parachutes in the plane — and the wings just fell off. And for good measure, when Max opens the emergency exit, it turns out to be the bathroom.

By going to Vegas, I'm hoping to keep the plane in the air long enough for Max to find the real exit. And if he doesn't, and everybody goes down in flames, I'm just hoping that I'm far enough away from the plane that when it crashes and burns, none of it hits me.

Not likely, but in Vegas you have to think positive.

My wife Monica hates planes. She once told me, "I love to fly —but why do they have to leave the ground?"

Hey, don't ask me. Men far smarter than I have been left with their mouths hanging open in the wake of Monica's logic. I tell myself, she's smart — she just doesn't like to flaunt it.

After checking in to the hotel — the Holiday Inn on the Strip — Monica's still not feeling well. I deposit her in the bed, and take a quick trip to the casino. No fucking around for me. I'm going to blow up Max's five hundred dollars faster than a herd of Al Qaeda terrorists cut loose in New York City with bombs stuck up their asses.

I make the pilgrimage to the Gamblers' Holy Land about three times a year. This isn't my first desert screwing, and I'm kinda hoping it ain't my last.

I still don't know how they do it. They promise you a great time, wring you out for every dime you were crazy enough to bring with you, then send you back home flat broke. But when you get back, you still tell everybody about the great time you had and how "Martha even won $90 on the slot machine!" Somehow, everyone fails to mention the $9,000 they blew after they got drunk and tried to play high-stakes poker.

Vegas breaks so many people—especially tourists. If you're from out of town and get cleaned out so bad you can't afford a way back home, the city's so smart that their Chamber of Commerce keeps a ticket fund available to front you the cost of a ride home. Seems they figure that's cheaper and safer than having a bunch of broke and pissed off out-of-towners running around. Besides, they want you to get home safe— so you can earn more money and run your dumb ass right back to Vegas.

Me, personally? I'm not like everyone else: I have a system. I already know that if I want to strike it rich overnight, I might as well stay home and play the lottery. Why go to Vegas? The odds of hitting it big playing Lotto at home are about the same. And with Lotto, I only have to put up a few dollars to find out I ain't getting shit.

The biggest problem with winning money in Vegas is getting out of town *with* it. It's almost a law of nature that you can't physically leave Vegas with more money than you came with. And if you are one of the few lucky ones who do, you must *never* return again!

Really, it's a proven fact. I tried for years. But now I accept that it's futile to try and leave with any money. So my attitude is that I'm here to party! So, if I get lucky and win anything, I just blow it on purpose. Therefore "When in Rome, do as the Romans do"….or is that "when in Vegas, do as the Vegans do"? Whatever it is, I'm all in.

Five hours after landing in Vegas, and three hours on the

blackjack tables, I'm doing and feeling pretty good.

No angry words from Monica on the cell phone, so she's probably asleep. The combination of the flight and desert heat was kicking her ass. I told you she's lazy — and that's a good thing because I'm ready to step it up a notch.

Max's five hundred dollars has netted me a cool eighteen hundred dollars. But that's no surprise. I always come in hot.

It's time to leave the Strip and get down to some *real* gambling. My favorite is Shaw's Palace Casino, Night Club, Hotel, Shopping Mall, and — get this — Child Day Care Center. All under one roof.

The gambling is serious, the tables are fast, and there's no tourist screwing up the rotation. Nothing fucks up a game faster than some fruit loop from Haskell, Oklahoma, who has no clue about the rules in a game of Twenty-One. Who *doesn't* know how to play blackjack?

Before I go into Shaw's Palace, I need a drink. I'm at a red light in my rent-a-car: a brand-new, all white Ford Crown Victoria. A police car if there ever was one, but I had to take it as part of the contest package.

I look over to the left and spot a bar—the *Happy Snake Eyes*. The parking lot is less than half full. I need a toot and a drink and this looks as good a place as any.

As I pull into the parking lot and get out of the car I hear tires screech, and the sound of a large horsepower motor, making that unmistakable sound, then —*BAM!*

A black Lamborghini Murciélago seems to just jump into the space next to mine, damn near taking the Crown Vic's door out - and me with it. I never see it coming. It's black, faster than Superman, and the drunk fuck driving it doesn't even have his headlights on. I'm hot now.

"Hey pal, what's wrong —can't find your brakes?"

In a kinda sing-song way, he says "Sorry Mee-ster."

Let me guess: he's not from Canada.

"Jour not *policia*, are ju?" he asked, peering at my car.

"No. It's a rent-a-car. Had to take it—free. You know." Don't want anyone to think that I would *voluntarily* drive a Crown Vic.

"I'm thirsty," declares the Lamborghini driver. "How

'bout I buy ju a drink?"

"Thirsty?" I have to peep into the Lamborghini's window. "You look more like *drunky*. You think it's a good idea drinking and driving that rocket ship?"

"I'm ok. Ju want a drink or what?"

It's obvious that talking common sense to this guy isn't going to make a difference. So, what the hell? I take him up on his offer. "Ok, here I come. Where you from anyway?"

"I from Colombia! Ju could tell, huh? Damn, I been working on my accent."

"You have? What are you trying to do? Sound more Colombian?"

"Real funny, Mee-ster. I thought I was doing pretty good."

"Oh, you're understandable, and by the way, my name's 'Mann.' What should I call you?"

"Call me whatever ju want," Lamborghini replies, "but I only answer to 'Nesto'."

"OK, Nesto-from-Colombia. I'm ready for a drink! Let's go."

Not long after we sit down at the bar, two things make themselves apparent. First, Nesto's having one hell of a time trying to pronounce my name. That's probably related to the second fact, which is that he was already pretty well shit-faced when we sat down. Now after a few more drinks, Nesto is really feeling no pain — or much of anything else.

He starts to talk, telling me things. Things that, if they're true, he shouldn't be sharing with anyone, much less a complete stranger. "So, Nesto: you expect me to believe your brother is the head of the Quintana drug cartel?"

"That's right, my friend."

"One of the biggest cartels in the world?"

"It is *the* biggest, my friend. But don't believe everything ju see on jour American TV and newspapers." Nesto gives me a long, drunken stare. "All cartels are about the same, give or take a few hundred million. We all take turns at the top. It's jour government that decides who's gonna be the big, bad wolf every few months."

"The American government?" This guy is truly drunk, but this sounds interesting. "How's that?"

Nesto gets a big smile on his face. "If ju are from this country," he says, "then ju know how this government works. And if ju know how it works, then ju don't want to know the answer to that question."

The drunker Nesto gets, the worse his English gets. At this rate, I'd probably understand him better if we talked in Spanish, though I don't understand a word of that, either. I wasn't buying his cartel story, but what the hell. It doesn't matter anyway. He's buying the drinks and he's pretty entertaining — so I just go along with the flow.

"If I'm not being too nosy, tell me something. What are you doing in Vegas? Spending some of those millions?" I almost want to laugh at my drunken new friend.

"No, Maw. I'm in town on official beezness."

"My name, for the twentieth time, is 'Mann' not 'Maw'— and *what did you just say?*"

Nesto blinks his eyes in the way that only someone who's had too much to drink does. Then after he's sure what he's gonna say, and trying to focus on the thought, he leans in a little unsteadily and says "I here to fix a sale, my friend."

"Damn! Cartels working out of Vegas. Now *that's* different."

Nesto shakes his head unsteadily. "No, Maw, not out of Vegas. I'm here because another one of jour rich American beezness man, he needs money."

In my head, he's beginning to make sense. "You know, Nesto—I understand your words, but I'm still not sure I get it."

The Little Voice in the back of my head says, *"You better hope you never do."*

I can tell Nesto is getting tired of my questions. He's probably having a hard time keeping up with his own story.

"I make this quick and see-mple." His tone is very patient, if very drunken. "Someone in America need what jour brother in the White House calls…umm, *como se dice? Ah* — a 'bail out,' — *sí?*"

Nesto starts to laugh. His glass dips, spilling booze. He's pretty well wasted about now. I can't help but think about

Al Pacino in *Scarface*. The scene when he's drunk in the restaurant, talking, and tells everybody, "say good night to the bad guy." Nesto even looks a little like him. He damn sure sounds like him. "So, you told me this much. You might as well tell me the rest."

"Ju don't want to know, my friend. Besides, I don't come here to talk!" He jumps out of his seat, points towards the backroom, then slams a very large bankroll on the bar. At the top of his lungs he yells, "I come here to gamble!" Everybody in the bar looks up and cheers. "Hey Maw, I hear there's a big poker game going on back there. Ju in or what?"

"No, Nesto. I can't cheat good enough to play poker. I'd rather give my money to the blackjack gods. That's my game."

"I don't see no blackjock tables in here, Maw."

"Well, to tell you the truth, I was headed next door to Shaw's Palace Casino."

"OK, my friend — ju go count cards. I'm go pully aces out my chew."

We both have a good laugh at that—whatever he said. He

stumbles toward the backroom, stops and looks back at me, then says, "Hey, Maw! I like ju. Call me tomorrow. I fix ju up with my baby cee-ster. She's a real bitch."

Before I can ask him how I could contact him, he's disappeared down a hallway, headed to the backroom.

I figure what the hell, let him go. Story is probably bullshit, anyway. And boy—what a story! Quintana drug cartel, U.S. Government, big American company bail out, his baby cee-ster…he can't really think I would fall for that much crap.

The thing is, it's never good to try and con somebody when you're drunk; you always mess it up and come out looking like a liar. Nesto was pretty well fucked up, but I never caught anything that made him look like he was lying. What difference did it make? He didn't give me a way to contact him anyway.

I get up, tip the bartender, look at the door and yell loudly, "Let's go gamble!" I was almost embarrassed—that is, until everybody in the bar screamed back, 'Yeah!"

Las fucking Vegas. The Little Voice in the back of my head said, *"That was a close one."*

Walking out the Happy Snake Eyes, the first thing I see sitting right next to my rent-a-Ford is Nesto's low-slung, evil, black Lamborghini. I don't know what — but there's *something* about this guy.

I came in hot, and I'm still hot. Walking out of Shaw's Palace, I can see the light on the horizon. It's 4:45 a.m., the streets are still dark, but the skies are telling the vampires it's time to run for cover.

No problem for me. I'm like Wesley Snipes: I'm a day walker.

The all-nighter at Shaw's served me good, with three grand of my own money, and the eighteen hundred parlayed from Max's five hundred dollars at the last casino. All total for the evening's earnings: eighty-five hundred dollars. Not bad for first night out.

I pull out of the casino parking lot and shoot up UNLV Boulevard toward the Strip. I'm sitting at the same stop light as last night; I look over to my right, there's Nesto's Lamborghini, still sitting in the bar parking lot.

I look straight ahead, light turns green and I hit the gas. I'm outta here.

No, I'm not.

I'm turning the fucking wheel right into the parking lot, right back into the same parking spot as last night, right next to the Lamborghini.

As I'm getting out of the rent-a-Ford, the Little Voice in my head gets out of bed, looks around and starts in on me. *"Mann, how in the hell did we wind up back here? Are you serious? If you're not going to listen to me, how about I go find someone else to look out for? This is why you never have any money when you leave Vegas. I'm serious: you go in there, I'm never talking to you again."*

And just like that, I'm back in the Happy Snake Eyes.

Vegas never sleeps. It's about 5:00 a.m. and inside the Happy Snake Eyes people are talking, music's playing, slot machines are singing. I don't see Nesto at the bar, so his poker game is probably in hyper-drive right now. I grab a drink from the bar and head to the back room.

This is just like in the movies: I walk through a beaded curtain, make a left, and then head down a short hallway. I enter a room thick with cigarette smoke, a single low - hanging light over a poker table. Chairs are knocked over. Nobody's at the table. A door standing wide open leads out to what looks like the alley. This sure as hell ain't right.

Little Voice is on duty. *"Mann, I don't like the looks of this! Get the hell out of here. Now!"*

I head towards the back door as Little Voice scolds me. *"You're not going to listen to me, are you? Oh, brother, here we go again!"*

I move slowly and carefully as I ease up to the back door. Voices are coming from out back; they don't sound happy. Standing at the doorway, I take a quick peek around the corner, and yep, there's Nesto being held up against the wall in-between two trash dumpsters. Five guys are all over him. They're big, mean, seriously pissed off — and if they are not Mafia, I'm a Russian ballerina. What the fuck now?

I don't know if this is cartel shit or backroom poker shit, and I don't really want to know. What I do know is that they don't know I'm here, so I'll just stand still and listen for a second. If this is cartel shit, I'm so gone—it'll be Denver before I stop moving. If this is poker shit, maybe Nesto got caught "pulling aces out of his chew."

Another quick peek. They've got him pinned against the

wall and it looks like they've already tenderized him. There's a guy on each side holding an arm. I can see Nesto's mouth is bleeding, and in my head I can hear him say, *'Maw, thees no look so good.'*

A guy with a fat pinky ring is standing to one side. His suit looks like it cost more than I have in my pockets. He nods his head toward the guy right in front of Nesto, then— POW! He drives his jumbo-size fist deep into Nesto's gut. I hear the rush of air before Nesto coughs, then — splash!—he pukes all over the guy's shoes, earning him another fist in the face.

I don't know what the problem is with Nesto — but it sure looks like they're willing to kill him. If they don't, at this rate, he'll still be walking bent over for a month.

The pinky ring guy says, "Listen, you little Mexican or Colombian fuck! We were nice enough to let you come and lose ten large to us. We even gave you a five large marker, so you could keep playing. Then we waited patiently for 'your cee-ster' to show up and cover the money you lost."

He stops talking, looks around at the rest of them. The others all laugh, and I can tell that he's the boss.

"But then, you fucking wetback" — he gets right up in Nesto's face— "you tell *me* in front of my people here to suck your dick, and that I'll get my money when you say I will —and until then, to sit my fat fucking ass in my seat and play poker, because I'm starting to sound like some bitch you used to screw…and now, you puke all over Big Paulie's new shoes."

POW!

Nesto catches another right in the ribs. Pinky Ring Guy leans into Nesto's face. "That's right: I. Remember. Every. Word. That. Came. Out. Of. That. Little. Nasty. Spick. Mouth."

Now that I know what's happened, I feel better about being there — but I'm not so sure about Nesto's future.

I'll bet all the money in my pocket that Nesto was so drunk, they cheated the shit out of him. By the time he woke up to what they were doing, he lost his temper, and started shit-talking — in between shots of whiskey.

Not the best idea, especially with these goons.

The boss guy's talking, and it ain't sounding good. "Now, Mr. Ricardo, or Poncho, or whatever they call you. I let you call your sister three times, and she's still not here. You can't pay me my money, and you can't buy Paulie here another pair of shoes. What do you think I should do?"

Nesto mumbles something that I can't make out. But I know it was the wrong thing, because Mr. Puke Shoes lets him have another one right in the face. Then the boss guy continues.

"Now Mr. Smart Mouth, this is what you're gonna do. You're gonna get down on that fucking ground and lick that shit off of Big Paulie's shoes. And if he doesn't like the way you tongue-shine his shoes, I'm gonna blow your fucking brains out."

He pulls out the biggest snub nose .357 I've ever seen in my life and puts it up to Nesto's ear, then says, "Either that, or I'll just blow you away right now."

I hear the gun hammer click. I reach in my pocket and pull out the cash that was just making me smile a few minutes ago, and step into the alleyway.

"I'm sorry fellas, I was looking for the bathroom. Any of you seen my drunk Colombian friend? I'm supposed to give him some money, then take him home to his very rich, very powerful drug cartel brother. I think you guys may have heard of him? Lanceo Quintana!"

Everybody pulls out their pistols and point them at me. I hear that Little Voice again, and it says, *"Aw, fuck!"*

Mr. Pinky Ring asks, "Who the fuck are you?"

"I'm Mann — Mann Walker. I'm here to pick up Mr. Quintana."

As I count out five thousand dollars, I'm saying a prayer in my head. Don't ask me why I gave my real name; it just came out. It's not like they're the police.

"So, 'Mr. Mann,' is it?"

"No. Mr. Walker; Mann Walker. My father said he's not raising a boy, he's raising a man."

"That's real nice. Tell your father I said so— *if* you get to see him again."

"I'm in no hurry, he passed away years ago."

"Well, you might get to see him a lot sooner than you think."

My Little Voice won't leave me alone. *"Real nice move there, brother. Now what?"*

I'm thinking as fast as I can. I look at Nesto lying in a ball on the ground and I say the only thing that comes to mind. "Oh, I see Mr. Quintana has fallen down. Can I tip you nice fellas for helping him up? Say, oh, about five thousand dollars, maybe?"

I hold the money out in front of me. Mr. Pinky Ring takes a couple of steps towards me. He looks at the money and says, "He didn't fall down, we *knocked* him down. And he don't owe five thousand dollars. He owes ten thousand dollars."

"*Ten* thousand!"

"Yeah, ten thousand! He insulted me, and he ruined Big Paulie's shoes. And now you're wasting my time—so it's about to become *fifteen* thousand. What's it gonna be? And cut with the bullshit."

They're all looking at me. They all have the guns pointed at me. Nobody's smiling.

"OK, this is the deal. I'm not here from his brother, I just met him earlier tonight. All I got on me is eight and a half thousand — take it. The guy's a long way from broke. He's just a little drunk, and his people are pissed at him. I know he's sorry he fucked with you fellas; give him a pass. Take the dough and let's get out of this alley. It's getting light. The cops are bound to see us, and I know you guys don't need the trouble."

"First off, Mr. Mann, it's *you* who don't need the trouble. What we do in the dark, we do in the light. *Capiesce?*"

He's right in my face now. His breath stinks like shit cigars dipped in garlic, he's patting me on the side of my face, and more importantly, he's got that goddamn cannon of a gun jammed right against my dick. He's almost whispering.

"Second of all, *brotha* — the cops?" He looks around. The rest of them give a little laugh on cue. "The cops, *they-don't-see-us*." He snatches the money from my hand, looks at it, and then hands it off to one of his other guys. "You must really like this guy or something. This money yours or his?"

"Mine."

He steps back and tells the money holder, "Give this guy a C-note." Mr. Pinky Ring points his stinking cigar at my face. "Go buy yourself some new friends; your old ones are gonna get you killed."

One of the guys that the boss man calls 'Lenny' speaks up. "Boss, it's getting late, don't forget that thing we have to take care of in Reno."

That seems to put Mr. Pinky Ring's focus on other things. He says, "Oh shit, I almost forgot, thanks to these two assholes." With a quick nod of his head, the group of thugs turn to go — but not before giving Nesto a few good kicks.

Right before walking through the door, he stops and stares back at me with the coldest look: there's no doubt that he's a killer. His voice is cold as his look. "You come out here with pennies in your fucking hand, dropping names like I'm supposed to jump and run. Well, here's a name for you: *Cus Barlow*. And I don't give a fuck about no fucking 'cartel.' Fuck him and his brother! He can't even come in this country. Take that piece of shit laying over there and find somewhere else to play, because if I ever see him again, I'll cut his head off and use it for a hood ornament."

He turns and walks back inside The Happy Snake Eyes. The guy behind him has to add his two cents.

"Yeah, I'm gonna use it for a salad bowl!"

Not to be bested, Mr. Puke Shoes says, "No, no —I'm gonna drink a margarita out of it!" Walking back inside, they all get a good laugh out of it. The door slams, and I could still hear them inside, busting a gut.

My Little Voice has to have the last word. *"Vacation, huh?"*

Nesto probably wouldn't look this bad if he fell out of an airplane at 30,000 feet. These guys could teach Officer Spriggs and the Denver Police Department a thing or two about busting a guy up. To be honest, Nesto really should go to the hospital but he says that's not happening, and take him to his hotel.

Looking at him, the first question I have is one I can't hold in. "How we gonna walk into a hotel and you look like this? Your clothes are covered with blood, and your face? Oh, brother — your face! What hotel are you at, anyway?"

"Ceeth-zar's Palathe."

"Did you say 'Caesar's Palace'? Between your accent and that fat lip, I can't tell what you're saying!"

"Jes, my friend, Ceeth-zar's Palathe."

"You're going to walk in Caesar's Palace looking like that?"

Nesto looks down at himself. His shirt is covered with blood and puke; his lip is twice its normal size, and he's got the beginnings of a black eye. He's still lying on the ground so I can't tell if he can even stand up straight. I doubt it. But he answers me with an attitude.

"I thspend a lot of money there; they take care of me."

I help him to his feet, and just like I thought, he can barely walk. We finally head out the alley, taking the long way around. There's no way we're going back through the Happy Snake Eyes.

When we get to the parking lot, Nesto gives me the keys to the Lamborghini. Fuck it: the rent-a-Ford can stay. Getting him in the Lamborghini with busted-up ribs was a bit of a problem — for him, anyway—but once inside, he was able to stretch out.

"So do I have to ask, or you going to tell me how you got yourself in that jam?" Trying to start this thing was a puzzle. Nesto pointed to the start button; I pressed it and

BOOM! "I got a friend back in Denver with a Ferrari, but it doesn't sound like this!"

I look over at Nesto. He's clearly not feeling my enthusiasm right now, so I try and ease it out the parking lot and head up UNLV Boulevard towards the Strip. Finally Nesto speaks.

"They sheeted me."

"They *what*?"

"Sheeted me. They sheeted me, ju know…"

"Oh — they *cheated* you! I guessed that much. Don't you know better than to get in a private game with a bunch of people you don't know? On top of that, you're totally drunk! If I knew you didn't know those guys, I would have at least hung out with you."

"I never been there before, I couldn't win a hand. They kept laughing after every hand, so I knew something was wrong. The one guy, I think they call him Lenny—he was one of the guys holding me against the wall."

"Lenny, huh? He looked more like a 'Lurch'. Nesto, you don't know how lucky you are to still be alive."

"He kept getting up and going behind me, said he was getting drinks."

"Well, if you knew they were cheating, why didn't you just get up and leave?"

"I could have, but I just wanted to teach them a lesson. Ju know, beat them at their own game. Mr. Big Shot—that guy who took jour money? He kept calling me names, like 'wetback', 'grease ball'— ju know, sheet like that!"

"Yeah, Nesto—looks like they saw you coming. Set you up real nice. Speaking of which, I hope you weren't bullshitting me about your brother. You got beat out of ten thousand dollars back there, and I just handed over damn near nine thousand to save your little happy ass."

"Yes, Maw, thanks for that. Ju real good people. Why ju do that anyway? Ju just met me."

"I don't know Nesto, something about it didn't set right with me. I just couldn't stand there and let them kill you and *they* were the ones cheating! I mean, why would they give a guy they never met before a five-thousand dollar marker? Because, my Colombian friend, they couldn't lose. They were cheating, hoping your money would show up so they could keep screwing you all night. By the way, why didn't your money show up?"

"Because I never send for more money, that's why. I didn't need any cash, I thought I could play my way out the hole. But..." Nesto gives a half-assed gesture.

"'But'? 'But' my ass, Nesto! They were cheating — you couldn't win!"

"I figured that out, but I still wasn't giving them any more money."

Now I'm pissed. This guy isn't making any sense, and talking crazy as well. I just took one hell of a chance just to save a nut, and I let him know it. "Are you crazy or something? You know what? Fuck it! I don't care if you are suicidal. I don't care if you don't have a penny to pay me back! And you know why? Because until I get my money I own this Lamborghini, that's why!"

"Maw..."

"What!" Nesto is giving me a contrite look.

"It's a rental."

I'm stunned. "What? You piece of shit! So you *don't* have

any money?"

"Maw, I didn't say that. I said I wasn't giving *them* any more money, OK? Now pull over."

I stop the car on a side street. The sun is up. It's 6:15 AM, it's already 85 degrees, and the heat is starting its daily sweat check.

Nesto tries to reach behind his seat, but his ribs ain't having it. "Maw, look behind the seat. There's a bag back there; pull it out."

I pull out a shoulder bag; it's heavy as hell and pretty warm to touch, since the Lamborghini's engine is right behind us. "So, the car isn't yours," I say as I hand the bag to Nesto.

"No, Maw, I don't live in the U.S. I'm just here all the time. I told ju last night I'm here on official beezness."

"It's 'business' not 'beezness,' Nesto. We gotta work on that accent."

He takes the bag, opens it, and then hands it to me. I take one look inside, and my mouth flies open; I can't help myself.

"Oh yeah! That's what I'm talking about! So how much is it?"

"I think about a hundred and seventy-five thousand," says Nesto calmly, "give or take ten thou."

The bag is full of stacks of hundred-dollar bills. Then it hit me. "You dumb fuck, you had all this cash in the car, and you let them beat on you like that over a few thousand dollars? What's your problem — you got a death wish?"

"Fuck them! I no scared to die!"

"Well, *I no scared to die* either, but I also *in no rush* to die, Nesto!"

I couldn't be sure whether he's crazy, or it was just an honor thing with him, but I could tell that he wasn't kidding. I figure it's best I get what he owes me and keep it moving. "So, do I take what I need, or what?"

"If ju want jour money, I give it to ju —but I got a deal for ju. Let's get to the hotel and I'll tell ju what I got for my new friend. Ju ok with that?"

"OK, let me think." I look in that money bag again. It didn't take me twenty seconds to give him the answer he already knew was coming.

"Uh, yeah, I think I got time to listen to you."

My Little Voice is back and talking. *"Just when I was about to give you credit for a job well done…"*

Pulling into the Caesar's Palace parking lot, Nesto has me stop by the side door. He's talking on the cell phone to somebody named Lester. A few seconds later, the side door opens and a bell captain comes out, pushing a wheel chair.

Nesto points at him and tells me, "Maw, this is Lesther. He's the bell captain at Ceeth-zar's Palathe. He's the man to know, and he takes care of me when I come to Vegas."

We help Nesto into the wheelchair. He was really beginning to feel that ass-kicking now.

"No hospital for you, huh," I joke. "Real tough Colombian."

I smile, but Nesto ain't feeling me. If anything, he's probably re-thinking his earlier strategy back at the Happy Snake Eyes. Lester tells him that the doctor is waiting for him in his room. I look at Nesto, and I guess he can read my mind.

"I told ju, Lester is the man to know. Take the car around to the front; the doorman will take care of it. I'm in Room 8700. It's the Honeymoon Suite."

"The 'Honeymoon Suite'. Ain't that cute! Where's the bride?"

"Haven't found her jet, but don't worry. I know where a real nice whorehouse is."

"I bet you do!"

"Ju better hand me that bag, just in case."

I reach in the car, pull out the bag with the cash. I still can't believe how heavy the money is. When I get to Nesto sitting in the wheelchair, I lift the bag up real high over him, then let it drop right in his lap.

"Owww! Ju *peen-chee cabron!*"

Lester fights back a laugh and covers up Nesto with the blanket, celebrity style.

His head and face is covered up, so he looks like an old

lady with a large purse in her lap. They go through the door, leaving me standing on the side of Caesar's Palace by an emergency exit. I'm standing by a shiny black Lamborghini with both doors up in the air. Anywhere else in the country, this would look strange.

Not in Vegas.

I really need to talk to Monica. Jumping back in the Lamborghini, I take the car and zip over to the Holiday Inn. Everybody at least once in a lifetime needs to scream down Las Vegas Boulevard in a Lamborghini. As I pass by, it seems like all the men have tears of jealousy in their eyes, and all the females are stopping to look at me with wide-gapped legs and their tops off.

Well, it looks like that to *me*.

It doesn't take but a minute or two to reach the hotel. I walk in the room, and Monica is so used to this type of routine from me, she's not even upset. I hope.

She quickly starts in on me.

"Babe, I know you, and when you hit the streets you're always trying to do more than you have time for. In Denver I'm ok with that: that's home. But out here, we're supposed to be on vacation. When I don't hear from you, well you know, I get a little scared."

"I'm sorry, babe. I'm OK." And I really am sorry to make her worry.

"Well," says Monica, her tone changing suddenly, "if you're OK—where the fuck you been all night?"

So much for her not being upset. I start with the old favorite, and as it came out my mouth, it sounded like a bunch of bullshit—even to me. "You're not going to believe this one, babe!"

I tell myself "what the fuck," I grab my shaving kit and take out the fake bottom. I pull out a fat baggie full of Colombian marching powder. Between snorts, I try and tell Monica about last night's adventure. And tell her everything — everything *except* the guns, the mob, and the cartel. You know I had to re-arrange the story a little bit. She worries too much.

All she really needed to know was: "I found a rich guy behind a bar, he was hurt and I helped him out." And with that, I take off my clothes and head to the shower.

I hear a couple of sniffs—and they aren't from

crying—and then her footsteps outside the shower curtain. I peep outside the shower, and I see her standing there with no clothes on, just staring at the curtain. I pull it back to let her in.

Stepping in she says, "Sounds like a lot of crap to me! Mann, I'm not letting you out of my sight until you prove it."

"Don't worry babe, I got the proof sitting in the parking lot!"

She looks up at me. "I love you, you crazy son of a bitch."

"I know," I reply, smiling at her, "I know. How could you not? Now come here." One thing about Monica, she knows how to drain me and recharge me at the same time. After having a gun —a very big one, I might add — jammed against my dick a few hours earlier, I found a new appreciation for it, and expressed it quite well with Monica.

She was very happy and impressed with my newfound genital appreciation—so much so that she asked, "Wow, babe! What's got into you?"

"Oh, I just missed you, that's all," I said, pulling her close.

She had no idea that I almost became the new version of the headless horseman.

Monica ordered room service; we ate, got dressed. I called Nesto, and he said he was trying to regroup.

"I figured ju took the car on a pussy hunt."

I smiled. "Not exactly. How are you feeling anyway?"

"Tree bruised ribs, sew on the lip, and my head is killing me. But ju know, fuck them *pendejos!* I have a harder time at the whorehouse!

"Well, Nesto, I don't! Unlike you, I'm not into the pain thing. When I do go to the whorehouse, I don't play hard to get with their money – *Oops!*" No sooner than I said it, I realized that Monica was listening —and she let me know right away that she heard it all.

"What did you just say? Mann, who are you talking to? Did you go to a hoe house last night?"

"No, no, babe! It's the guy I told you about!"

Nesto is on the other end, asking questions. "Who the fuck ju talking to, Maw?" I forgot to tell him about

Monica.

"Don't trip, Nesto, it's my wife."

Monica is not happy about now. "So *now* I'm your wife!"

"Wife! Ju got a wife? Poor guy," snickers Nesto.

"Was I your wife last night?" Monica is standing stark naked with her hands on her hips, glaring down at me.

"Ju didn't tell me ju was married! And I was gonna hook ju up with my babe cee-ster. She's a real bi-"

"Yeah, yeah, I know, Nesto," I reply. "Yeah, I know — she's a real bitch."

Monica totally misunderstands the conversation I'm having with Nesto. "*Bitch?* Who are you calling a bitch?"

"No, babe, not *you*!" Things are going bad, fast. "Oh, fuck it! Nesto, I gotta call you back."

"OK. Can ju be here in two hours?" I look over at Monica, who now *is* in Full Bitch mode.

"I'll make it one."

"Good! We gotta go somewhere."

Considering the last 24 hours with Nesto, I have to ask. "Where?"

"To get rich, my friend!" That was the right answer to grab my attention and pep me up a little.

It took a while, but I manage to calm Monica down. I have to admit, it did sound bad. When we leave the room, she's still tight as a boxer before a prizefight. I'm not too worried: I got that black, four-wheeled trump card in the parking lot.

Just like I thought, she about jumped out of her clothes when the valet pulls the Lamborghini around, gets out, and holds the door for me while the other valet holds the door for Monica. She looks over at me with the sexiest smile I've ever seen on her.

"I told you I met a rich guy last night! I gotta go meet him here in a few, so I'm going to give you some money. You can either hit the casino or go shopping." I handed her two thousand dollars.

She looked at me, then at the money, then back at me.

I grinned at her. "What? You're fucking with a high roller now, babe!"

"I'll be fucking with a *dead* roller if you're up to something, Mann. I promise you: I'll put you, this car and any chicken-head bitch I catch you with in the E.R.!"

I just smile and tell her, "It's nothing like that, babe." To try and get her mind off *that* subject, we zoom up and down Las Vegas Boulevard a few times.

At the same time, I'm attempting to get that big, nervous lump down my throat: those gap-legged, topless females are back. I have to admit the damn car is sexy as hell. When you hit it just right, the car hollers, making goose bumps stand up on your arms.

I whip up in front of the Mandalay Bay Hotel. The Lambo is doing its thing—black paint shining, the engine talking. Monica is loving it. The valet heads for my door, but I wave him off and point to Monica. I push a button and the door goes up, like only a Lamborghini does. Seems like everybody going in and out of the hotel stops to see who it is.

Monica takes her cue. She steps out of the car, head up, ass out—she's fine as hell when she wants to be, and today she is on point! She leans back into the car and gives me a '10' on the Wet Kiss meter. Then as she's walking away from the car, she says, "I got my fucking eyes on you."

God knows why I love her; one day I wish He'd tell me why I do. She turns on her heels and struts it hard into the hotel. I see a few people not sure who they're looking at, then I hear *click-click*. First they get a few pictures of Monica, then they turn their cameras on me.

I could get used to this. The attention and car get the best of me, and I spin tires burning out of the parking lot. Must be my lucky day.

Back on Las Vegas Boulevard, I do my best not to look at the now completely-nude "super models" lining both sides of the road. The temptation is getting a little too close.

Speaking aloud to myself, I say "I gotta get out of this thing! Where is Caesar's Palace?"

I spot the hotel and make a beeline to it, pulling up in front of a valet. They're all over me like a pit crew. The doors open and getting out of the Lamborghini, I stretch my legs and look around.

Everything is back to normal: no more super models, all the women are fully clothed and don't give me a second look. I glance back at the Lamborghini. It's not a car, it's some kind of fantasy chamber. The valet hops in and takes off. I'm glad to see it go. I see Lester standing by the valet stand, and he waves me over.

"Nesto's cool," he says. "A little busted up, but he heals fast."

"'Heals fast! Has this happened before?"

"Well, nothing quite like this, but you know Nesto."

I shake my head. "No, I don't know Nesto!"

Lester hesitates for a moment. "I hope you know what you're doing. Anyway, he's waiting for you upstairs. You know the way up?"

"I'll find it."

Jumping off the elevator, I find his room with no problem. I stop at the door to take a listen— not to the room, but to the Little Voice in my head. I can always count on a little bit of wisdom when I'm about to cross an unknown threshold.

But, nope, not a word. I don't know if it's a good or bad sign. Who knows? My Little Voice must be back in the bed, sleeping - and that's something I'll need to do, soon. I haven't closed my eyes since before I left Denver.

Right as I'm about to knock, the door swings open. We both kind of jump. She looks at me, I look at her. "Who are ju?"

Oh, shit – that accent. This must be Baby Cee-ster! And I mean, *Ba-bee!*

I clear my throat. "Hello, I'm Mann."

"Maw." She calls out to someone in the suite. "Hey, Nesto! Ju expecting a 'Maw'?"

I can hear Nesto's voice answering her. "It depends on what maw it is."

She looks at me. "What Maw are ju?"

"No, my name isn't 'Maw,' it's 'Mann'; Mann Walker. I'm the one who helped Nesto out of a jam this morning."

"Oh, *ju* the guy who saved Nesto! Please come in!" This woman is *beautiful*. I swear, I am so hoping this isn't

Baby Cee-ster.

She leads me into a large front room, and over on the couch is what looks like the mummy. It's Nesto, and he's wrapped from head to toe. I gotta tease him. "For lack of a better word, brotha, it looks like you got beat the fuck up!"

"I know it looks worse than it is," replied Nesto. "Every time I try to take this sheet off, my cee-ster over there puts it back on."

I laugh. "No more back room poker, huh!" By the look on Nesto's face, I knew right away I had just fucked up.

"Poker? Poker! Ju didn't say anything about no *peen-chee* poker! Ju say it was some gangbangers, trying to car-jack ju!" She stomped out the room, cussing furiously in Spanish.

"Sorry, Nesto! I guess I let the cat out of the bag."

"Don't worry about it. She's always bitching about something. She acts like she's the oldest."

I'm thinking about what Nesto just said: "She acts like she's the oldest." I gotta ask.

"Is that who I think it is," I ask, hoping I sound casual.

"Jeah, Maw—that's my baby cee-ster."

Uh-oh. "Monica gonna kill me," I mutter to myself.

"What did ju just say?"

"Nothing, not a thing." I'll cross *that* Monica-Bridge when I get there. "Where do we go from here?"

"Maw, ju good people—I like ju. What ju do back home?"

"I'm in the business. I'm pretty sure I've probably sold some of your stuff before in the past."

"I figured as much, I knew we had something in common." Nesto peers at me. "Ju want to try it on a bigger level?"

"I haven't thought about it. It took me a long time to get things just right, you know what I mean? But thanks to a friend, I might have to make some unscheduled changes."

"What's wrong? Somebody talking to the *policia*?"

"No, just a friend pissed off at dirty cop, but he said he's taking care of it."

"How ju say it? 'Famous last words.' "

I hope not, but I know Max, and there's no telling what to expect with him. I don't say as much to Nesto, but he can see it on my face. I try and change the subject.

"So…what are we doing here? I'm still eight big ones in your pocket, and I'm supposed to be on vacation with my lady."

"If ju like, I give ju the fifteen grand that Mr. Big Shot wanted to end my life for last night, and ju could leave now. But if jour as half as smart as I think ju are, I can help ju get ten time that much, in only couple of days."

The Little Voice in the back of my head returns. *"Take the money and run like hell! Mann, we don't need this. If you do this, I'm never talking to you again."*

"So – Nesto…*ten* times as much?"

"Yes. And that's only the beginning."

The Voice is trying to reason with me. *"The beginning? Oh, yeah—sure it is. Mann, let's get the hell out here. Now, please?'*

I smile at Nesto. "I'm all ears."

The Voice has only more one thing to say. *"Oh, fuck!"*

CHAPTER 3

"OK, OK – I'm coming! Who the fuck is it?"

"It's me! Can I come in?"

"Bill?"

"Yeah, it's me!"

"What the hell, why are you at my door? You in some more trouble?" Max snatches the door open, takes one look and almost slams it back. "Bill, what the fuck is your problem? What are you thinking — that I'm the Salvation Army Rescue Mission? Look at you, you're really losing it! Come in here before one of my neighbors sees your ass!"

Max glances behind Bill. "Oh, shit— what the fuck are you doing with *her*!"

"Hi." She gives a quick grin.

"Yeah. 'Hi'. Bill, follow me: we need to talk!"

Max quickly ushers Bill and companion into his condo, slams the front door, then turns to the pair in front of him.

"You — *young* lady — have a seat. I've got some PopTarts in the fridge, and you can watch cartoons if you want — they still come on Saturday morning?" He gives Bill a hard look, and practically drags him into the bedroom.

"Bill! Bill, you better listen real carefully to me. It took a lot of cash, leg work, and ass-kissing to clean up that fiasco you created at the Montville Hotel. I had to bribe the front desk clerk so they would take your name off the registry, and you don't want to know how much that cost! I had to pay off the maid to clean up the room and not go tell the hotel security that the room was covered in wall-to-wall cocaine."

Max looks ready to toss Bill out the condo window. "Then there's that little pervert bell boy who somehow managed to pop up with his hand open, too! And let us not forget Miss Nicky! To keep her happy, I'll be in debt for a very long time." Max stops to catch his breath. "Hey! Why aren't you at work? And why do you have the head D.A.'s crack-smoking daughter with you? And why in the fuck did you bring her over *here*?"

Bill seems to be thinking carefully about how to answer. Then he finally says, "I was up all night at a motel with Anna."

"Anna? Oh, is that her name? Here's a better question for you, Bill. How *old* is Anna?" Max's face is flushed and sweaty with anger.

"She's almost seventeen."

"Seventeen, huh? And how 'most' is 'almost'?"

"Her birthday is in March, so she's almost 17!"

Max stares directly in Bill's face. "OK, Bill—look at me. This is good ol' Max talking to you. You know, Crazy Max, the nutty DJ that will do just about anything, right? Now if there's something that old Max *won't* do, then it's pretty fair to say the rest of the world shouldn't even think about attempting them, you know what I'm saying?"

Bill nods.

"Ok, so. Let me put it this way, Bill: *fucking the Head D.A.'s underage druggie daughter* is at the very top of the 'Things I'd Never Do' list!"

Bill opens his mouth to answer.

"No, No, Bill, the only thing I want to know from you right now is why you are over here with that crazy little bitch, and not at work?"

"I got Day-Day to cover for me," mutters Bill.

"*Day-Day?* He doesn't even work at the station. He's a fuckin' intern from the local high school and he's the one that should be screwing little Miss D.A., not your old ass! And if her birthday is in March? Well, this is June — which means she's not 'almost seventeen' — it means she only turned *sixteen* three months ago! Have you totally lost your mind?"

"She only looks young. She's smart—funny, too. I know girls twice her age that don't know half the stuff she does."

"No, no," replies Max, "she's not smart, she's not funny—she *is* strung out, and so are you! You have to take her home right now. How long have the two of you been running around?"

"A few days, give or take." He frowns a bit. "I don't know, I guess I lost count. She moved in with me."

"She moved in with you? Then why were you at a motel last night?"

Bill is speaking to Max as if he were slightly mentally deficient. "Well, I got to thinking: when she came to my place, she took a cab. What if her father could somehow trace the cab and get my address— and came looking for her? I didn't want to be at my home with her getting high."

"Dammit, Bill— Even you know you're out of line!" Max's urge to toss Bill off his condo balcony is growing. "My God, we're so fucked!"

Bill is silent for a moment, then he asks a question. "Max? You got some stuff?"

"Are you for real?" In Max's mind, Bill making an exit via the balcony is beginning to sound better with each passing minute. "If it weren't for the fact that I gave you your first hit, I would throw you out on your ass, and call the cops myself!"

Bill is still looking at him, waiting for the possibility of a quick hit.

"No, no, I take that back," mumbles Max. "Let me think: what would Mann do? Think Max, think! Fuck it! Now *I* need a hit!"

He digs through his drawer, and comes up with a baggie of white powder. "Good old Mann. I'm glad that I saved this before he left for Vegas."

"Vegas? You got this blow from the guy we gave the trip to? That's cool." Bill would high-five anybody who gave up the white powder.

"Bill, don't you ever repeat that to anybody. I'm going to hate myself in the morning, but here. Take this shit and go in the back room with Little Miss Poison Ivy out there. Do whatever it is that you do: I don't want to know. But don't either one of you leave this condo! I can't afford to have the two of you running all over the city, half out your fucking heads. *Especially* if they're out looking for her." He picks up his car keys and wallet. "I gotta go somewhere. If you need anything, *call* me and I'll bring it to you. Neither of you go anywhere: Do. You. Hear. Me? Good!'

"Max…"

Max sighs. "Yes?"

"Thanks. I'm sorry if you think I fucked up."

"Think? Ha! Just don't try and go anywhere. And do me a favor: Stop thinking that you're smart as they come. When you're high, you are the dumbest son of a bitch I've ever met."

Max takes a small bit of coke out of the baggie, then gives the rest to Bill.

"One last thing, Bill. Let's go out here so I can ask Anna a few questions. You cool with that?"

Bill nods his head, and they both head into the front room.

Max starts. "Hi, Anna. You OK? Hungry or anything?"

"You can stop talking to me like I'm some fucking six-year old. I know what's up. This ain't my first rodeo! Ok, it may say '16' on my birth certificate, but a bitch knows how to handle herself."

Max can't tell how much of what she's saying is an act and how much is for real. For now, it's probably best to let her think she's in control.

"Ok, I guess you do. So, Anna: what's up with your dad? I know he's has to be worried about you. Have you talked to him?"

"Fuck him."

"Damn!" Max is shocked at her reply.

"That pervert, he ain't gonna do shit," replies Anna. "You're just like him. You're on the radio, talking all this crazy-ass cool shit. But when it comes down to it, you're chicken shit, a fake. Just like my father!"

Daddy issues, thinks Max. "Why do you call him a fake?"

"All my life, all he ever talked about is bad people, drug dealers, rapists, perverts, and bank robbers. I guess he thought if he told me all the screwed-up shit they did, it would scare me from being curious about that lifestyle. All it really did was make me that much more curious." Anna sounds like an accident waiting patiently to happen.

"Alright — if you know about the laws and how your dad is, then you must also know that if he finds out about you and Bill, he's gonna hang Bill's ass out for the wolves."

"Hang Bill? For what?"

"For what? Thought you said you were smart! Anna, you're not old enough to be out after midnight without a chaperone in this state— but both of you are using cocaine, which is a felony in this state last time I heard. As if that's not enough, he's also screwing you, and you're under legal age — *another* felony here in the fine state of Colorado."

Max is on a roll, and puts on a fake announcer voice: "*But hey, boys and girls — who isn't doing something stupid nowadays? I'd say heck, what's a couple of little felonies? There's just this one other small thing that's troubling me a little…can you guess what that is?*" Max is beginning to sound like a daytime TV game show.

"*Surprise! You're the head D.A.'s underage daughter! So — can we please see what prizes are waiting behind Curtain Number Three for our fabulous contestants?*"

Anna's arms are crossed, her hip is out and she has a sour look on her face, but Max is just hitting his stride.

"*Well, first off, we have six months of intense therapy for victims of child rape, followed by out-patient drug rehab, at your Aunt Mathilda's avocado ranch in sunny southern California. And when you finally get back home, all the love and support of the community for you, you poor abused little girl.*"

"Max, that's a bunch of bullshit. I don't even have an aunt–"

Max cuts her off. "But wait, there's more!" He strides over to Bill and points at him.

"*We can't forget about Bill here — dear old Bill. First off, you'll get all busted up by the police for being a child molester—and since it's the D.A.'s daughter we're talking about, they'll really let you have it. As a matter of fact, they'll probably damn near beat you to death. Then you'll sit in jail for months while the whole thing is played out in the press, on TV, online websites— you name it. And while that's happening, you'll have the pleasure of having your ass stomped out daily by the homeboys in jail. No one they like cozying up to more than a child molester, you know.*

"And because it was the D.A.'s daughter," Max points back at Anna, *"you'll lose in court and go to prison for a long stay with an even badder group of 'boyfriends'. If you somehow manage to live through that, don't forget what's waiting for you outside when you're tagged by Americans everywhere as a piece of shit sex-offender. No one will want to rent you an apartment or hire you. So — now that you know what we have planned for you —ding-ding-ding! — Come on down and get your prize!"*

Bill and Anna are laughing so hard they forget the trouble they're in.

"You're cool Max, just like on the radio! But…" She leans in real close to Max, looks him straight in the eyes, "I guess you didn't hear a word I said. My father, he's a bigger phony than you are. He ain't gonna do shit to Bill. I'll bet my sweet little young ass on that!"

"What makes you so sure?"

"Hah! I thought I was supposed to be the naive one! Well, don't worry your little brain. I got this one —don't I, Bill?"

She gives Bill a quick grin. "Now I heard you tell Bill we can kick it in your extra bedroom. Well, where is it? Come on Be-ill, I'm ready! Did he give you the stuff?"

Max asked, "Did you just call him 'Be-ill'?"

"Yea, that's what I call him. Shit, you guys think he's a nerd or punk. Hell, that's my Be-ill. And what am I, babe?"

"You're my ill-Be," grins Bill. He sits down next to her and kisses her hard on the mouth. Max can't believe that this is the very same guy he gave his first line of coke to just a few months ago. Bill and Anna whisper something to each other, then Bill gets a crazy smile on his face.

"Hey, Max! You want to see something really sick?"

"What? It can get sicker than this?"

Bill and Anna crack up, but Max isn't amused. He was serious.

Bill says, "OK, Max close your eyes. No, really! We ain't gonna hurt you."

Max sighs loudly, then slowly closes his eyes, hoping beyond all hope he's not going to regret it. He sits with his eyes closed for what seems like forever. Then he hears Bill.

"OK, Max. Open sesame!"

Max opens his eyes, and jumps back at the same time. "Hey, Bill! That's on you! I ain't going out like that!"

The couple burst out laughing again. Anna is standing right in front of Max, with nothing on but her shirt and panties.

"What a chump," she says. "I knew you were full of shit, but I didn't know you were gay to boot!"

Bill grins. "Max, relax —she ain't tryin' to rape you! She's just trying to show you something. Now sit down."

Max looks at the both of them, and slowly sits down. Whatever she's trying to show him, he wishes she'd hurry up and get it over with.

Bill looks excited, and says, "Ok, Maxie, here it comes!"

Anna starts dancing from side to side while she's pulling down the top of her panties. Right in the middle where the pubic hair should start, Max can see what looks like letters from a fresh tattoo. He tries to refocus his eyes, and he makes out the words. He's still trying to understand what he's looking at when it hits him.

The words, "PARTY KILLS" are as plain as day. Max leans back and looks up at Anna. She sits down and slowly opens her right leg. On the inside of her thigh, it says "LET'S." Then she opens the left leg, and there's more writing. This time, Max reads "DIE." Max thinks to himself while reciting aloud what he's just read: "PARTY KILLS. LET'S DIE."

Before Max can begin to put it together in his head, Bill says, "Sick, ain't it? We got it tatted last week. Max! Don't trip—we're in control!"

Anna nods her head towards the back bedroom. She gets up and walks down the hallway.

Max is still staring where Anna was sitting, and he hasn't blinked.

"I told you she ain't no fucking kid," Bill grins, as he heads to the back bedroom and slams the door.

Max is sitting alone in the room. *'Whatever's going on in that little girl's head, it runs a lot deeper than dope,'* he thinks. *'She's just running, just like everybody else who gets high. Getting high, thinking she can outrun the ugly truth.'*

After a few minutes, Max becomes aware that there are noises coming from the bedroom. He does his best to shut them out. He was ready to get away from these two a long time ago, but they wouldn't let him. They may have kept his legs from walking out the door, but his mind was long gone.

◆────────────◈────────────◆

Nesto, you falling asleep?"

"No, Maw. Just thinking."

"About what?"

"My little problem."

I gotta ask. "And that is?"

"I got this rich guy – *really* rich guy. He's so rich he thinks he don't have to pay his bills, because everybody loves a rich guy, right? This rich guy, he loses a lot of money on Wall Street. He's not broke but he's greedy, so he tries another investment – and BAM! He loses his ass on that one, too. He's still not broke, but he's not so quick with the money anymore. Along comes his big, rich friends. They tell him they're investing in a billion-dollar hotel in Vegas. It's gonna be the biggest, baddest hotel ever built. Each investor puts up about 50 million apiece, and in a few years, they'll watch the money come rolling in."

Nesto takes a deep breath. "The rich guy has the money to invest, but he don't want to use his dough – well, not *that* much, anyway. So he gets wind of a deal that this big shot computer CEO pulled a year or two ago. Ju know the one —with the peace sign on the back: Peace Computers. Remember when they were supposed to be bankrupt? Then just like *that*: they were back in the black.

"Well, the company president Darrel Fench did what everybody does nowadays when in need of a quick cash injection. They find a Colombian like my brother, order a shipment of cocaine, sell it and live happily ever after – or until they get broke again."

"Nesto, Darrel Fench pulled Peace Computers out of bankruptcy selling dope?"

"Yep."

This can't be right. "Bullshit! I've been selling this shit for years – something as big as that, I would have heard about it. It would have been impossible to keep that a secret."

"You don't know shit, Maw."

"Nesto, I knew about the Air Force flying C130 transport planes packed with cocaine into the country, long before the press did. I knew about the drug lords controlling the New Orleans police force. I knew about the giant warehouse in L.A. that kept half the West Coast in cocaine!"

"And how did ju find out about all this stuff?"

"For a couple of them, I was in the know because of the people I deal with," I reply. The other, well, it was just a matter of good business practices. If my supplier is consistent with good product, then I try to cut out the middle man by finding out who his supplier is. That way I get a better price. If you look hard enough, even if you can't reach the guy at the top, you still manage to find out who he is."

Nesto started to clap, then says, "What if he don't have no sales over here?"

"What do you mean by that?"

"Jour boy Darrel Fench has a company that sells product, worldwide. And it just so happens he sells computers in England. The British coke habit is not too far behind the Americans, ju know. But it's a lot harder to get it in over there. The British are more honor-bound. Trying to bribe a British official is risky business; they'll set ju up in a heartbeat. It got even worst with the terrorist shit. The British just weren't playing that shit when it came to their borders. 'No' *meant* 'No'! But it was a gold mine for the one who could get large shipments in. And leave it to the nerdy computer geek to pull it off."

"Ok, Nesto, now did Darrel Fench get British customs in his pocket?"

"He didn't get anybody in his pocket," said Nesto. "His computers are so popular over there, he walked the shit through their Customs on his reputation alone. Every time a shipment with his logo on it showed up, the British wanted the computer products bad, they were like, 'fuck the red tape' that everybody else has to go through. Nobody ever thought there could be a connection between Peace Computers and the sudden surge in coke."

"Wow, Nesto. Is he still doing it??

"Hell no! Why should he? He got his company out of debt and passed the ball to next broke billionaire."

I'm trying to keep up with Nesto's explanation. "What do you mean, 'passed the ball'?"

"It's still going on. It's kind of a running joke with the rich. Any big American company that gets hard up for cash — if they already ship products into the British market, they get with my brother or the local competition, get a few thousand pounds of blow, put it in a shipping container, slap their American brand name and flag on it, put it on a boat to England, and in thirty to sixty days, they clear a tax-free hundred million or so."

"So what's with the rich guy that won't pay his bills?"

Nesto's smiling face changed in a blink of an eye with the question. "This fuck sends for one hundred keys. My greedy brother, in a rush as usual, sends the shit up here. They put it in this rich guy's ranch house, right outside of Vegas. Everything is right on schedule. Then the guy gets cold feet, says his buyer has backed out of deal."

"So, sell the shit to somebody else, right?"

"That's what we all think, but my genius brother gets impatient and send him a message: *pay up or else he'll have his head at the end of stick,* or some dumb shit like that. The old fuck gets scared and run to Europe. He sends his own message: he says that he has other business in Europe to attend to, so *"please come and remove supply from his property".* If it's still there when he returns from this trip in about 180 days, he have the American government remove it!"

"Ain't that a bitch? So I guess that's where you need my help to pick it up?

"Jeah, Maw! There's been so much noise about this whole thing, I don't even know if the shipment is safe."

"Nesto, I wish you could say my name right." The conversation is disturbed by Nesto's phone ringing. Again, I'm left alone with my own thoughts. Listening to Nesto converse in Spanish, a thought pops into my head: I'm a little worried about what his answer is going to be. Right then, I hear Baby Cee-ster behind me.

"Ju hungry, Mr. Walker?"

"No, I'm fine – and it's 'Mann', ok?"

"Mann…like a *man*, right," she replies.

"Yeah, that's it. And that's a lot better than your brother says it."

She's a real looker, that's for sure. I don't know why she's not on the cover of somebody's magazine. Trying to keep my cool, I ask her, "You enjoying Las Vegas?"

"It's ok. I've been here before, so ju know, it's the same old stuff. Everywhere I go, the men are like horny dogs."

Looking at her I can understand the reaction, but I have to stay cool.

"That's too bad. Maybe you need an escort." *Why did I say that?*

She smiled. "Maybe so. Who do ju think I should get to do that?"

The way she leaned toward me when she spoke made my blood pressure jump. She was causing me to lose my common sense, so I reply just like a junior-high schoolboy.

"Well, if it's something important that you need to take care of, maybe I can make sure you're safe."

She bats her eyes and says, "I like that. I bet nobody says anything nasty to me with ju on my arm."

On her arm. How did I just do that? Note to self: remember to take foot *out* of mouth before putting foot *in* mouth. I can hear it now: "*Woman puts cheating husband, drug kingpin's baby sister, and black Lamborghini in hospital. Film tonight on the 10 o'Clock News."* Where is my Little Voice now?

"I have a lot of catching up to do -- but like I said, if there's no one else, I might be able to help you stay safe." I'm not doing a very good job of helping myself. The smile on her face and the look in her eyes would make most men look to the heavens and say "thank you!"

All I can think of is, "Now I lay me down to sleep."

Nesto is off the phone and on the move: a welcome sight for *several* reasons.

"Maw, hand me that shirt over there; we gotta go. Leta, leave him alone – ju can eat him up later if he can get away from his other maw-eater."

"That's not funny, Nesto! His name is 'Mann,' not 'Maw'! And what did ju mean, 'his other maw-eater'?"

"Oh, not a thing, my lovely cee-ster." Nesto gives me a look, shakes his head and breaks out laughing. "Maw, let's go. I'll let ju know more on the way."

"On the way where?"

"The ranch house."

RENO, NEVADA

"Please come in, gentlemen. I trust your journey from Las Vegas was pleasant. Mr. Singleton will be with you in one moment." Singleton's butler Carleton politely show Cus Barlow and Lenny to the library.

"Tell this guy to come on – Cus Barlow don't wait for nobody. I flew up here on a charter flight, and it's waiting to take me back to Vegas. And it ain't free, *capiesce*?" snarls Barlow.

The butler nods as if he gave a fuck, and as he leaves the room, wonders what kind of business Mr. Singleton could have with these ill-mannered people, with their oversized rings and semi-gloss suits.

Lenny frowns. "Hey, boss – who is this guy? Look at this place. The books in here look older than the both of us put together."

"He's just some old fruit with more money than he knows what to do with. Put that book down, Lenny – it's probably worth a fortune!"

"That's right, Mr. Barlow, it is quite valuable. I think I paid two hundred thousand dollars for it a few years back. It's worth well over a million dollars now."

Arthur Singleton had silently slipped into the room through a side door.

"And I assure you gentlemen that they can't print more money than I know what to do with. Also - 'Lenny' is it? – Mr. Lenny, I'm not a 'fruit', as Mr. Barlow so crudely put it. I just have particular tastes. When you've lived the kind of life I have, let's just say that the mundane Las Vegas blonde or the exceedingly obnoxious redhead showgirl just doesn't pique my interest."

Cus Barlow rolls his eyes at Singleton's words, then says, "Yeah, right – it's your world. We're just here to take care of business. Your people in Vegas showed me the stuff from the ranch house. Good stuff, too – how'd a guy like you come across it?"

"This is not a matter that you need to be concerned with. I assume you're here to finalize your offer?"

Singleton's exaggerated hand gestures and proper way of speaking are getting the best of Cus Barlow's patience. "Finalize, yeah, yeah – Lenny, give him the bags."

Lenny heaves two flight bags on the desk in front of Singleton. He opens one and dumps stacks of money out on the desk.

"Mr. Lenny, that's not necessary. I trust all fifteen million is there."

"Well, that's how we do it where I'm from," says Barlow, snapping his finger at Lenny, nodding for him to sit down.

Barlow starts in on Singleton. "Here's the deal, Singleton. It's not fifteen – it's TEN million. And before you get your panties in a bunch, I've been around a long time and I know a thing or two about this type of shit. You bid high – I bid low: we meet in the middle."

"Well, Mr. Barlow, on the phone we agreed to *fifteen* million!"

"We, Mr. Singleton, are no longer on the *phone.* If this ain't good enough for you, then fuck you! Get the dough, Lenny, we're out of here."

Singleton's nose-in-the-air attitude has dispersed, and Barlow is taking pure pleasure in seeing this asshole feel the heat a little.

"Here now, wait a minute, gentlemen! I guess under the circumstances, I'll concede to this new offer."

"Yeah, I thought so," barks Barlow, "because if you had me come all this way to turn down my money, then all I was going to do was go back to that fucking farm or whatever it is, and take that shipment myself!"

"It's a ranch house, Mr. Barlow, and I'm not one you want to take lightly, so watch your mouth, honey."

"*Honey*? You fucking faggot! I'll show you…"

"Boss! Boss!" Lenny catches Barlow just in time. A split-second slower, and Barlow would have had Singleton by the throat. "Boss, we did what we came to do; let's get outta here. Remember where we're at; this is Genelli's turf. We shouldn't even be up here."

Barlow calms down. He straightens his jacket and pats his hair in place. "Lenny's right. We're leaving. Singleton, tell your people we'll have somebody over there to pick up that shit before midnight."

Singleton shakes his head. "No! You keep off my property. I'll have my people load it up and they'll bring it to you immediately. I'll need a destination."

Barlow jabs a finger angrily in Singleton's direction. Lenny senses the worse and starts to stop Barlow again.

"…Boss…"

"It's OK, Lenny. All right, Singleton, it's your world." Barlow's eyes get that cold look in them again, then he says, "But you better not make me show you mine. Lenny, give him the address. I'll be waiting in the limo. I need some air; it smells like faggots in here."

Lenny writes down a Las Vegas address on a piece of paper, throws it in Singleton's face and walks out.

The front door slams, and a side door by a bookshelf slides open. Carlton walks in carrying a Walther PPK nine-millimeter with a silencer on it, and places it on the top of the money. Then he begins to rub Singleton's shoulders.

"Arthur, I'm sorry—I mean, Mr. Singleton. One more step and Mr. Barlow and his friend would have been missing the tops of their respective skulls."

"Yeah, Carlton, thank you. Remind me never to get involved with this drug thing again. It has a fair return on the investment, but it's entirely too messy."

"Mr. Singleton…"

"Yes, Carleton – and stop with the 'Mr. Singleton'; it's just the two of us."

"Ok, Arthur – *what* investment?" They both start laughing.

"By the way, Arthur, what about the Colombian – what's his name? Lanceo."

"Carleton, to use a phrase from Mr. Barlow: *Fuck him!* It's my understanding he's barred from entering this country. And if he does, I'll have the Feds on him so fast…You know the director of the FBI? Well, he and I were an item at one time. But he's nowhere near the man you are. Now Carleton, take one of these bags upstairs: I want to play with the money while you play with me. I'll be up shortly. I have to call the ranch house with this address."

By the time Lenny climbs in the limo, Barlow is finishing off his second shot of whiskey.

"Boss, that was a close one!"

"What the fuck, Lenny? Why did you stop me? You heard the way that pussy tried to talk to me! You don't have to worry about Genelli. He'd look real bad trying to start a war because I busted up some smart-mouth faggot!"

"It wasn't Genelli I was worried about."

"Well, what the fuck – I know you ain't scared of some goddamn fruit, are you?"

"I guess you didn't see it, Boss. When I dumped the money on his desk, I looked at that side door Singleton came out of."

"So fucking what, Lenny! Did you see a bunch of fags with ninja suits on?" Barlow is pouring another shot.

"No, Boss," replies Lenny, "but there was somebody on the other side of that door — and they had a pistol with a silencer on it. I looked right at it. When you went for Singleton, it was pointed right at your head."

"Why the fuck didn't you say anything?"

"Because I know you would have gone for that hog leg of yours, and you wouldn't have made it. Besides, I'm not sure if there was only one gun on us."

As the limo pulls away from the house, Barlow remains silent. Lenny can only guess what's going through Cus' mind.

"Good move, Lenny, not letting me know about the gun behind the door. After we get the stuff from his people, believe me, Singleton is a dead man."

Lenny can't believe they're leaving without Singleton's head separated from his body – and this is when Lenny realizes how much Barlow must really need this shipment.

Getting in the Lamborghini was a major problem with Nesto's busted rib, making entering and exiting the small exotic car a long, painful, drawn-out task.

Looking at the small space in which he had to bend himself to enter the car, Nesto had enough.

"Fuck it. Let's take a cab to get jour white Ford. Is it still at the bar?"

"Yeah, I hope so. Where do we have to go after we get the car?"

"It's a little area right outside of town, about an hour away."

"Is that where the ranch house is?"

"Jeah. My people called me: the guy that delivered the stuff to the house is going to meet us at the truck stop on I-95. He knows a back way to the property."

Mann looks at Nesto. There's something different about him. Gone is the smiling face and don't-give-a-fuck attitude that he gave off last night.

"Nesto, what's with the shoulder bag? This sure don't feel like money."

"Just a few equalizers, just in case." Nesto smiles as he taps the shoulder bag full of weapons.

"What do we need all this for? I thought you said the rich guy wants you to come get the shipment off his property."

"That's what he said, but if there's anything I've learned in this business, it's to hope for the best, and keep a loaded pistol real close. What's the matter – ju getting scared?"

"I'm never scared – I just don't like surprises."

"Well, if ju don't like surprises, I'd better get this out the way: It's not one hundred keys, it's more like five hundred keys." Getting into the cab, Nesto looks back to see Mann standing on the curb, stiff as a light post. "What's the matter, Maw? Ju look like one of those statues at Ceeth-zar's Palathe."

Mann swiped the sweat from his forehead, not sure if it's from the Vegas heat or from the information he's just learned. "It's not 'Maw,' it's '*Mann*'! And if you have one more 'surprise,' I'm out of here, OK?"

"OK Ma-*an*. I just didn't tell ju because people start to freak out when I talk big numbers."

"Oh – and one hundred keys ain't big enough??"

"Uh…I didn't think so."

"Nesto, you've been doing this too long."

Riding down Las Vegas Boulevard, they both fall silent. It's hot, the cab driver won't turn up the air conditioner, and all their worries are making their cases known.

Nesto is really getting tired of playing trouble-shooter for his brother Lanceo, who doesn't do anything but sit at home in Colombia, counting money and giving orders.

Mann is getting the feeling that he's really getting in too deep. The ever-present and protective Little Voice in his head hasn't said a word in hours. Mann reads that as either he's already dead and doesn't know it, or he's already dead and can't bring himself to say it out loud.

Either way, he's officially fucked.

Mann throws a wad of cash at the cabbie, and gives Nesto a good shove as the Colombian gets out of the cab. Mann is behind the wheel of the Ford, in reverse and rolling before Nesto can get his door closed.

Nesto finally gets himself straightened out in his seat and stares at Mann. "What's the rush? Take it easy, Maw!"

Mann, keeping an eye in the rear-view mirror, says, "I guess you forgot what happened there last night. It's obvious that's their hangout, they probably own the joint. Don't you think we have enough shit to worry about? If not, I can turn around if you like. It'll be your head they'll be eating salad out of."

Nesto reaches in his shoulder bag, and pulls out an AR-15 fully automatic machine gun.

"If ju do turn around, it won't be my head that will look like tossed salad."

Mann looks at Nesto holding the gun up, then grabs the barrel, pushing it back down.

"Put that fucker away! It's daylight out here! How many of those do you have in that bag?"

"We have two AR-15's, two nine-millimeters, 4 clips, and 4 hand grenades."

"*Hand grenades?*"

"Don't look at me! My cee-ster Leta packed it."

"What – no cheese and crackers?"

"Hey, she's familia, and my familia is *cartel*. It's all we know, ju see, and she just doesn't want us to get hurt. She's just doing what she thinks is right."

Hitting I-95 South, Nesto sits back and tries to let his body recoup. He's gonna need to be at his best very soon.

Max is finally getting over the shock he experienced at his condo at the hands of a 16-year old and a nerd. He's run all over Denver with nowhere in particular to go.

He has taken rides around the city in the past. Whenever Mann has a major problem, he'll pick up Max and say something like "we need to take a ride." Then after an hour or so of just riding, Mann will turn to Max and just come up with a solution to whatever their problem is. Mann will say, 'Max, we need to do this or that,' and from start to finish - *problem solved.*

The problem today is, he isn't Mann, and after hours of driving away a hot summer evening, he hasn't come up with shit except an empty gas tank, and a numb nose.

Max needs to get some gas and get back to his place to check on Bonnie and Clyde.

Landing on a small, private runway, the twin-engine Corsair taxis up to a waiting limo. Cus Barlow and Lenny step off the plane and get into the car.

"Lenny, does your brother-in-law still stay in Reno?"

"Yeah, Boss – when he's home - but him and my sister are always out in the middle of nowhere. He's still doing demolition for drilling companies, when they need a big hole blown in the ground or the side of a mountain. I think he's set off more explosives here than he ever did in Afghanistan."

Cus smiles at Lenny's answer. "Well, Lenny, I think I want him to set off one more. Get him on the phone ASAP."

"I'll call him right now, Boss, but you sure you want him? I mean when he makes things go boom, they *really* go boom. I think that's why my sister likes the black SOB so much; she gets off on blowing up shit."

Cus is still smiling when he says, "Either that, or she's scared the crazy bastard will blow her to kingdom come if she tries to leave him."

Lenny turns to Barlow with phone in his hand. "I got him on the phone; we're in luck, he's at home."

"You tell him to stay by the phone; we have a quick job for him. Call the boys and see if they heard anything about my shipment."

Covered in sweat and hundred-dollar bills stuck to his body, Arthur Singleton and his part-time lover/full-time butler Carlton lie naked in bed.

"Carlton, you're fantastic. What say we spend the summer together in Paris? I can see us now…" The phone rings and Singleton reaches for it. "Hold on, let me get this call – don't *you* move a muscle."

Singleton's pretty sure he knows who's on the other end, and the voice on the phone confirms he's right on the money.

Cus Barlow's voice rumbles in Singleton's ear. "OK, Singleton -- is my shipment on the way to the address we gave you?"

Barlow is at his wits' end, and Singleton knows it. He can't help but stoke Barlow's fire for being so disrespectful earlier.

"Oh, it's you. I should have known. Yes, I have the address, and yes, they're going to bring it tonight. But please understand they will have to load it, and there is such a thing as 'travel time'. We can't just beam it over like an episode of 'Star Trek'! I don't understand what type of people you're used to dealing with, but I'll have you to know, Mr. Cus Barlow, that my reputation is worth far more than any petty business affair you and I have.

Now you're just going to have to wait until they get there, and just because you're such a contemptuous person, I hope they get delayed in traffic. Now stop harassing me, or I'll have the authorities at your doorstep!"

Singleton slams down the white and chrome old-fashioned phone receiver as hard as he can. Wiping the sweat and shit-eating grin from his face, he turns and speaks to his butler. "Carlton, pack my bags -- we leave tonight!"

When it finally registers that Singleton has just slammed the phone down in his face, Barlow's voice goes instantly from a rumble to a full-blown roar. "That little prick-eating weirdo! I'm gonna take his gay ass out in the desert and stick his head in an anthill! Then I'm gonna shove a stick of dynamite up his ass, tape a magnifying glass to it, then I'm sit gonna sit there and eat popcorn and make that faggot butler of his watch his faggot master get chewed up by ants — and get his ass blown off all at the same time. Where the fuck is my shipment!"

Lenny just watches as Cus tears up the house, and knows that if Singleton were only a few miles closer, Lenny would be looking for an anthill in the desert.

Riding in a four-wheel drive van bouncing down a dark and deserted dirt road, Nesto and Mann listen to Nesto's guy Rico. They managed to drive the Rent-A-Ford two hours out of Vegas to a truck stop to meet Rico. As they travel through the dark with no headlights, Rico fills them in on everything he knows.

"I know this area pretty good, like the back of my hand. I grew up out here. Before the rich people came and built all these ranch houses, the planes used to come at night and make drops. I learn how to drive in the dark when I was just a kid."

"So ju said the shipment is safe," Nesto asks.

Rico gives each of them apprehensive look before answering. "As far as I know, one thing is for sure: the Feds aren't around. I can't be sure about anybody else."

"How do you know the police or the DEA aren't watching the place?"

"Those guys are so stupid. You see, there's nothing in the desert. So if I see a lot of tire tracks around out here, or planes flying all low back and forth, I know they're on to somebody. They couldn't catch a rattlesnake bite if they walked around out here barefoot."

Rico stops the van, gets out and signals for them to follow him. In a low voice, he tells them the ranch house is just over the ridge; they're a couple hundred yards away. As they come to the top of the ridge, Rico pulls out an Army-issue, night vision single-lens binoculars. He lies down on the ground and focuses on the house in the distance. "There's somebody behind the house. Looks like they're loading boxes."

"How many people do ju see?"

"Looks like about six. Did they know we were coming?" Rico says.

"No, why?"

"I'm pretty sure those boxes are full of your stuff."

Mann asks, "Why do you think he'd be moving it? You think he found a buyer?"

Nesto gives Mann a puzzled look, then says, "I don't know – last time we talked to Singleton, he said he was in Europe. He said that we'd better come get this shit before he calls the Feds. I talked to my brother this morning; he's been trying to reach Singleton all week with no luck. What do ju think, Rico? They're not Feds, are they?"

"No…I recognize two of them – they work at the ranch. I think that other guy hangs out at the truck stop. He'll do anything for a buck."

Mann takes a look through the binocular to check out the scene, then says to his partner, "Either they're stealing it for themselves, or the rich guy has a buyer. I just thought of something, Nesto. So the rich guy's in Europe, right? What's to keep him from selling the stuff, coming back from Europe maybe a month from now, and playing dumb?"

Puzzled, Nesto replies, "What ju mean, Maw?"

"You know he said that he's in Europe. He already said to come take your stuff back. What's keeping him from selling it and telling you, all he knows is the shit's gone, and he figured that you guys picked it up. So he pockets the money — and if you and your brother start to put the pressure on him, he keeps his promise and calls the Feds.

"With the kind of cash that dude has, I'll bet he's got connections all the way to the White House. "He'll come up with some bullshit story about the cartel trying to threaten him, so they can use his ranch house to move drugs."

Rico jumps in and says, "Whatever is going on, if you guys don't do something – and fast – you can kiss that shipment goodbye. I'm sure somebody over there is packing. It looks like four workers, plus the two guys talking on the side of that van. I'll bet those two are the guards."

The three of them wait in silence for a few minutes, until finally Mann asks the question that they all knew came next. "So fellas, what's the plan? Nesto? Rico? How are we gonna do this? It's either now – or never."

Nesto puts his hands out to his side, with a baffled look on his face. "Mann, I don't know. I'm a general. I always come in after the shooting, talking sheet and taking names. I am not a foot soldier."

Mann looks at Rico, who returns the look with a blank expression, saying, "Well, *I am* a foot soldier. I get on my feet and go in the other direction."

Mann sees his dreams of shoulder bags filled with cash fading with each passing moment, until the Little Voice in his head kicks in. "*OK, Mann – looks like it's up to us!*"

In response to his silent partner, Mann replies aloud, "Hey, my friend is back!"

Staring curiously at his friend, Nesto says, "What did ju say, Mann?"

"Oh…nothing. Just thinking out loud."

"Come on, Maw, this ain't the time or place to be losing it."

"No, no – I'm fine. I just got an idea. Rico – how long will it take you to drive back down that road and come up the front side of the ranch house?"

Rico shrugged. "Just a couple of minutes, I guess."

"With your headlights out," adds Mann.

"Maybe five minutes, at the most."

"Ok, take the van. Go around to the front, so you're coming straight at them. I'll call your phone. Stay on the line until you hear from me. Creep up on them slow and quiet; we'll be watching.

"When they hear you coming, they'll start around the front of the house. That's when I tell you to hit it. Hit the high beams and punch it! Come straight at them fast and hard. At the same time, we'll creep up behind them when you hit your lights. We'll start yelling, 'D.E.A. – you're under arrest!' They won't know where we're coming from or who it is. I'm sure that the workers will run for it. If we're lucky, they'll all shit their pants and haul ass."

Mann can see Rico running the plan through his mind. "Pretend we're the Feds...not a bad idea. But what if they don't run?"

Looking at Rico, Mann considers his question. He points at the satchel full of guns and asks Nesto, "Are you any good with those things?"

"Ju don't have to be any good with an AR, Maw. Ju just point and squeeze."

Mann grabs one of the guns from the bag. "Rico, you take this AR. Nesto, you take that other one. I'll take the nine-millimeter and the grenades. If they try to fight – Nesto, you spray them with everything you got. We need to scare them. Hopefully they'll think there's too many of us to try and fight. Rico, you hit them with short bursts, and force them towards us. If we can't shoot their asses into running, I bet these hand grenades will make them see things our way."

Looking at the grenades, Mann tells Rico, "You have to stay low. Remember with those headlights on, you're going to be the only target they have. If it gets too hot, put that van in reverse and get out of there. Now - are you guys ready?"

They both look at Mann with shock on their faces.

"Ju in the Army or something," says Nesto. "Where in the fuck did that come from?"

"Why? You got a better idea? I'm all ears."

"Like it? I *love* it! Ju want to go to war with me? Hey – *say hello to my little friend.*"

Mann shakes his head at Nesto. "Take it easy, Scarface. Don't forget what happened to *him* at the end of that battle."

Rico is gung-ho, running to the van and taking off down the pitch-black road. Mann hopes he doesn't disappear forever; he still can't figure out how Rico can see in the dark without any headlights.

"Nesto, you ready?" Mann and Nesto slowly start to make their way over the hill.

"OK, genius: What's wrong with this picture?" Mann's friendly Little Voice is back. Looking around, Mann questions the scene in his head: What *is* wrong with this picture?

Then it hits him. More like, his eyes finally open to the problem: Nesto is wearing a bright, white shirt, just like his own. On top of this little detail, Nesto also has a large white bandage on his head. They couldn't be worse prepared for the situation if they had tried.

Mann grabs Nesto by the arm. "Hold on a sec, Nesto. Take that shirt off and lose that head bandage! Don't look at me crazy. It won't be hard to put a bullet right through your head with all that white on."

Nesto looks down at himself. "Oh, sheet! What should I do?" In the middle of the desert, there's not much mud or camouflage around.

"Take it and scrub it on the ground. Get it real dirty – and hurry up! Rico will be coming soon and we still need to get a lot closer."

Nesto goes to work on his shirt in the dirt. Mann starts to do the same, then simply tosses his shirt away. Nesto puts his shirt back on, the white glow seemingly gone.

Mann calls Rico on his phone. "Hello, Rico - where are you?'

"I'm just now getting to the front gate. I have to go slow. This road is pretty bad. If I rush it, they'll hear me way too soon."

"Ok. Take your time. We're still trying to get in position. If they act like they hear you, I'll let you know, so stay on the line."

Mann and Nesto spread out about twenty feet apart, making their way toward the house like they were really ready for battle. Mann can't believe they're really going to try this. He can barely see Nesto in the desert dark. The two of them are right about where Mann wanted them to be, and he's about to let Rico know that they were in position...when Mann hears something that almost makes his heart stop.

Nesto's cell phone starts to ring. Nesto drops his gun, trying to find his phone. Mann looks up the hill towards the house.

"Nesto! Get down! They're looking this way."

It is too late. One of the security men points a flashlight right at Nesto, as his not-so-white shirt picks up the light like a neon sign. Mann yells into his phone, "I don't care how far off you are, Rico – hit it, and I mean NOW!"

Mann can hear the sound of the van come to life, but it's nowhere near enough to have the effect he was hoping for. The sound of the van engine is suddenly replaced in Mann's ears by the terrifying sound of machine gun fire.

Nesto hits the ground just in time. Mann can see the light trail from the tracer bullets passing right over Nesto's head. Without thinking, Mann yells out, 'D.E.A.! Drop your weapons!"

Instantly, the ground and air around Mann is infested with bullets. He finds himself kissing the ground. It seems the closer he gets to the ground, the faster the bullets come. Things have gone real bad, real fast.

Hearing a crazy man's scream, Mann looks over to see Nesto jump up with his gun firing non-stop, running straight at the shooters behind the ranch house, spraying bullets everywhere.

Mann knows Nesto's going to run out of ammunition and get caught out in the open. Nesto's making ground – he's got one of the shooters penned down under the van, but the guy is trying to reload.

Mann catches sight of one of the shooters ducking inside an open doorway behind the house. The guy peeks out, fires on Nesto, who gives out with an anguished scream and goes flying through the air, almost making a complete front flip before crashing face-first into the ground.

Mann's heart is racing. Nesto is hit — and he's face-down and in the open.

Mann takes aim and, taking a deep breath, he squeezes the trigger. With one shot he nails the shooter in the doorway. The guy under the van is doing his best to take Nesto out, using bullets to chew up the ground in front of Nesto. Mann figures if Nesto isn't already dead, he will be if Mann doesn't do something *soon.*

If Mann stands up, he's a sitting duck. The shooter has an automatic, and he's taking turns shooting at Mann, then back at Nesto. Every time the guy shoots in Nesto's direction, Mann can see him flinch.

Suddenly, Mann sees a bright light come up behind the van and— BOOM! — Rico slams right into the shooter's vehicle, full speed. Mann is sure they can hear the sound of the crash all the way to Vegas. The van is knocked over on top of the hill, with the rear axle catching the shooter that was hiding under the van.

Mann watches as both shooter and van fly through the air for a good fifty feet. Both the vehicle and the shooter look as if they're flying in slow motion as the man's body slowly descends to the ground, then in a sickening sight, the van lands right on top of him. The whole thing comes to a rest about two feet away from the spot where Nesto is laying.

There's dead silence for what seems like forever. All Mann is aware of is his own heavy breathing. Carefully getting to his feet, he makes his way over to Nesto's body. He can tell Nesto is alive, but not *how much* alive. The van nearly landed on top of his friend; Nesto is completely buried by the dirt and trash kicked up by the wreckage. Mann grabs a handful of Nesto's shirt and pulls him from under a combination of dirt and what looks like the twisted remains of the bumper. Nesto is painfully holding his side; his shoe is missing and his foot is a bloody mess.

Looking at Mann, Nesto asks, "Did we win?"

Mann lets out a large sigh, then replies, "You ok? You hit anywhere else?"

"Hit? I'm hit? Where?"

"Looks like in the foot, Nesto."

Nesto looks at his foot just as the pain confirms Mann's statement; he starts yelling bloody murder. Mann takes a good look at Nesto's injury: there's a ragged hole right through. "If this is all you got, you're pretty goddamn lucky."

He suddenly realizes they're missing someone. "Oh, shit – *RICO!*" Mann runs up the hill to Rico's van, and can see his friend slumped over the wheel. He almost comes to a complete stop at the sight; Rico moans, then kind of flops out of the truck's door. Mann runs over to him; Rico's face is covered with blood. Actually, *everything* is blood- red: his nose is sitting to one side, and the only thing that looks almost normal is his eyes. Rico looks at Mann, then tries to talk through busted lips.

"Did we win?"

"Rico. You ok? Did they hit you?'

"No. I hit the van so hard, I'm sure I broke both my wrists. And my face hit the wheel....but did we win?"

"Yeah, yeah, we won, I think we--" Just then Mann hears a gun hammer click. He looks up.

It's the shooter from the doorway: white as a sheet, he's holding his stomach, and blood is pouring from between his fingers. It's obvious to Mann that he won't make it to the next sunrise....but he still has his pistol trained on Mann's head.

Mann hears his friendly Little Voice. *"Oh, fuck! Why didn't you check to make sure that the coast was clear? Shit, Mann – we can't go out, not like* this*!"*

The guy in the doorway smiles and Mann can almost feel the bullet leaving the gun's barrel. Then an explosion fills the air. Mann jumps from the sound of a machine gun. He doesn't feel anything – but the guy from the doorway is now face-down, and clearly dead.

"I got ju, ju fuck! Hey, Maw—ju all right?"

All Mann can see is the top of Nesto's head; he's still lying on the ground and waving his AR in the air, yelling, "Ju wanna fuck with me? Ju wanna *fuck* with ME!"

Mann quietly shakes his head, thinking, "*Scarface is back*." Then it hits him: Nesto, Rico and Mann had counted six men. Only two are dead – where are the others? Trying to hold back panic, Mann's eyes look everywhere as he asks Rico, "Can you get up?"

"Yeah, I think so…but look at my hands." His left hand is bent all the way back to his wrist, and the right is flopping around like it's not part of his body. Mann can still hear Nesto ranting, *à la* Scarface.

"Nesto! Be quiet! I think there's still four of them missing." Instantly Nesto shuts it down, rolls over onto his stomach and starts scanning the area with this AR. "Nesto, can you walk?"

"No, but I can crawl – and I'm not getting up until they are *down*. Maw! In the garage doorway! Somebody's still in there. I can see the shadow moving."

Mann yells out, "I don't know who's in there, but I've got a hand grenade. If you don't want your asses blown into the next life, you better come out, real slow."

There's an uncomfortable silence, then Mann says, "Fuck it! I pulled the pin on this thing, since you don't think I'm for real!"

This time, there's a voice; it sounds *old*. "Ok, ok, my friend. I'm no enemy. I just come here to get some money in my pocket!"

An old man comes slowly walking out, hands in the air. Looking straight down at the ground. It's obvious that he's no threat. Mann's about to knock him down when he sees another pair of hands behind the old man.

Pointing the gun, Mann yells, "Get on the ground, both of you!"

"No problem. It's just my grandson. We ain't no enemy."

Unsure about the two of them, Mann is contemplating shooting first and asking questions later. He doesn't want to get shot like Nesto, and damn sure doesn't want to get killed. His head is on a swivel, and every little sound or movement makes him jump.

"Ok. Old Dude, there were four of you. Where the fuck are the *other* two? And if you want to live, you better say the right thing."

Without looking up, the old man clears his throat; when he speaks, his voice shakes nearly uncontrollably.

"Miguel — he's the house man. He tried to shoot it out with you. He's in there on the floor. One of you guys shot him right in the head. He's dead."

"And the other one – where's he at?"

"I don't know – he's lives in town, over by the truck stop. He's like us – he just came out here to make some money loading the van with those boxes."

Mann hears Rico's voice calling out, "Over here, Mann!"

Mann looks at Rico. He's trying to point under the van he was driving. Mann bends over, looking under the vehicle. He can barely make out the sight in the dark, but it turns his stomach. Rico starts talking again.

"When the shooting started, I was way down the road. Then you screamed over the phone to hit it. I punched the gas but I forgot to turn on my headlights. I was almost to the house when I remembered to turn them on.

"I pulled the light switch, and there was Floyd running down the middle of the road. My lights hit him the same time my truck hit him. He was probably looking back, trying to get away from the shooting. We never saw each other!"

Nesto manages to make his way over to the other men. He's kind of leaning on his good leg, but still has his gun trained on the old guy and his so-called grandson.

Looking around, Nesto says, "Damn, what a mess. Where is the closest neighbor?"

"A little over half a mile," Rico answers. "It's pretty spread out." "Ju think they heard us?"

"Well, if anybody's home, they probably think World War III has just started!"

Mann thinks about Rico's answer, then asks him, "What do you mean, if anybody's home? Why wouldn't they be home?"

"These are vacation homes for the rich and famous." says Rico, "It's summer."

"So? I don't get it."

"How many people take summer vacations in the desert?" Rico asks sarcastically.

"I guess not many. Think it's possible no one heard us? No one's on their way out here to check?

"All that fucking noise, somebody is calling somebody somewhere. Mann, you and Nesto need to decide what you're going to do. There's only one sheriff in this area this time of year, and he's probably over in Silverton County. Most of the people in this area live there. If somebody did call this in, it'll take him at least an hour to get out here."

Not much of what has happened since he arrived makes Mann think there's an ice cube's chance in hell that they might be able to pull this off. But Rico's latest information gives him a ray of hope – along with the thought of the money they'll be counting if they get away with this shipment. Mann's thinking fast as he can; no one else has said a single word.

"OK, everybody come on, give me some help here. What can we do to buy some time?"

Even though there's blood and swelling on Rico's face, the others can see Rico's not on the same page as Mann.

"Buy time for what? Let's get the fuck out of here!"

"Listen, Rico – I didn't come all this way and damn near get my ass blown off to walk away empty-handed. That van is full, but thanks to you, it ain't going anywhere. We need to get that shit out and moved into– Oh, shit!"

Mann looks at Rico, the other van is trashed, too. Mann is going for his black belt in cussing — when he thinks he hears a small voice say, "Leave the stuff in that van, and tow it out of here."

Mann had forgotten all about the old man and his grandson. He looks at the old man, who promptly points to his grandson. They both stare at the youngster who repeats himself with a shrug and a 'know-it-all' air:

"I *said* to just leave it in the van and *tow* it out of here."

"And how do we do that," asks Mann.

"There's a tow truck in town," says the boy. "Me and my friends sometimes steal it and ride around in it. The old man that owns it goes to bed before the sun goes down, so he never knows we have it. Let me and Grandpa go get it. I'll bring it back so you can tow the van away."

"Away? Away, *where?*"

"Grandpa's house. He has a big barn in the back, and there's nothing in it."

Mann isn't sure about what he's hearing, but if the kid's right, it's the best idea that anybody's come up with, and time is running out fast.

"What time is it?" Mann asks. "How long have we been talking?"

"About fifteen minutes."

"How much time do we have?"

Rico is eager to go and quickly answers. "Not enough."

Mann ignores him, trying to figure a way to make this work. "What's your name, kid?

"Donnie."

Mann walks over to Nesto, who has taken a shirt out of the van to wrap his foot. He looks like hell, but seems to be ok. Mann kneels down by his friend. "What the fuck – I guess I blew it. It sounded like a good plan when I thought about it."

Nesto's holding his injured foot. "It was a good plan," he says, "until my phone screwed us."

"The phone didn't make any difference, Nesto. You saw those guys. They weren't giving up shit without a fight. I was hoping they would get scared and run."

Nesto interrupts Mann. "Did ju run?"

"Run away? Well — no. Why?"

"Right. That's my point! You don't give that kind of job to anybody. Those guys weren't pussies; they know what they were doing, and they knew the risk."

"I guess you're right, Nesto. Kind of like us."

"No, we're not like them. They're pawns. They do what somebody else tells them. We –well, *ju* — ju make things happen, and ju don't even want the job! That's what's makes ju special – separates ju from the rest. Look what ju did in the alley last night for me. That was classic! I had a front row seat. I couldn't believe my eyes. There's no way either one of us should have walked away alive. But ju make it happen."

The pint-sized general interrupts sharply, turning Mann and Nesto's heads. "Well, you two need to make something happen right *now* — 'cuz it's gonna take at least 20 minutes to get there and back with the tow truck."

Mann says, "Go, and take Rico with you. Is there a doctor in town?"

Rico replies, "Don't worry about me. Get me to the truck stop. I'll call my cousin on the way there. He'll be waiting to take me to the hospital in Silverton. Mann, can we talk before we make a move?"

"What's up, Rico? I'll make sure you get a cut if we make it out of here."

"Listen, Mann – I'm not worried about that. I know you're a fair dude. The thing is — I know how to make sure you get enough time to get out of here. I'm sure I can buy you all the time you need."

"How you gonna do that? Don't tell me you're going on some suicide mission."

"Hell, no! Just trust me and give me those grenades."

"*What?*"

"You need time?" Rico stared directly at Mann. "Then I need those grenades — *now.* I need to be at that truck stop as fast as possible."

"What about the tow truck?"

"If I don't beat the sheriff to the truck stop, it won't matter. I'll call you if we don't make it in time."

Mann and Nesto watch Rico, the old man, and the kid get in the old man's station wagon. "Nesto, I told gramps that we'd give him $10,000 if he gets Rico to the truck stop before the sheriff gets there and brings the tow truck back."

Nesto looks at Mann, with a puzzled look on his face. "Why do they need to beat the sheriff to the truck stop?"

"Not sure— and at this rate, the less we know, the better."

Getting in the car, the old man slides over and lets the kid drive. Rico's in the back seat with both arms hanging in the front of his shirt like they're in a sling.

The kid fires up the motor. Mann shakes his head at the sight of the old man hanging on for dear life as the kid spins the wheels, hand grenades in his lap, tearing down the road in an old station wagon that's twice his age.

CHAPTER FOUR

Sitting in the living room of their house behind the Happy Snake Eyes, Lenny seems to be uncharacteristically antsy. "It's almost twelve o'clock, Boss – you think we should go out to the ranch house?"

"No, Lenny, we ain't going anywhere, be it the ranch house or the whore house, dammit! Now call that fucking brother-in-law of yours!" Cus Barlow is just as antsy as Lenny, and Lenny doesn't waste a minute of time dialing the phone.

"Here, Boss – he's on the line; his name is Antwan."

"Hello, Mr. Antwan? How would you like to make five large for one night's work? Hey, Lenny – you hear this? He says the work's no problem, but the price— we have to negotiate!" Lenny reflects on Cus' phone negotiation skills, then shakes his head.

Cus just laughs.

"It's twelve forty-five in Denver Colorado! You're listening to KBPO, Denver's only rock-and-rap station. Hope you're having a good Sunday morning – I'm your Saturday night party-hardy host, DJ Tone. We'll be back with more music after these messages. But first, I'd like to send a shout out to our morning DJ, Max! He's been under the weather since his rooftop — how would you say — exposure. But if you're listening Max, give us a call. We want to hear from you! You're still the top—"

Max shuts off the radio with a finger punch to the switch. "Fucking little punk! 'DJ Tone,' my ass! He's been laying to get my morning spot ever since I came over from 95FM-The Cam."

Almost screaming at the radio, Max continues to talk to himself. "Thought he had it, until old super DJ Max showed up to save the day. Then they dropped his ass to the 10PM-to-sunrise spot. And if I've got anything to say about it, that's where he's gonna stay."

Max is sitting in his front room in the dark, staring at the radio. He's been home for over three hours. His plan was to come in here, get Bill and Anna out of his bedroom and, if possible, out of his life.

But when he got there, the house was dead quiet. He went to the bedroom door and listened for a minute. He heard what sounded like snoring and thought to himself that he should leave them alone: the sick fucks probably need the rest.

But deep down inside, he was really scared. Of what, exactly, he wasn't sure. Not Bill. Who could be frightened of Bill? The more he thought about it, the harder it was to admit to himself. The real source of his fear, the doubt rumbling inside is...*Anna*. That kid...or little girl, or whatever she is. She reminds him of somebody, somebody he once trusted. But he damn sure didn't trust Anna, or ill-B...ill-B? Ah, he gets it now. B-ill/ Bill is sick for Ill-B: Sick Bitch Anna.

Max begins talking to himself again. "Oh, brother, Max, you've done it this time. This is really some sick shit. Who the hell is this chick? I need to talk to Mann...Oh, shit! I can't call him and tell him about this crap. He's gonna be so pissed!" Max clears his nose and wipes the sweat from his forehead.

"I know what I'll do. Little Miss Fast Ass in there is so smart – I'll see what she thinks we should do. Maybe when Bill sees she's not so bright, he'll come to his senses and help me clean up this goddamn mess. If his stupid ass hadn't gone back and got caught up with that little demon, I wouldn't have a problem in the world."

Reaching in his pocket he pulls out a baggie. "I'll just do a couple of lines —then it's time for the sick B's to get the fuck up."

Max fixes his nose. He's been snorting non-stop since he left earlier. It doesn't help he found a bag of powder stashed in Mann's Mercedes. Being around Mann as much as Max does have its perks — especially when you know the location of Mann's stash spots. Clearing the powder off his nose in the mirror, it dawns on Max who it is Anna reminds him of.

"I'll be dammed! She's an underage female version of Mann! Only thing is Mann's a good dude – a really good person – but this little chick is bad, a real evil mothe---"

"Hey, Max!" Max about jumps out of his shoes when Bill walks up behind him.

'What the--?"

"Oh, I'm sorry, Max – I didn't mean to scare you. Who are you talking to? Why is it so dark in here, and where is Anna?"

Bill's last question makes Max's head whip around. "What do you mean, 'where's Anna'? She's not in there with you?"

"No, I thought the two of you were out here talking!" Bill running through the house proves what Max already knows: Anna's gone.

Max is pissed. "Oh shit, I can't believe this! Why'd you have to mess with her? All the dope-loving, sex-crazed, eighteen-and-over groupies that I have to fight off just for concert tickets – and you have to hook up with Poison Ivy!"

In a total panic, Bill yells at Max. "She's not here, Max? What did you do? Where did she go?"

"I didn't do shit, Bill! I don't know where she went. Hell, I didn't even know she was gone until you just came out of the room."

"Max, we gotta find her. How long have you been back?"

"I don't know…I think I got back about nine-thirty…maybe ten o'clock."

"Fuck, Max – it's after three in the morning!" Max could see the panic in Bill's eyes. "What if somebody grabbed her?"

"If somebody did grab her, I feel sorry for them," Max smirked.

"That's not fucking funny, Max. Wait – I'll call her cell phone!"

"Yeah, call—NO! Bill, *don't call!* Wait a minute…What if she thought about what we talked about, and realized that the best thing to do is to go home?

Bill looked puzzled. "Why would she do that?"

"Well, so she…uhmm…so she wouldn't get her *Bee-ill* in trouble. Look Bill, she's the D.A's daughter, so she has to know how this is gonna wind up. You said it yourself: she's a lot smarter than her age. She's trying to save your ass, Bill!" Max hopes what he's saying is right, if not, at least somewhere close to the truth.

Bill has the sorriest look on his face. "No, Max, you don't understand! I need her!" Bill looks and sounds like he's as young as Anna, and it pisses Max off.

"Listen Bill, wake the fuck up! You keep doing this sick shit, and you're gonna end up in prison, and take me and Mann with you! She's too goddamn young for you; sooner or later it's all gonna go bad, and she's gonna run that fat, know-it-all mouth of hers to save her own ass — and fry the three of us at the same time! Come on Bill, we are the adults here."

Max puts his hand on Bill's shoulders. He's sure that his speech is enough to make Bill at least think about the facts – and hopefully, slow down. "She's pretty and all that, but she's all messed up in the head. We're supposed to be trying to get her help, not getting her high and screwing her, living out some fucked-up high school fantasy."

"You don't care, Max. All you want is for her to be gone."

"Well, uhm… *Yes*."

"You're full of shit, just like she said. What if, right now, somebody's got her tied up and is raping her?"

"Believe me, Bill, if there's somebody getting raped, it ain't that chick," smirks Max.

"You think she'll rat on you and your dope connection. That's all you give a damn about, isn't it, Max? Anna's not like that. But you know what? If something does happen to her, and you don't help me find her, I'll make damn sure that everybody gets screwed!"

Max jumps in Bill's face, and punches him square in the mouth. Bill stumbles back and trips over the hallway table, with Max on top of him in a blink, grabbing Bill by the throat.

"Bill, you rat fucker — don't you ever talk to me like that again. You have *no* idea what you're dealing with!"

Bill is still new to this lifestyle, so the drugs and drinking haven't taken a toll on his health: he's still in pretty good shape. He tosses Max off of him like a rag doll, sending Max flying. Before Max knows what's happening, Bill is on top of him with one hand full of Max's windpipe, and his other hand pulled back in a fist.

"Max, I don't give a fuck about you or your connection! I do know this much—you got me started down this road that night at the concert! The only reason I like it is because I met Anna." Bill's face is getting increasingly red and sweaty. "You know more about this life than I do, Max, so I'm telling you—you're gonna stay with me until we find her and make sure she's safe. And I know for damn sure she's not at her father's place."

The entire time Bill's been talking, he's had his large hands around Max's throat, continuing to squeeze tighter and tighter.

"Ok, ok, Bill! I can't breathe. We'll find her. Just — let me up, dammit!" Bill slowly backs off. Max sits up, still coughing and trying to catch his breath. "Damn, you're a strong S.O.B."

"I played college football at BYU, all four years. Could have made the pros, but just wasn't fast enough." Listening to Bill, Max notices his friend's physical size for the first time.

"What position did you play?"

"I was a safety, defensive back field, but that was ten years ago."

Still sitting on the floor, Max looks at Bill, who walks away from Max with a certain look in his eye. It's clear to Max that there will be no compromise about what Bill's next move will be.

"Ok. It's obvious nobody's gonna talk you out of finding Anna. So I'll make you a deal. I'll help you find her, on one condition."

"Which is?"

"When we find her, if she's home or some safe place, trying to get herself together—we do the right thing and *leave her alone*. Deal?"

"Deal. But if she's in *trouble*, you're gonna help me save her. No matter what we have to do."

Max thinks about who they're talking about, and knows they're in for it. As much as he doesn't want to agree, he knows he has no choice. "Yeah, I guess so."

A funny thought pops into Max's head. "Here's come Captain Save-A-Hoe, and his trusty sidekick, Max!"

Bill is puzzled. "What's that supposed to mean?"

Max sighs. "Never mind, Bill—I forgot, you're from Salt Lake City."

Bill goes back to dialing Anna's number. "There's still no answer. I told you something's wrong!"

"Relax, Bill, we'll find her. So did she say anything while the two of you were in the bedroom? I mean anything about leaving, or something that she needed to do?"

"Not that I can think of. I mean I was pretty buzzed, and tired, too, so I can't remember everything."

"Yeah, I see. So let's start at the beginning. How did you two manage to hook back up after that night at the Montville Hotel?"

Heading towards the door, Bill looks back at Max. "I'll tell you about it in the car. We need to find Anna."

Driving around Denver in Mann's Mercedes, Bill tells Max about Anna calling the radio station, asking for him. She left a message about doing a concert, and needing promotional information.

"Max, I thought it was a legitimate call, so I called the number back. I had no idea that it was Anna. She said she'd been thinking about me, and could we meet. At first, I told her 'no dice, I'm done with that night and everything that had happened', and asked her not to call me anymore."

"So if you did that, why are we cruising Denver streets right now, looking for her?"

"It's hard to describe, Max."

"Try me."

"Well, at first, I thought she was some crazy, mixed-up kid, looking for attention by acting out."

"She *is*, Bill...I think."

"You *think*? See? Even you! You can tell, too. There's something about her, Max."

"I'll tell you what it is, Bill. You're a naive country boy from Salt Lake City, and she's a born control freak, probably just like her father—speaking of which: what's up with that? I get the feeling from the way she talks about him that he's done something to her, you know what I mean. Is Denver's D.A. a fucking pedophile?"

"I thought the same thing, Max. She really hates him. When I finally asked her, she said he's never touched her, but then she says that he's *worse* than a pedophile."

"What can a dad do to a little girl to be considered *worse* than a child molester?" Max frowns. "And what's the deal with her mother? Bet she's one of those rich chicks, all messed up on prescription drugs."

"No, nothing like that. Anna told me her mother passed away when Anna was a kid."

"She lost her mother when she was a kid? That says a lot. Because she's *still* a kid."

Bill shook his head. "No, she's not. Yeah, I mean, she is a little young, but she knows what to do, you know."

"Hell, no, I *don't* know! And you need help, Bill. I didn't know that *you* were that fucked up!"

"No, Max, not like that!" Bill shakes his head. "I mean, yeah, she's no virgin. But I'm talking about how Anna is with people. Even you and me, she's not *really* controlling. It's not like she *has* to be in control. It's more like you can't help yourself —you *let* her have control, and she knows what to do with it. Max, have you ever known anybody like that? You know what I mean: always has the answer, always one step ahead of everybody else? "From the time we met at the station up until tonight, she told me what we were going to do and how it would play out. Just like she planned it all. Take today: it was her idea to come over here. She said, 'let's go over Max's, get some blow and kick it. I'll bet he'll be cool with it.' That's what she said, Max - and look what happened."

"Well, she got everything right—except the 'cool with it' part. Bill, why couldn't you hook up with the Nicky chick? She's just as risky, the wife of a cop —but at least she ain't the D.A.'s underage daughter!"

The car remains silent long enough to get Max's attention. Bill seems to be somewhere else in his head. Max is about to ask *what's the problem* when Bill suddenly yells, "Max, turn the car around! I know where she's at!"

◆─────────◈─────────◆

Retired Special Forces Captain Antwan Rose, and two of his friends, also Special Forces [Retired], take up their respective positions around the Arthur Singleton estate, located right outside of Reno, Nevada.

"Tact One, you read?"

"Loud and clear; side door covered."

"Roger Tact One. Tact Two: you a go?"

"That's a 4x4 on contact; front door is covered. Cap, I got movement in front. Looks like one male putting luggage in trunk of limo. Now he's returning to house."

"Tact One, move on house. I got your six, Tact Two, disable limo. Now MOVE!"

Antwan and his men go into action with the speed, stealth and precision that reflect their years of training. One flash-bang grenade later, Singleton's butler Carleton is on the floor, hands and feet trussed up with zip-tie cuffs, ears still ringing, and eyes only able to make out human figures standing over him. They resemble military by the way they're dressed, but his head is still spinning from the flash grenade —he can't be sure.

Also, the rifle pointed directly in his face makes it hard to pick any other clear point of focus.

"Tact Two, how's it look upstairs?"

"It's all quiet up here, but there's a guy up here with a gun in his hand and his brains all over the wall behind him. What do you want to do, Captain?"

"Come on down, Nate. We're cleaning up right now. Let's get the fuck out of here."

Standing over Carleton, Smitty asks Antwan, "What do you want to do with him?"

"That all depends on him. Mr. Bar— uh, I mean *the customer* said there should be two large flight bags filled with cash around here somewhere. And if *Mr. Belvedere* here wants to see the sun rise tomorrow, he better start talking and pointing—real fast. We're already behind schedule, and you know how I feel about tardiness."

Smitty leans down to tell Carleton a story about the captain. "Dude, if I was you, I'd start talking, and fast. Captain here has a thing about being late. He says if you're late, you're dead. In Afghanistan, the enemy nicknamed him, 'The Truant Officer." He'd wait for a company of enemy troops to pass by, and those troopers that were lagging in the back, he'd take out. He would say, "That's what they get for being late."

Carleton's eyes shift from Smitty to the Captain, then back to Smitty— who smiles at Carleton, then drags his finger across his throat, as he nods his head towards the Captain. Carleton looks at Antwan's black face; it looks like he's never smiled in his life. His stare is blank and ice-cold. Carleton looks at him and starts to shake. He points at the desk, pleading, "Over there on the desk. Please take it!"

Antwan jerks his head in the direction of the desk. "Take a look, Smitty."

"Woo, yeah! It's here alright! How much is it supposed to be?"

"I don't know—just grab it, and let's get out of here."

"OK, Cap—but didn't you say something about two bags? There's only one here."

Turning back to Carleton, Captain Antwan Rose gives him a look that burns right into Carleton's flesh like hot ice. Gritting his teeth, Antwan snarls. "Ok, Slick—now *you* are late. You wanna make up that time by telling where that other bag is, or you wanna be early for Judgment Day?"

When Antwan raises his rifle, Carleton knows without a doubt they care about nothing but the money. Even though he's as close as he's ever been to getting himself killed, he's still trying to figure out a way to get the cuffs off his hands.

Carleton knows that he's waited too long to let it all go now. The other bag's in the car; if only he'd grabbed both of them at the same time, he'd be long gone by now. They would have found Singleton upstairs with his brains blown out—an obvious suicide—and Carleton would have the ten million dollars and the rest of his life to spend it. He needs a distraction in the worst way.

Almost overcome with anger and disappointment, Carleton steadies himself, then in a calm voice says, "It's upstairs."

"Where?"

"In a wall safe."

Captain Antwan Rose doesn't trust a word Carleton is saying, but time is passing fast; the captain truly lives up to his reputation: get in and out, fast as possible. If you're late, you're dead.

The captain looks at Carleton. "You better know the combination."

Carleton feels he's found a ray of hope. The longer they think he can get them into the wall safe, the longer he has to find a way out of there with the money. "Uh, yeah...I know the combination."

The captain calls on his radio. "Nate, you still up there?"

"Roger, sir."

"What are you doing?"

"Cap, there's money all over the bed up here, but it has this guy's brains all over it. I'm trying to get the shit off. Blood or no blood, I'm not leaving this much cash behind."

Antwan turns back to Carleton. "Where's the safe?"

"Behind the headboard."

"Nate, check behind the headboard: should be a wall safe there."

"Cap, you need to get up here. It's all fucked up!"

Antwan readjusts his aim at Carleton's head. "Ok, Slick – what's the combination?"

Carleton sticks his hands out. "Take these off."

"You're pissing me off, Slick… *what is the combo*?"

"Listen, I *have* to go upstairs with you. The safe has a laser fingerprint ID on it. I have to put my finger on it before it will accept the combination. And my name's not 'Slick,' it's Carleton."

Antwan lowers his gun, then says, "Smitty, cut this fucker loose…just the ankles will do for now. The wrists we can cut upstairs. Hey *Carleton*, you try any dumb shit and POW! Now let's get a move on: I'm feeling late. Bad shit happens to people who are late."

Climbing the steps, Carleton's not sure what he's going to do, but he has to get these cuffs off. The other bag of money is in the car, and the keys are in his pocket. All he needs is a little break.

At the top of the stairs, Nate calls them. "In here, Captain! Look."

Walking in the bedroom, Antwan looks at the body of Arthur Singleton in a heap on the floor, where Nate pushed him off the bed. The far wall is covered with blood and brain matter, and the unmistakable smell of death has already made itself known.

"Whoa! Fuck, *Carleton*, so explain this one."

Carleton's brain is racing a million miles a minute. Lucky for him, he already knows what to expect when they walked in the room.

"He's—he's my uncle, and he was sick with cancer. He said that he wanted to die, and would give me a fortune if I helped him do it."

"So what did you do? Help him hold the gun to his mouth?"

"No, I couldn't do it. He got mad and told me to take the money and get out: he'd do it himself."

Antwan taps Carleton on the chest, then says, "Ok, Slick: hold that thought. Where's the safe? And —Nate, what's the problem?"

"The safe is over there. Look Cap—the top of his head is all over it."

"Well, wipe that shit off and open the safe door!"

"Come on, Cap—I had enough of that shit in Afghanistan. He's got to open the safe anyway: let him do it."

"OK, *Carl*: get over here. Nate, cut him loose and watch him." Nate cuts the wrist cuffs.

"Now getting back to your story, Carl. If he told you to take the money and get out, why is there still a bag in his safe?"

Carlton wasn't ready for that question, and it showed. Nate takes a step back as Antwan starts to bring his gun up. Right then, Smitty pops into the room.

"Sorry, Cap—I had to piss like a race horse! You should see the bathroom in this place."

Antwan and Nate look at Smitty, right as Carleton drops his shoulder and drives it into Nate's chest with all he's got. Nate falls back over a footstool, and Carleton fights to keep his balance. He spins off Nate, pumping his legs as hard and fast as possible, and throws himself through the bedroom window, head first.

Foop!

The report from Antwan's silenced rifle explains the burning punch Carleton feels in his thigh. The bullet's impact spins him through the air, and he falls awkwardly. When he hits, it's hard: half on the roof, half on the windshield of the limousine. The intense pain takes his breath away, but he manages to fight off the shock and rolls off the hood of the car.

Knowing that at any second, another bullet is going to tear into him again, Carleton's mind and his body are in lock-step, moving with unnatural speed. The car keys are in his hand almost before his feet hit the ground, and his other hand is finding the door handle and pulling it open while he propels his body behind the steering wheel. With each successful move, he feels more driven to pull off a harm-free escape.

Antwan and Smitty tear down the stairs. "Don't kill him! He knows where that other bag of money is!"

Hearing the Captain bellowing that order is the only thing that keeps Nate from shooting Carleton through the top of his head. Nate realizes that Carleton is going to try and drive away in the limousine. In a panic, he runs after Antwan and Smitty. At the top of his lungs, Nate is yelling, "*No*! COME BACK!"

But Carleton is almost home free— he just has to push in the key.

He looks at the front door of the house. The front door starts to open slowly. Just as it does, Carleton turns the key in the ignition and …

KABOOM!

Antwan, Smitty and the front door fly backwards through the house. Glass, chairs, tables, grandfather clock—anything and everything that wasn't nailed down in the front room are now against the far wall. Super-heated air and flames rush in through the door.

Nate, who was halfway down the stairs, is tossed in the air by the blast's concussion. He lands hard at the bottom of the steps, leg bent behind him.

The front door — torn clean off its hinges — flies into Antwan's face, driving his body into Smitty. Along with the door, the two men fly back into the hallway wall. Smitty is smashed between Antwan and the wall; Antwan's head snaps back, knocking out all of Smitty's front teeth, and the wall crushes his lower vertebrae.

The limousine is now only two wheels and half of a front grill, sitting in a burning black crater.

For fifty feet in a semi-circle, burning hundred-dollar bills float to the ground.

"Nesto, how long have they been gone?"

"About five minutes longer than the last time ju ask. What the fuck, Maw, relax! Ju gonna hurt jourself!" Sweating like a mad man, Mann puts the last of the boxes from the house into the van.

"That's the last one, Nesto. I found an ATV in the garage: if they ain't back in ten minutes, I want you to get on it, and ride off down that dirt road we came up on."

"And what ju gonna do—stay and fight?"

"No, asshole. *I* am on two good legs. I can run off into the underbrush."

"Then do what? Get caught? Maw—we're in the middle of the desert: there's no place to hide. If *la policia* get here before the kid and Grandpa get back, I say we hide out. And when the cops get out of their car, we jump them, take the car and drive back to the truck stop."

Mann freezes in his tracks. "Truck stop? Truck stop? Oh, shit I forgot! Hold on, Nesto, I gotta call Rico!" Dialing Rico's number, Mann watches as Nesto gets up and limps into the garage.

Inside Nesto looks at the man they called Miguel; either Mann or the grandfather has put a box over his head. There's still blood all over the floor. Nesto only has one shoe on, and tries to hop around the bloody floor. He manages to make it to the ATV and hops on it, thinking about Mann's idea. He can still hear Mann outside, talking a mile a minute. Sitting on the ATV, Nesto tries to ignore the pain in his foot. Other than Mann's phone conversation, it's quiet.

Nesto closes his eyes and wishes he were somewhere else— anywhere but here running around like a trained killer cleaning up for his brother.

He is aware that Mann isn't talking anymore. Silence settles around Nesto like a warm blanket. He opens his eyes, and sees Mann standing in the doorway, looking at him sitting on the ATV.

"I see you're thinking about getting out of here on that thing," says Mann.

"Jeah, I'm thinking about it. I'm also thinking about getting caught with all this sheet. And ju know what? *I'm* not leaving, *we* are leaving. The hell with it, Maw! Let's just get this thing started, get on it and ride the fuck outta here while we still can.

"Ju did *good* Maw, it's just ju gotta know when to cut and run! I already tried to hang on too long the other night. If it weren't for ju, I'd be dead. Come on, help me get this thing out of here, and let's go! I'm *cartel*: there's plenty more where this stuff came from."

Mann gets a crazy look on his face, his eyes bug out and he starts talking crazy. "The hell with that! You said I could do anything! I could make it happen, and I'm *gonna* make it happen, even if I gotta take the fucking cops hostage and trade them for a helicopter outta here! You hear me, Nesto? We're going big—we're going *prime time!*"

"Oh sheet, Maw! Ju are losing it! Come on, snap out of it, I'll give ju money or more dope— just don't try this! *Por favor!*"

Unexpectedly, Mann busts a gut laughing at Nesto. "I was just bullshitting you! I just talked to Rico. They beat the cops to the truck stop. The kid and grandpa are on their way back with the tow truck."

"So?" Nesto replies, "The cops are still gonna get here before we can get clear of this place."

Mann's still laughing. "At first, *you* were the one who wanted to shoot cops and all that crazy shit. Now, when it comes time to do what you say, you want to act like your common sense is making a comeback. But it doesn't matter, Nesto. I wish I could take credit for this one, but Rico came up with it."

"What one?"

"Rico and his cousin are at the truck stop right now. Rico just called the sheriff's office. He said there's a big fight at the truck stop. A couple of drunk truckers are beating the crap out of everybody."

"That's only gonna slow them down for as long as it takes them to figure out it's a bullsheet call. Then they're really gonna know something's up!"

Mann, still sporting a big grin, replies, "Yeah, and that's all we need."

"Jeah, ju are losing it. A whole *five* minutes, if that much? Maw, we're gonna need at least a good thirty minutes' head start. Let's just get on this ATV and ride down the highway so we can meet the kid and his grandpa. Let's get the fuck outta here! Why the fuck ju have that crazy look on jour face? What's so goddamn funny?"

"It would be easier to show you than try and tell you; I just wish we were at the truck stop right now."

Nesto is getting irritated. "I just wish ju'd tell me what the fuck is going on!"

"Ok, ok, Nesto! Rico and his cousin are waiting at the truck stop for the cops."

"Ju already told me that!"

"Yeah, but — before they left, Rico asked me for a hand grenade. When the sheriff stops to check on the fight, Rico and his cousin will just drop a happy bomb in their car, and BOOM! No more sheriff car."

Nesto just shakes his head and says, "And ju want to take credit for that sheet! They're gonna blow up a cop car at the truck stop with a hand grenade? Ju said ok to that plan? Maw, Rico and his cousin are half-ass crazy! They'll probably throw the hand grenade *in* the truck stop! Why didn't ju tell me about this before now?"

Mann's phone starts to ring. Before he answers it, he looks at Nesto and says, "Surprise! Either way, Nesto, here we go. It's Rico on the phone now. *Hello, Rico?* "

Speeding through traffic, Max is following Bill's directions, and asks Bill, "Where do you think she's at? Nicky's? Why would she get up and sneak off to Nicky's? I'm not going anywhere near that cop's house and neither are you!"

"I didn't mean *at* Nicky's house, Max. She's probably *with* Nicky."

"So which one is it—*at* Nicky's or *with* Nicky? Does it really matter? Or is it that—let me guess— Nicky is somewhere using Anna to get more dope? Or is it the other way around? What's really going on, Bill, because

I'm really starting to hate even having you in the car with me."

"It's neither, Max. Anna is probably trying to get Nicky to change her mind."

"Change her mind? Change her mind about *what?*"

"About you and me."

Max is still flying through traffic, but he hasn't taken his eyes off Bill. "You and me? What the fuck did *we* do? Oh, shit—don't tell me. Does this have anything to do with that night at the hotel?" Again he asks, "Goddamn it—about *what*, Bill?"

"Yeah, Max—Nicky wants to blackmail the two of us."

Still not looking at the road, Max drops his head at Bill's answer. They both jump at the sound of an oncoming horn. Max has let the Mercedes-Benz drift into approaching traffic. Bill reaches over and wrenches the steering wheel, getting them back on their side of the road with only inches to spare.

Feeling like he's been sucker-punched, Max goes off. "That little *bitch*—the both of those *bitches!* Mann warned me—I swear, he told me that Nicky-bitch was a snake!"

Trying to get Max to calm down, Bill replies, "I know it sounds bad. But it's really not her fault, Max. Nicky needs help and this is the only way she could think of to get it."

"Bill, are you really that stupid? She's trying to screw us over, and you're talking about her like she's a poor, homeless orphan. On top of that, your sweet little underage piece of ass is in on it, too!"

Max continues to drive, but not as fast as before. He seems deep in thought, and simply stops talking. Bill is hoping that the storm has finally passed, just as Max asks, "So how is this supposed to go down?"

"Nicky is like Anna's big sister," replies Bill. Max gives him a quick side-eye to that comment. "Anna says that Nicky's husband and her dad hang out together. She says the cop that Nicky's married to is always over their house. That's how Nicky and Anna first met each other.

"Anna's been getting into trouble at school and not coming home at night. Anna's dad asked if Nicky could talk to her or something, because Anna doesn't have any females in the house to confide in."

Max shakes his head. "It still doesn't make sense to me. What's blackmailing us gonna get them?"

"Anna tells me that she and Nicky are just alike. They both grew up with no mother; they both hate their fathers. And they need to get away from their situations. But neither one of them has any money."

"What's so bad about Nicky's situation," scoffs Max. "That cop took her nasty ass off the street, married her and takes good care of her, from what I hear."

"Anna said Nicky told her he's crazy, beats her and shit like that. Nicky found out some really bad shit about him and his police work. She's scared that he's gonna do something to her, like *kill* her!"

"Well, Bill, right now that doesn't sound like a bad idea. Matter of fact, I'm damn near ready to help him."

"Max, how come you know so much about Nicky?"

"Let's just say I've got a good friend who gave me a bio on her. She's bad news, Billy-Boy—the worst. That 'woe is me' shit that she's selling you is just that: *shit!* So tell me: why is Anna trying to talk her out of their little blackmail plan now?"

"It sounded cool at first, according to Anna. The both of us working at the radio station…you're on the radio, talking with the mayor, and me handling all the big name concerts in town. Everybody sees you driving around town in that Ferrari! Nicky and Anna figured they could get at least a couple hundred thousand out of us."

Max sighs. "The dealer I bought that car from told me: The car's a lot of fun but it would keep me in trouble. He was right. And a couple hundred grand? I don't know about you, but they'll be lucky to get a good buzz out of me. I'm broke, Bill."

Bill gives Max a look that says he doesn't believe a word that Max just said. "Yeah, right, Max. Anyway, Anna told me that's why she called the station and asked for me. Then she came up there and waited in the parking lot for me. She and Nicky were gonna get me in another hotel room, take a bunch of pictures, then hit the both of us with the blackmail. Nicky even went back to the Montville Hotel and talked the bellboy into saying that he'd seen the both of us having sex with Anna and Nicky, and forcing them to get high."

Max's blood-shot eyes bug out. "The bellboy was going to sell us out like that? That little motherfucker! I gave him a thousand dollars and an ounce of blow to forget that night ever happened. Damn! Where do they get these snakes from?"

"Anna and I were supposed to go to some hotel over by the Denver Tech Center so we could get high and mess around. But I couldn't find any blow, and you were missing."

"Oh boy, lucky me! So then what happened, Bill? You couldn't find me, so that little problem fucked up their whole plan?"

"Well, not really, Max. We rode around for a while, then we went to the movies and she fell asleep next to me." Bill's face gets soft. "After the movie, I told her we could try it again tomorrow if she'd like, but that I had to get home and get some rest. Said you and I had that big meeting at the station the next day.

"She asked me if she could hang out with me just a little longer, because she didn't like it at home. We went to my place. We talked some more, and I fixed something to eat. When I came out of the kitchen, she was sound asleep. So I covered her up, and I went to bed. When I woke up the next morning, she was still asleep. I left some money on the table and a note. I wrote that she could stay if she liked, and to call me when she woke up."

Max stared at Bill. "Well, ain't that some Lifetime Channel shit! And it doesn't bother you that this little bit—, well, this 'girl' is trying to screw us inside out?"

"That's the thing, Max: it's not her, it's Nicky!"

"Are you sure?"

"Yeah, I'm sure! When I got home from work, Anna was gone. I didn't hear from her until the next night."

"Yeah. Well, vampires do tend to come out at night," Max muttered.

"Stop with the jokes, Max – she ain't no blood sucker!"

"OK – but you said it, not me. I'm still trying to understand how you figure that she's such an angel."

"When she finally showed up again," replies Bill, "she told me the whole thing was a set-up. She knew where to get some stuff all along. But after we talked, she didn't want to do any. She told me she never met a guy who was nice to her and didn't want something in return. She told me that Nicky had the room set up with listening devices and hidden cameras, and was really pissed at Anna when we didn't show up. Max, she told me that she just couldn't do it to me."

"Bill, this Nicky chick is a real live one. I hope you know at this rate, none of this is just going to go away. Not without somebody getting screwed."

"That's why Anna is trying to talk Nicky into leaving the two of us alone."

The radio DJ shoots Bill a look. "The 'two of us'—as in you and me, or you and Anna?"

It takes Bill entirely too long to answer, and Max knows whatever he says, it's coming from the bullshit that's been put in his head by Anna. Finally, Bill's feeble answer comes out.

"To tell you the truth, Max, I'm not trying to leave you out in the cold. The way Anna and I figured it, if Nicky leaves Anna and me alone, she won't have any reason to mess with you."

"*And they lived happily ever after!* That's bullshit, Bill! Nicky is like an STD. She doesn't care who she infects, as long as she has a nice warm body to cling to. She's a parasite: she will always need a host. If she was smart, she'd sit back and let her nut-job husband keep doing the crazy shit he's been doing and sooner or later, it's gonna catch up with him in the form of a bullet through the head, or a long prison sentence. Then she gets everything. But she's too stupid. She can't wait. She wants to do what she wants to do, no matter who gets fucked in the process. But she can't, because he keeps her under his thumb. Bill, I've been trying to keep a lid on this, but this is getting above my pay grade."

"What do you mean by that, Max?"

"What I mean is, they're trying to play hardball, but when you do that, the *real* hardball players come out. Understand this, Bill: when you try to throw shit on people, you can't help but get shit on yourself. Sometimes people throw shit back, and the kind of shit these people throw don't stink, it kills!"

"Who? Like your 'friend', Mann?"

Max knows he has no choice but to tell Bill the truth. He hopes that it will make Bill realize how serious this is.

"Yeah, Bill, like Mann. He's a lot closer to this than you could ever guess. He left town so I could clean this mess up, but all I've managed to do is let it get worse. Right now, he's in Vegas, having a nice quiet vacation and thinking that when he gets back, I'll have everything under control. Bill, I can't call that dude and tell him about this. I promise you, it won't end well for either one of us. We have to put our heads together and fix this, before the WMDs get involved, and I mean it!"

Rushing to a call about gunfire over by the ranch house, the local sheriff on duty pulls his police cruiser off I-95 and slides to a stop at the Lucky 95 truck stop. In a flash, he's out of the car, and through the door, expecting the worst. He's responding to the call of a drunken fight at the truck stop and he's ready for battle. When Deputy Peter Tucker rushes in the door, everyone in the truck stop looks at him exactly the way he's looking at them.

Whatever the problem is, Sheriff Tucker realizes in a second that it isn't a fight — and it doesn't take long to find out what the problem is. Moments after the sheriff enters the truck stop, KABOOM!

Everyone inside hits the floor…then total chaos ensues.

Miles away, Mann hears the distorted noise over the phone. Still trying to talk to Rico, he gets the details he needs, then hangs up. Mann looks for Nesto, and finds him outside of the garage.

"Hey Nesto, it's—"

"I know, I heard it."

"What do you mean, 'you heard it'?"

"While ju were in there, talking on the phone and fooling with that ATV, I heard a low thump, coming from the direction of the truck stop. So I guess they pulled it off. What's the deal now?"

"Rico's cousin had to do it. Rico said that his wrist hurt so much that he couldn't hold the hand grenades. They almost killed a cop."

Nesto immediately starts cursing in Spanish. "I told ju it was a bad idea! Now are we getting the fuck out of here? They hurt a cop! I don't want anything to do with the sheet that gonna come down after this!"

"Relax, Nesto—it wasn't a policeman, it was the *dog*. Surprise!"

"Ju mean a police dog? Damn, that's a relief! So did they put the car out of commission?"

"Oh, yeah. Rico said the sheriff pulled up and ran in the truck stop. Rico's cousin drove up next to the sheriff's car, and was about to throw the grenade in the open window when they heard the dog in the back seat, barking.

"They didn't know what to do next. His cousin said a prayer for the dog, then rolled the grenade under the front of the sheriff's car. They took off down the road and—BAM! Rico said the front the car came off the ground, the doors blew open and the dog flew out. The last time Rico looked, the dog looked like a drunk, staggering down the middle of I-95."

About ninety miles northwest of the ranch, in a house across the alley from the Happy Snake Eyes Bar, Cus Barlow and Lenny Salvo are their usual un-calm and un-collected selves.

"Hey, Boss—look at this."

Coming out of the bathroom, cursing into his cell phone, Cus stops short to see what Lenny's taking about on the TV.

"What is it, Lenny? All I see is the same reporter talking about the same tornado in Oklahoma. I don't give a rat's ass about Oklahoma, or any goddamn tornadoes!"

"No, Boss! Look at what it says across the bottom of the screen."

"Look, Lenny—I'm busy trying to find my shipment. I don't have time for this shit! Just tell me what it says." Barlow turns and starts into another room. Lenny reads aloud from the CNN ticker going across the bottom of the screen.

> *"CNN News is getting unofficial reports that capital investment and real estate tycoon Arthur Singleton has been found dead of what appears to be a self-inflicted gunshot wound. An extremely large explosion also has occurred on his estate destroying Singleton's limousine and*

caused severe damage to Mr. Singleton's mansion in northern Nevada, just south of Reno."

From the other room, Lenny hears Cus before he sees him.

"Holy shit!"

"What do you think, Boss?"

"Get that brother-in-law of yours on the phone. He'd better have my money. I told him to get my dough, and knock off this Singleton guy—but to do it *quietly*, and no trail. I know he's your sister's husband, Lenny, but if he's fucked this up and fingers start to point every which way, then he's got to go!"

"I know, Boss," replied Lenny, "I'm calling now. Still no word on the shipment?"

Cus' frown gets deeper. "No, nothing yet. Call Big Paulie. Tell him to get some of the boys and head out to Singleton's ranch house. But don't go all the way up there—just call me when they get close."

◆————————◈————————◆

Grandpa and the kid pull up in an old Ford tow truck. The kid is still behind the wheel. Mann walks up to the window and looks at the old man.

"Sorry it took so long," wheezes out Grampa, "but this ain't the fastest set of wheels. Oh, brother—what a night!"

Mann nods. "How do the roads look, Pops?"

"Headed this way, the roads are empty… but down by the truck stop all hell has broken loose. You two better rethink trying to take that van full of dope that way."

"Why's that, Gramps? We're just passing by in an old truck. Who's gonna take notice of us?"

"After your friend blew up the police car, the whole town is in the streets. There's no way the tow truck pulling that van is gonna sneak through all that action, and somebody not ask a question or two. My grandson was just starting up the tow truck when the blast went off. I'm not sure, but I think the old coot who owns this truck was woke up by the blast. So you damn sure ain't gonna tow this here van onto my property now."

Mann stands looking dumb-founded.

Nesto scoffs, "Ju guys didn't think about all the attention the blast would bring, did ju?"

The old man kicks back in, "You'd be a damn fool to try and tow this thing through there right now!"

Looking at the old man, Nesto asks, "What if we just stay on the highway and tow the van all the way back to Vegas?"

"Yeah, good idea, Nesto!" replies Mann.

Again, the old man gives the bad news. "You still have to drive by the truck stop! With all that's going on down there, do you want to chance that the old man that owns this truck - or somebody else - spots you? There's going to be a lot of other sheriffs flying up and down I-95 in about 30 minutes."

"I thought you said there was only one sheriff in this area," said Mann, squinting at the grandfather.

"Yeah, that's right: I did say that there is only one sheriff in this area. But three other counties are less than an hour away. You guys *blew up a sheriff's car!* How long before the place is crawlin' in lawmen? Hell, by sun-up, they'll have the helicopters out."

"What if we hit 95 South? Where will that take us?"

"That's no good, either. That only takes you to open country in the middle of the desert. If somebody spots you and decides to pull you over, you're sitting ducks. And neither one of you look like you belong out here."

"And there's no way we could lay low here until tomorrow night?" asks Mann.

Everybody looks at Mann like he's crazy.

Incredulous, the kid yells, "What did you just say?"

Nesto echoes the boy's astonishment. "Maw, even the kid knows that's a real stupid idea!"

Gramps continues with even more bad news. "Even if you could lay low, your friend over there has a hole blown clear though his foot. It won't be long before that thing gets infected. Then his foot will be history, if not his whole leg."

Hearing the old man's diagnosis on his injured foot brings panic to Nesto's face. "Ok, fuck this, Maw! Let's get moving!"

The kid is still pondering the problem, then calls out. "Hey, Grandpa, I have an idea." The kid and his grandfather huddle up and start talking really low.

Mann watches as they seem to be debating the best plan of action. He can't help but wonder why the grandfather, who is definitely Mexican or American Indian, has a grandson who is, without a doubt, African-American.

More than that, the grandson is fully equipped with an East Coast swagger, a Chicago White Sox hat on backwards, and a pair of Jordans on his feet. He also seems to be quite at home with the criminal element.

Mann looks at his watch and starts to say something, but then the kid and his grandfather break their huddle.

The kid speaks first. "Mr. Mann, you said if we got Rico to the truck stop before the sheriff got there, you would give us ten thousand dollars."

"Well, yeah, I did say that, but I can't give you a thing if we can't get out," replies Mann.

"That's OK, you can keep the ten thou — because the price just went up. *Way up*."

Nesto lets his anger and frustration fly. "I've had all the bullsheet I can take, Maw! Ju gonna let them squeeze us for more money, and we can't even get the fuck outta here?"

"I'm feeling you on this one, Nesto," Mann replies. "I'm ready to say the hell with it."

The old man jumps in, "No, no; you misunderstand. My grandson was raised back East. Sometimes he forgets where he's at and thinks he's back the big city. Let me explain. On the way to the truck stop, Rico told us what's going on. He also said how much that load in the van is worth. My grandson and I have an idea how to get the both of you *and* that van out of here."

Nesto rubs his hand over his face. "Oh, brother! Who do we have to blow up this time, Maw?"

"Be quiet, Nesto. I don't see you coming up with anything."

"What? I said let's get on that ATV and get the hell out of here a long time ago! Don't ju tell me I'm not---"

Mann is enraged. "Bullshit, Nesto! If it weren't for you keeping my money, I wouldn't be—"

The old man steps in between Mann and Nesto. "You both better calm down. We're running out of time." The grandfather then nods to his grandson, who runs over to the tow truck and starts backing it up to the van.

Gramps continues. "Here's how we can help each other. Like I said, Rico told us about the value of the shipment. Now—understand we don't want any money tonight, but when you bring Rico his cut, we want one hundred thousand dollars."

"Oh, sheet! For *what?* Getting us caught?"

"No, Mr. Nesto—that doesn't make any sense. If *you* get caught, how do *we* get paid? No. First thing we need to do is hook up the van to the tow truck. Then you two are gonna drive down that back road you used to sneak up here. About a half-mile or so, there's a fork in the road. You're going to turn left onto Old Miners' Road, headed west. It's 2:30 now. So pulling the van with this old truck, using that beat up road…it should take you until sun-up to get to Route 6. You got that so far?"

Mann and Nesto try to repeat the instructions, which both men have totally screwed up.

Gramps sighs and shakes his head. "Never mind. I'll draw you a map. Look, when you get to Route 6, you'll turn right, headed north. You'll be on the other side of Silverton. Route 5 takes you around Silverton and back onto I-95. You'll come out on the other side of Silverton and all this mess. Come here, and see how I drew it up for you."

Again, Nesto is the first to question the plan. "Are ju serious? One hundred thousand dollars—for *this*?"

Mann quickly backs Nesto. "He's right, Gramps. That does seem like a lot just for directions to another road that we could have probably found ourselves."

"Wait a minute, guys. The money ain't for directions. It's to guarantee you make it."

"Ok," replied Mann, "now we're talking. How you gonna do that?"

"Me and my grandson are going into the house and watch TV."

Nesto is already hot. "What the fu—"

Grandpa keeps talking. "We're gonna watch TV until the sheriff gets here. Then we're gonna tell them some guys we never saw before asked us if we could load some boxes for a few dollars. Then while we were loading up the truck, some guys in a black Cadillac pulled up. A couple of gangster-looking guys got out. Then they all started to argue about how somebody owed somebody else a lot of money. The shooting started, and I took my grandson and ran into the house, hiding under the bed for a long time after the shooting stopped. When we finally came out, we found all this mess. My grandson and I were so scared, I had to cover his ears to keep him from crying from all the noise. He's only thirteen but he's not right in the head, if you know what I mean. The poor little guy…"

Both the kid and his grandfather look at Mann with big puppy-dog eyes. The kid starts talking again, but this time he's not so sharp.

"Mis-ster Policeman, can you make your car go 'Eerrr, Eerrr', like on TV? Them bad guys, they go bang bang."

Then he promptly digs in his nose. Both Mann and Nesto crack up.

"Maw, I think we should let the kid handle the shipment. He'd probably get a better price than either one of us!"

"Yeah—that, or we wind up working for him! OK, grandpa, you got a deal. You have a cell phone?"

The old man gives Mann a "Duh!" response. Mann backs off.

"Ok, sorry. When the sheriff gets here, call me and let me know if it looks like they're not buying your story. Let me know *right away*, ok?"

"Ok," replies Gramps.

Donnie is listening to every word, then asks, "How long before we get our money?"

Mann has to smile at the kid's business sense. "Don't worry, kid—I'll make sure to pay you! I don't want *you* looking for me. OK— Nesto, get in the truck. Me and little Al Capone here are gonna hook up the van. It's already ten to three. It'll be morning before you know it. We better step on it.'"

"Hello? Where's my dough, Antwan? And what the fuck happened up there?…I thought I told you 'nice and quiet'! The people on the news said that they felt the explosion over a mile away. I know for your sake, this better not come back on me, you black son of a bitch!...What?...I don't care if you can't hear out of your left ear!...Where the fuck is my money!"

Antwan tells Cus Barlow what happened: finding Singleton dead, and some guy who claims to be Singleton's nephew trying to escape with the money. "Mr. Barlow, I know this isn't what you wanted, but you never said anything about another person trying to pull the double-cross. I got one bag of money, and the other bag was in the limo when it blew!"

"How do I know you're not trying to pull a double-cross yourself, and keep half the money," snarled Cus.

"Mr. Barlow, just check it out. The police said they found burned up money everywhere. How much money was that bag anyway?"

"Five million hard-earned dollars, and if I don't get my shipment, I'm taking it out on every fucking body! You *capiesce?* Now get the rest of my dough down here, now!"

"Lenny, you talk to him!" Barlow tosses the phone at Lenny, then turns back to the special report on CNN.

The reporter continues to give information on what appears to be a staged suicide and car bombing. Officers are not commenting on the reports of human remains found in the wreckage of the bombed-out limousine.

Barlow throws the remote control at the TV, then snatches up another phone, calling his boys on their way to the ranch house.

"Hello, Paulie—where the fuck are you guys?...Well if you couldn't find Ike, why didn't you just come and get Lenny?...Never mind...You're just now leaving Vegas? It's almost three-thirty. Dawn's coming — so step on it! I need you in front of that ranch house in an hour, you hear me?" Barlow hangs up on Paulie and throws the phone on the couch. "Lenny? Lenny!"

Cus is bellowing at the top of his lungs. His face is red, and his blood pressure is only half as high as his anger is right now. Lenny, being used to Cus Barlow's outbursts, runs into the room.

"What is it, Boss?"

"What did your brother-in-law say?"

"He told me he'll try and get here by tonight. I told him that it better be sooner than later, but two of his guys were hurt really bad in the explosion."

"Goddamn it, Lenny, you said he knew what he was doing! So why was the explosion so big?"

"He told me that his men put the wrong charge on the limo. He had a small one for the car and a big one in case he had to blow the house. Boss, what's this shit about Singleton already being dead?"

"I think that fag butler pulled a double-cross on Singleton. Antwan told me he said he was Singleton's nephew. But the description of the nephew he gave me sounds like the butler. If your brother-in-law didn't show up when he did, that double-crossing piece shit would have walked with all ten million. If I don't get my shipment, I'm up shit creek, because half of that ten million belongs to the Santos Brothers."

"The Santos Brothers?! Boss—what are you gonna do?"

"I'm not sure, Lenny, but if I don't come up with their half in either cash or blow, that fat piece of shit Bruno Santos is gonna start a war."

Mann never thought driving and talking on the phone could be so difficult. But even though the road is washed out and looks like it hasn't been used in fifty years, it's still not as hard to navigate as it is trying to talk with a *Very-Pissed-Off* Monica.

"...I know, baby, it's just that I had my phone off...no, NOT so you couldn't bother me...it was so some people that were looking for my friend wouldn't hear it ringing. I can't tell you over the phone...Listen, Monica, we're about to be real rich...No, baby, I'm not bullshitting...What?...No, no, don't do that...OK, soon as I get back to Vegas...No, I'm still in Vegas...I mean, I'm right outside of town. I should be there, say about 6:00 in the morning...NO, I am NOT at a whorehouse...Yes, I love you, and no, I am not loaded."

Nesto is laughing so hard, he's about to have a heart attack. If it weren't for his injured foot, he'd be having the time of his life watching Mann try to talk his way out of the shit-pile he's in with Monica.

The Old Miners' Road has been around since Vegas was a watering outpost for the Pony Express, and because they're towing the van, they're lucky to be doing twenty miles an hour. Mann and Nesto are bouncing around in the truck like two tennis balls in a metal trash can.

"What the fuck, Maw! We're bouncing around so much, I think my foot's bleeding again."

"Here, use some of the stuff I got out of the house. Wrap it up tight, put it up on the dashboard. Try and keep it elevated."

"Maw, we're being tossed around this road too much. I can barely stay on the seat! The hell with it, I'll be alright. I already called Lester. When we get to Vegas, he'll meet us at my room. He knows what to do."

"He EVER go home?"

"He's home now. I have his cell number. Taking care of people like us, Lester makes more dinero in a week than most people do in a month. If I want to screw one-legged hooker on the deck of – *como se dice?* – 'aircraft carrier' - for the right price, Lester could make it happen in the same day."

Mann gives Nesto a doubtful look, asking, "If he's so good, why didn't you call him when we were stuck out here?"

Nesto shakes his head. "I wish I could, but he won't do it. When I first start to deal with him, he warned me. He said he could get me in and out of any place, or any situation. He can even get me out of most bad circumstances—but don't call him if the wolves are already snapping at my ass. He said if they're already on me, then it's too late….Hey Maw, ju alright? Ju hear a word I said?"

"Yeah, I heard every word you said, and it got me to thinking. I'm just…I don't know. Every time I try and avoid shit like this, it seems to look for me, and before I know it, I'm in the middle of a shit-storm! Then there's Monica. She doesn't deserve to have to worry about whether I'm coming home in one piece, or if I'm coming home at all."

Mann can feel his next headache, waiting patiently for a good time to strike. "I'm sure you already know that was her on the phone just now. She told me that she just won ten thousand dollars on a lucky bet, playing craps. And you know what she said? Everyone there was happier than her because the person she should be sharing this with was nowhere to be found."

"That's fucked up, Maw; ju are a real piece of sheet," replies Nesto, laughing. "No, I'm just kidding, but ju know how this life is."

Mann sighed. "Sometimes I feel like I have another lover. There's never enough of me to go around. No matter how hard I try, I can't seem to satisfy everybody."

"So, don't let it get ju down. If ju were as bad as they make it seem, I sure they wouldn't be waiting for ju either. But the hell with all that right now. How much farther do ju think we gotta go before we're off of this washboard ju call a road?"

"I don't know, but when we went over the top of that last hill, I could see some lights over that way. I'm pretty sure we're almost to Route 6. Nesto, check if the radio in this thing works."

Nesto turns it on, and of course it's on the country music station. Nesto looks at Mann, then keeps turning.

"Wait, Nesto—turn back! Right there!" The voice on the radio has that classic country twang. What Mann thought was the news station turns out to be the local hell, fire-and-brimstone religious station.

> *"What's going on out there, folks? Police cars are getting bombed, some rich guy earlier today kills himself, and then his limousine blows up. And all this right here in Nevada! I'm telling you people, if you don't know what it is, I'll tell you: it is God's holy wrath! The Devil is on the loose and—"*

Mann overrides the radio preacher's voice. "That's more than I can handle right now. Please find a news station. I think that guy was talking about us!"

"Ju damn right, he's talking about us. Unless ju know somebody else riding around, blowing up sheriffs' cars."

"Look over there, Nesto. I think that's Route 6, and just in time. It's sun-up, and I didn't want to be on this backroad in the daylight."

Nesto tunes the radio into a news report.

> *"Good Morning, and this is PR News. Last night, sometime between 2:30 and 3 a.m., in Silverton County Nevada, just sixty miles outside of Las Vegas, somebody threw an explosive device under a Silverton County Sheriff's police cruiser.*

> *"No one was hurt except a police dog in the back seat of the police car. The dog narrowly escaped with his life jumping out of the back seat when the doors blew open. The police say they have no leads, but have Interstate-95 Southbound closed, and are searching all vehicles as part of their investigation. Earlier, neighbors had reported what they said sounded like a major gun battle just south of a Silverton truck stop.*

A police spokesperson had this to say: 'We don't know if this is the work of them Taliban fellas, but the bombing definitely was a set-up. Somebody called in a big fight at the truck stop, but when the officer showed up, there wasn't a problem. That's when the K-9 officer was attacked in the car. As soon as we get air support, we're gonna check out a report about a gun battle just south of here!' "

"Yep, we're famous now," said Nesto as the radio starts up a local savings bank jingle. "Maw, I hope ju know what jour doing!"

As soon as Mann pulls the truck onto Route 6, a helicopter races overhead, zooming in the general direction of the ranch house. Mann and Nesto both watch as the helicopter disappears over a ridge.

"Oh boy, it's getting hot out here!"

"Be quiet, Nesto! I'm trying to hear what they're saying on the radio," responds Mann. The news report continues:

"...and this explosion comes on the heels of a mysterious incident in northern Nevada. Multi-millionaire Arthur Singleton was found dead last night of an apparent self-inflicted gunshot wound to the head. Police were drawn to his estate after

*a very large explosion rocked the affluent South
Reno suburb.*

*"Police are not releasing much information, but
it appears as if somebody placed a large
explosive device in Mr. Singleton's limousine,
killing a thus-far unidentified victim. There are
unofficial reports that Mr. Singleton owned
property just south of the Silverton County truck
stop which was bombed later last night. The FBI
have been called in to the investigation."*

"I don't believe it, Maw! That's the rich guy, the one who
just killed himself. That's the guy who owes the money
for this stuff!"

Mann took his eyes off the road and stared at Nesto. "I
thought you said that he was in Europe. Nesto, what in
the hell's going on?"

"I dunno, Maw!"

"Why isn't this guy in Europe?" Mann was puzzled.
"Why is he dead, and who blew up his car? Hey…I bet it
was your brother. Your brother found out he wasn't in
Europe and had him hit!"

"My *brother*? What? No way! My brother don't order no
hits. He's a rich, fat fuck like the guy who just killed
himself. Lanceo's got so much money, he don't know

what to do with himself. He should have retired ten years ago, but he's still a greedy fuck, and he's got me to do his leg work."

"So why did he call this Singleton guy and threaten him about not paying?"

Nesto chuckled. "He has to keep up a front, Maw. Everybody has to think jour gonna come and kill them if jour a dollar short on a million bucks. The only reason he even knew about Singleton not paying is because *I told him*."

The Colombian winced as he shifted his injured foot. "Maw, all that sheet ju hear about cartels cutting off heads and taking over Colombia—that's all a bunch of bullsheet. They bought and paid for Colombia a long time ago! Ju can thank America's cocaine habit for that one. Cartels are part of the world economy now. They lend money to small countries. They bail out big business like Peace Computer. That sheet on TV about cartels on the U.S. - Mexican border, killing up people and attacking the policia? That's not the cartels—that's a bunch of Mexican street gangs having turf wars! It's all *political*. 'Jour Government at Work'."

"Wait a minute," replies Mann, "how's the U.S. Government involved? Don't they want to stop all that shit?"

"Hell, no! Maw, it's about the border! If there's peace along the border, then a lot of people will say, 'Go ahead – open up the border and let them come and go as they please'—just like the U.S.-Canadian border.

"But the people in Washington, the ones who make the rules, and make all the *dinero*? *They* don't want it open. Matter of fact, they're scared that if the border opens up, they'll lose control. Don't ju forget, there's power in numbers. They're already feeling the scale tip out of their favor: look at Texas and California.

"So they keep starting *sheet* down there. Remember the guns the ATF sold to the so-called cartels about a year or two ago? It had some stupid code name…it was all over the news! That was on purpose: they sent some agents to buy drugs from one gang, then go to the other gang and tell them *'those other guys across town said ju guys can't sell stuff in this town – it's* their *town.'* So then ju Americans trade guns for dope with that second gang.

"Then jour U.S. Government sits back and watches the Mexicans tear each other to pieces…then they run back and tell jour people: *'See? Look at them! We can't let them in our country! If we do, they'll bring all this violence with them!'* And it's always this way, always along the border. Have ju ever asked jourself, 'why is that?' "

Mann's head is spinning, thinking about what Nesto's just told him: it had a very uncomfortable ring of truth to it, and was so much deeper than Mann wanted to contemplate.

Despite the beat-up van they are towing, they're making much better time since getting off the dirt road and onto Route 6. Wanting to break away from the deep political conversation, Mann looks over the road and says, "Nesto, speaking of borders, look at that sign."

"*Welcome to Silverton, pop: 20,000'.* Ok: where to now?"

Mann glances at a piece of paper. "The old man's map just says to stay on this road. It curves around Silverton and heads east towards I-95...Nesto, this is creepy: it's too empty. Why is it so—"

"Maw, it's Sunday morning. Ju ain't slept in how many days?"

Mann sighs and nods. "I lost count. Let's find a gas station and see what the locals are saying."

"Do you know what kind of car Nicky drives?"

Max and Bill pull into a hotel's large parking lot on Denver's south side.

"Yeah," responds Bill, "I think it's a Lexus. I'll know it when I see it."

"You sure they're at this hotel?"

"I'm hoping so."

"Why this one?" asks Max, scanning a row of parked cars, looking for a Lexus.

"Anna said that Nicky comes here a lot. She knows the front desk clerk, and they look out for each other."

"How we gonna find the right room?"

Bill sighs. "I don't know. I'm hoping we find her car, set off the car alarm or something. Damn, there are a lot of cars out here!"

Max gives Bill a look of disbelief, then reminds himself whom he's dealing with. "Bill – that's *not* what we want: a bunch of pissed off people looking out their windows this time in the morning. Have you tried calling the front desk and asking them if they have a Nicky, umm, let's see. Try 'Nicole' – see if they have a 'Nicole Spriggs' on their guest list."

Bill listens to Max's instructions, then dials the phone. "Yes, I'm trying to contact Nicky -- uh, I mean Nicole Spriggs – a Mrs. Nicole Spriggs. Do you have anyone with a room under that name?"

"Nicky or Nicole – which one, sir?"

"Do you have either?" Bill's voice is starting to crack and sound a little suspicious. He's hesitates and doesn't know what to do next. Looking at Max, he whispers, "They want to know who I am!"

Max rolls his eyes and reaches out for the phone. "Give me that thing." Putting on his in-charge voice, Max speaks to the desk clerk on the cell. "Uh, yes – I'm sorry! I had my little brother call while I parked my car. I'm trying to get in touch with my good friend Nicole. Some people call her Nicky."

The voice on the other end is beginning to sound a bit leery.

"If she's your good friend, why don't you know her room number?"

"Because she normally meets me in the parking lot," replies Max. "I just talked to her. She's supposed to be waiting on me to come up, but I've forgotten the room number, and she's not answering her cell."

Max is hoping the person he's talking to is one of the desk clerks that knows Nicky. He takes a chance and tries to appeal to what he hopes is their bad habit.

"Do you know her? If you do, then you know she's probably 'on one'...if you know what I mean. I've traveled all this way out here so she can pick up her, uhm, *stuff* from me, and I don't have any plans to come back out here. Could you tell me if Nicole is registered in one of your rooms" said Max, playing the annoyed connection man.

The voice gives off a small laugh, then says, "Yes, we are talking about the same Nicky, and yes, she's 'on one.' I seen her earlier, and she said she would bring me something down. But she ain't came back down. Probably up there trippin'. Let me connect you. If she don't answer, she's in Room 435. Hey, bro--" The voice on the other end gets real low, as if it mattered who might hear, then says, "Before you go up there, stop by the front desk and hook me up. Nicky was supposed to, but she's too goddamn greedy, and I can't leave the desk for another hour."

"Ok," Max tells the hotel voice, then hands the phone back to Bill. "Take this – the desk is calling the room now." Max can't believe what has just happened, and silently wonders, *is everyone getting high?*

The phone ring in Bill's ear a few times, then Bill puts it on speaker phone. He is practically willing someone to answer. Finally, Anna's voice comes across the line.

"Hello? Hello? Who's this?"

"Anna! Anna, it's me, baby, it's Bill!"

"Oh, Bill, where are you? How did you find me? Bill, I'm in trouble!" She starts crying and hangs up. Instantly, Bill is in a panic.

"Max, what room is she in? You heard her, she's in trouble!"

"Slow down, Bill – we gotta play this one cool. So she's 'in trouble'? She didn't say what *kind of* trouble?"

"No," replies Bill, already looking desperate.

"Take it easy," Max advises, "try and call her back."

Bill promptly gets Anna back on the phone. "Hello, Anna? What's wrong? I'm coming up, ok?"

"Don't come in the front way," whispers Anna. "Go to the back of the parking lot. I'll let you in the emergency exit."

Bill points toward the far end of the hotel. "Max, drive there: she's gonna let us in the back door."

Max frowns. "The back door, huh. Back doors mean trouble. Got beat up by a jealous husband at a back door one time."

"Max, I'm serious!"

"So am I." Max squints through the windshield. "There it is. Hey, is that her in the door? What has she got on – a night shirt?"

The car hasn't stopped, and Bill is trying to jump out. Max catches his arm.

"Bill, take it easy! We don't want anybody to see you running into the building. Here, let me park the car. Ok, now - take a deep breath." Bill nervously tries to slow himself down. "Ok, that's more like it. Now – let's just *walk* to the door. Come on."

Anna's no longer standing at the door, but it's still open. Max says, "The front desk said they're in Room 435. Let's take the stairs here. Did she say anything about...I hope we don't need a gun!" Patting his pocket, Max asks Bill, "You got a knife?"

"We don't need anything like that. It's Anna! She would tell me if we did need one."

They make their way up the stairs and enter the hallway. Max sees her first, then points her out to Bill. He takes off running towards Anna. When he reaches her, Bill grabs her off her feet and they both disappear through an open door Max walks in a couple seconds later, and Anna lets out a small scream.

"I didn't know you were with Max!"

"Yeah, baby," answers Bill, "if it hadn't been for Max, I don't think I could have found you."

Anna gives them both a sick look, then says, "I wish you hadn't!" She breaks down crying. Max doesn't like it: Anna's one of the tough ones, and tough ones don't cry easily. He looks around the room; it's a mess, but not a wreck like the Montville was.

Max hears water running and says, "Sounds like someone's in the shower…"

Neither Bill nor Anna answer. Max continues his room survey: there's a pile of dope on the nightstand with all the extras: pipe, lighter, razor, mirror, and of course, powder. Max's eyes stop on the powder.

"Alrighty, then! I see you saved a bit of breakfast for me!" Max takes his finger, dabs it in the powder, brings it to his nose and snorts. As he brings his finger down for a second one, his eye catches something in the trashcan. Max finishes his nose job, but never takes his eyes off the can. Anna is oblivious to Max, her head still buried in

Bill's chest. Not wanting to know, Max finally brings himself to ask, "Excuse me, but what's that?"

Anna looks up at Max, then down at the trashcan where Max is pointing. She really didn't have to, since she'd been watching Max's every move from the corner of her eye. Now that she knows what Max is looking at, she really starts crying.

Bill looks at Max, then asks him, "What did you do to Anna?"

"I didn't do shit! You should be asking her what the hell she's done," replies Max angrily.

Max picks up a pen from the nightstand that looks as if it had doubled as a snort straw. He uses it to fish a shirt out of the trash can, recognizing the garment as the shirt Anna had on yesterday at his house.

"Oh, my God! Is that blood?" Max blurts.

Bill snaps his head around and comes face-to-face with Anna's blood-soaked shirt.

In a calm and deliberate voice, Max asks, "Anna, is there something we need to know?"

He looks around the room again, then suddenly drops the shirt and runs into the bathroom. Opening the door, the shower has steamed up the room so much that Max can barely see. Reaching behind the shower curtain, he turns the water off and pulls the curtain all the way back.

Bill and Anna hear Max yell from the bathroom, and he stumbles back out, falling on the floor and landing at the foot of the bed. Max rolls over and looks up; both Bill and Anna are just staring at him with penetrating look. Anna's no longer crying; her head tilts to one side, like a puppy when it hears a strange sound. Bill is looking straight through Max.

In a shaky voice, Max asks, "Bill? Bill, you hear me?"

"Yeah, Max, I hear you."

"In the bathroom…you knew, huh?"

Bill raises his head, looking blindly at the ceiling, then answers, "I guess we don't have to worry about Nicky anymore, do we?"

Max is shocked by Bill's reply, but the calm in the room is infectious, and Max is overcome with an odd sense of relief. He doesn't know why, but the panic that had him cornered only a few moments ago has disappeared.

Slowly getting up off the floor Max replies, "No, Bill, I guess you're right. We don't have to worry about Nicky anymore. She's there in the tub, and she's white as the tub. There's a big cut across her throat, but I don't think there's a drop of blood in her ---." Max looks Anna directly in her eyes; they don't look like Anna's eyes at all.

"Tell me, Anna – how did Nicky wind up like that?"

Anna smiles, looking more like a child than Max had ever noticed before. "I killed her."

CHAPTER 5

"Mann, don't stop. I got a bad feeling, like they're in their houses, waiting for us to stop."

"Yeah, I know what you mean. It's just too quiet. It feels like a set-up. I've only seen two cars on the road so far.

"And there goes another helicopter. That's the third one in less than an hour. Boy, we got them stirred up out there!"

"Hey, a little town like this doesn't see a lot of action."

"I know – most *big* cities don't see their police cars blown up! …Hey, Maw, jour phone is ringing."

Mann was so preoccupied with looking over the area, he didn't hear the phone. Telling himself there's no way that they're stopping for *anything,* he cautiously answers his cell.

"Hello…yes, I can hear you….They are? You got your story together?...Ok, how many of them are there?....Hey, listen, Pops – if there's something wrong, like they don't believe you or ask about the tow truck, ask them if you can call your family to let them know that you're alright… If they do, call me and say you're scared but safe…..Got that?...Ok…Good Luck!"

Wiping the sweat from his forehead, Mann looks at Nesto and says, "Oh boy! That was Gramps on the phone, and he says there are two helicopters. One of them is landing; the other one is just circling overhead. There are sheriff cars coming up the road. I could hear them on the bullhorn, telling them to get on the ground with their arms spread."

"Yes, sir, ju want to talk about getting shit stirred up? Jour government ain't got nothing on us. I hope Pops and the kid can handle it."

"I'm sure the grandson can do it, and Pops – he's old enough that he knows they can't do anything to them: they'll be alright. *It's us* that I'm worried about. Turn that radio back on. We're good on fuel, so I'm putting my foot into it a little more. The sooner we're on the road to Vegas, the better. That road sign back there said the exit to I-95 is another 10 miles…Speaking of foot – how's yours, Nesto?"

"It was fine until ju just reminded me!"

"Oops. Sorry."

Cus Barlow and Lenny are stuck in front of the television.

"I better call Paulie and the boys – this is *bad*. The news! Special Reports! Police helicopters! I sure hope the boys don't do something stupid and get themselves in a jam!'

Dialing the phone, Barlow can't take his eyes off the TV. "Hello?.. Hey, Paulie, where are you at right now? ...Yeah, I know about the police and the helicopters. That's why I'm calling...I don't know what's happening...I don't think it has anything to do with our shipment, but somebody just blew up a cop car just a few miles away from Singleton's ranch house ..It's way too hot to even think about going out there. Turn around right now."

Cus puts the phone down and runs his hand through his hair, taking a deep breath.

"Lenny, get me a drink – Fuck it! Bring me the whole bottle! We need a drink. Paulie and the boys are ok. I'm kinda glad they got a late start. Otherwise, if they would got out of here when I first told them to, they would been in the middle of all that confusion! He said there's cops and helicopters everywhere! He can't take a chance on making a U-turn on the freeway with all that shit going on, so they're going to keep heading that way until they get to the Silverton exit. He said it's another five miles."

"That sounds good, Boss. If he's just coming up on Silverton, that's far enough away from the truck stop where they shouldn't draw any attention. Boss! Can you see Big Paulie, Ike and Bruiser in the Cadillac with all those cops flying around them?"

"Oh man, I didn't think about that! I bet Bruiser's ass is so tight, he can't fart."

Cus and Lenny have a good laugh. As bad as things were going, they had to find something to laugh about.

◆————————◈————————◆

"Look, Nesto! *'I-95 North to Las Vegas – 1 mile.'* I love it when a plan comes together. You wanna know where I got that saying from?"

"No, and I don't give a sheet either. Tell me about it when the plan is complete. I just wish I knew what was happening with the old man and the kid."

"Don't worry, they'll be ok. Look at all the traffic on the road — it's headed back the other way, and that police car that shot past us a minute ago didn't even give us a second look. All we gotta do is sit back and enjoy the ride! Cool?"

The confident look on Mann's face gives Nesto a small feeling of relief before he answers. Ok."

Mann glances at his partner's face, "You don't sound very happy. What's up?"

"Now I gotta find a buyer for all this stuff. It's a lot harder than ju think, and can really get dangerous."

"Buyer! I thought you were going to Vegas to host the world's biggest cocaine party!"

"Maw, you been dipping in the stuff again?"

"Well…"

Landing at the ranch house and ducking out of the helicopter, the cheap suit, dark glasses and clean-cut face were a dead giveaway: the Feds were on-site. The FBI agent walks up to the local sheriff, and in a matter-of-fact way says, "Hello, I'm FBI Special Agent Bowles. And you are…?"

"I'm Deputy Sheriff Watson, and I'm in charge here."

"Yes, of course you are. We're not trying to snatch the rug from under you. As far as we can tell, there's nothing up here that falls under federal jurisdiction. We were just hoping you wouldn't mind if we have a look around…See if anything up here ties in with the bombing at the truck stop. You do understand that, because there were explosives involved, we have precedence in that matter."

Sheriff Watson wasn't happy about that fact, but he knows there isn't much he can do about it. "Damn shame we can't investigate our own car getting blown up. I'll tell you what, Agent Balls…"

Bowles couldn't stand these country-bumpkin sheriffs, with their cowboy boots, .357's and a mouth full of *chawin' tabackee*. Sheriff Watson fit the country-boy stereotype to a tee: Tall with a barrel chest, tight jeans, cowboy boots and a ten-gallon hat – that, and plenty of attitude.

"That's Agent BOWLES, not Balls."

"Oh, I'm sorry! I thought that would be a compliment. *'Bowles'*, is it, uhm? Well, like I was sayin', your fellas got my car and my truck stop all to yerselves. Hell, man – that was my deputy they tried to take out. And my best trackin' dog. The vet says he's blind in one eye, and he'll probably never fully hear again. You see, it's a job to you, but to me, it's *personal*."

Agent Bowles was hoping they wouldn't bump heads. It's obvious he isn't going to get his wish. Bowles does his best to claim the situation.

"I understand your feelings about this, so what do you need from us? I'm more than willing to share any information that we learn with you, and I hope you will do the same. At the end of the day, we're on the same team, right?"

Sheriff Watson spits a large lump of tobacco right between Agent Bowles' feet, then says, "I don't care too much for team sports, but when I play, I don't sit on no fuckin' bench. You want help from me? Then you gotta guarantee that if the S.O.B. that tried to hurt my deputy, kill my car, and fuck up my best dog is a local, you'll stand down and let me at him!"

"Well, Officer Watson---"

"That's 'Sheriff'!"

"I'm sorry, *Sheriff* Watson, if there's something out there that can help the both of us, I'll keep you at the top of the list when I hand in my report."

"I guess you ain't hearin' me. I ain't no goddamn hillbilly redneck from Junction Fuck Valley. We're about 60 miles outside of Las Vegas, and I've been dealin' with hustlers, pimps, gangsters and highway men since you were sittin' on your thumbs and playin' with Hot Wheels cars. Now stop tryin' to tell me it's shine on my shoes when I know that it's shit! Either we got a deal like I called it, or get the fuck off of my crime scene!"

Bowles knows it's pointless to argue with Watson now. He gives in and agrees to the terms. Sheriff Watson gives Bowles a quick briefing on what they've discovered at the ranch house.

"We got four bodies; two of them locals. Two of them gunshot victims, and the other two look like they were ran down. We still got one under that van over there; he's one of the locals. We also have two locals alive. They said they were offered money to load a van with furniture, but before they had a chance to do any work, some fellows in a black Cadillac pulled up. They talked a few minutes, then a shoot-out started. The old man and his grandson over there – they said they hid in the house until the shootin' stopped. They're both a little slow in the head, know what I mean? Harmless."

Bowles looks at Donnie and his grandfather. They look dirty, scare and confused. Bowles decides he's had all he can take of these people, and takes a pass on interviewing them. Turning back to the sheriff, he says, "I'm sure you already have an APB on the black Cadillac. I have eyes in the sky. It's probably too late, but I'll tell you what: I can have my pilot run up and down I-95 and see if we can spot anything for you."

"You're right, by now, they're down a rabbit hole somewhere…but go ahead. I appreciate it."

Bowles gives the information to his pilot when he climbs back in the helicopter.

At the same time Agent Bowles and Sheriff Watson are going at it, Mr. C. L. Woods, the owner of the tow truck, is giving Mann and Nesto a blessing they would never know about. Mr. Woods is standing with a small crowd, outside of the yellow crime scene tape that borders the truck stop. Junior FBI Agent Taylor walks up to the edge of the tape, facing the crowd, and calls out in a clear voice: "Does everybody here live in this area?"

Most of the crowd indicates that they're local folks. Taylor continues. "That's good. I'm Special Agent Taylor of the FBI. I'm conducting an investigation into the bombing. We would like to know if anyone here has seen, heard or noticed anything unusual – maybe a new face in town, or a strange car. Anything other than the shooting that everyone heard last night. We already know about that."

None of the people step up to say anything.

"Nothing? Well, ok – we'd appreciate it if you would contact your local sheriff's department if you do see something that's not right, no matter now little you might think it is. Thank you and have a nice day."

Mr. C.L. Woods thinks about the question for a minute. Even though he had looked right at the spot where he left his vehicle the night before, he was in such a rush to run down to the truck stop, it never dawns on him that his green and rust-colored Ford tow truck is missing from the side of his barn.

"Max, slow down on that stuff!"

"Don't worry, Bill, if I do all of Anna's stuff - I still got a big baggie in the car. And it's almost full to the top!"

"That's not what I'm talking about—"

"Bill, I don't give a damn about what you're saying or what you think, because it's obvious you don't give a shit about me! I really don't think you give a damn about *yourself,* because if you did, neither one of us would be about to go to jail for complicity to a murder!"

Trying to reason with his friend, Bill replies, "We're not going to jail for murder, Max!"

Max holds the mirror of cocaine up to his face. "I'm glad that you're so calm, because you're going to need that calm when you're trying to explain this one to the cops— as they try and beat a confession out of you!" He does another very large line of coke, wipes his nose with his sleeve, and then continues.

"Anna, please tell me that you walked in on the murder, and all we have to do is take you down to the police station and you can tell them who did it. You can tell them who it is, and we'll be heroes. Then we can get our pictures in the—"

"Max!" yells Bill, "Stop it!! You know that's not what happened. You're sweating, so sit down, dude – you've done too much blow! You're starting to lose it!"

"I have yet to do enough as far as I'm concerned," replies Max. He reaches over for the pen snort straw on the night stand. "As a matter of fact--" With a knock on the room door, Max jumps and looks around wildly. "Was that the door, Bill?"

Anna runs to the door, looks through the peep-hole, and lets out a sigh of relief. "It's Pat - she works at the front desk!" Calling though the door, Anna says, "Pat, we're in bed. Come back a little later."

There's a moment of silence, then comes the reply. "Bullshit, girl! Let me in! You're not getting rid of me until I get mine. I know that guy came up here with the stuff. Come on, let me in! Goddamn it, you know I work here and have a pass key."

Max's eyes pop as he hears the door click. Anna yells, "Hold on, Pat, let me --" Before she can get another word out, there's a loud bang and the safety chain catches the door. Again Anna yells out, "Hold *on*, bitch! Wait a minute! Damn, you're pissing me off!"

Max runs into the bathroom and slams the door. Taking a quick look around the room, Anna points across the room and whispers, "Bill, the trash can!"

Bill jumps over the bed and grabs the trashcan with the bloody shirt in it. He runs to the bathroom door, opens it, throws the can in and slams it closed, right as Anna opens the front door to let Pat in.

Pissed, Anna looks up at the very tall Pat. "Damn, bitch! You can't wait or what? I was gonna let you in – I just needed to get dressed!"

Pat replies, "I don't know what you're so mad about. You get to sit up here all night gettin' high! You up here gettin' screwed, too? That must be why you wasn't tryin' to open the door!"

Pat looks at Bill, then says, "Who's this dude? You the one I talked to on the phone? Ah-ha! Bitch, caught you fuckin' the dope man! Where's Nicky? She in the bathroom doin' somebody else?"

Pat is a six-foot tall athletic blonde who grew up in the country with four brothers; so she knows how to get what she wants. She starts toward the bathroom door, screaming out to Nicky, "Come out of that bathroom, I want some blow!"

Bill jumps up so fast it startles Pat.

"Whoa, man! What the fuck? You ok?"

"Yeah, I'm ok, Miss – but what you're after is over here," replies Bill, pointing to the night stand.

Pat looks over at the table. "What is this? All I see is a mirror with some dust on it! I'm gonna stop hookin' you guys up with these rooms if you think they come for free. Nicky, get your ass out here! Your people are playin' games!"

She takes another look at the room: Bill is blocking her path to the bathroom, and Anna won't make eye contact with her.

Pat takes it all in.

"What the fuck is up with y'all – and what is that smell? It smells like a hospital in here! Where's Nicky?" Pat looks toward the bathroom door again. "Hey, Nicky? You alright in there?"

The door to the bathroom opens and Max comes out, closing the door behind him. He's been in the bathroom, alone with Nicky's dead body for a lot longer then he can handle. Looking at Nicky's face and her pale body has him shook up – and he looks it.

As he enters the room, Pat takes one look at Max and says, "Wow! Now who is this? And what have you been in there doin'? I hope you ain't on that meth shit. Because whatever it is has got you and the rest of y'all lookin' and actin' real strange. What's Nicky's problem? Why won't she come out of that bathroom?"

Max knows the longer Pat is in the hotel room, the harder it's going to be trying to keep her out of the bath. He has to get her out of the room, and her mind off of Nicky.

"How are you doing? I'm Max, and I'm the one you talked to on the phone. Nicky's alright. She's in there, just getting herself together. How much does she owe you?"

"Well, uh…I don't know. She just always takes care of me. I never put a price on it."

"Pat," says Max smoothly, "is there someplace where we can talk? How about let's go down to my car. I got some more stuff. I don't know, maybe I feel like treating you. Does that sound cool to you?"

Pat's unsure about Max's offer but she wants to get high, and there's something about Max that makes her relax. "I…I don't know…I guess. You sound familiar. Do I know you?"

Max looks up at her, and he hopes she doesn't know who he is. He's thinking to himself that she's not a bad-looking woman. Still looking up, Max asks, "How tall are you, anyway?"

"I'm six-foot even, and before you ask — *yes,* I played volleyball in high school."

Walking to the door, Max starts to feel better with each step. He couldn't wait to get away from Bill, Anna and Nicky, even if Nicky was already dead. Max is sure Anna will be the reason all of them land in jail, *if* they don't end up dead first.

Before leaving the room, Pat looks back at both Anna and Bill. They still have that spacey, far-away look their faces.

Pat yells over her shoulder. "Hey, Anna? You know checkout time is 11:00, right? That's less than an hour. What are y'all gonna do? Tell Nicky when she comes out of that bathroom, she needs to talk to me. This shit is gettin' out of hand!"

Max doesn't waste any time making it clear that he's in charge.

"Don't worry about anything, Pat. I'll take care of the room, and anything else you need. Let's go talk – that is, *if* you want to make a deal."

Max's statement puts a smile on Pat's face.

"That's more like it, honey. I like a man that knows how to take care of business!"

Walking out of the room, Max stops right before he closes the door. "Hey Pat, why don't you go the front desk and handle the room. I need to talk to Anna and Bill…and, uh, Nicky… about something. Ok?"

"Sounds good to me, sugah. You want I should get us a room, too, or are we coming back up here?"

"No! I mean, uh, yeah – yeah, get us a room. I don't feel like dealing with them in that room…you know."

"Ok, baby! I'll be waiting downstairs…hurry up." Pat spins around, looks back and winks at Max. He can't help but watch her walk away. Her legs go all the way up to her ears, and Max likes the idea of climbing all over a taller woman. She's probably a lot of fun, he mused, but she is also the *last* thing in the world he needs at the moment.

Max walks back inside Anna's room. Bill is sitting on the bed by himself and asks, "Where did Pat go?"

"She's gone to get me and her another room - and give you two another day. Where's Anna?"

Bill pointed to the other door. "She's in the bathroom, trying to wash the stains out of her clothes."

Max takes a second to reflect on their situation. He's still as mixed up as he was when he first came in the room. He needs to ask Anna more, and calls out, "Anna! What the fuck happened in here?"

Not getting an answer from the bathroom, Max changes his mind.

"You know what? Never mind. I don't want to know. On top of that, I don't have time right now. I gotta go down to the car and get the rest of that blow. That chick Pat is curious, but she's more interested in getting high. I'm going down to another room with her, and make sure she keeps her mind on the coke, and not Nicky and what's going on in this room. I'll be back when I'm sure Pat's not gonna come up here.

"In the meantime, you two need to decide what the hell you're going to do, and don't even think about running. You wouldn't last two weeks out there. You might as well face the facts: this ain't gonna go away. And the more you try to avoid it, the worse it is gonna be when they do catch you."

Max turns to leave when Bill calls out to him. Max turns around, and Bill walks over and tries to hug Max. He shoves Bill away. "Go hug your mother! You want to do me a favor? Get me out of this shit!" He stalks out of the room, slamming the door behind him.

Heading to the front desk, along the way Max is thinking hard and fast. Despite his best efforts, the combination of stress, fear, lack of rest and drugs (of course) has left Max with no idea of how to save himself or what to do next. Why *not* go in one of these rooms with that six-foot blonde, and make damn sure that she doesn't forget this day? He might as well have a ball: it'll probably be his last.

Flying north over I-95, Special Agent Bowles is looking through a pair of binoculars. Passing over the Route 6/I-95 junction, the traffic is pretty light in either direction. He sees a couple of police cars, one on each side of I-95, right before the Route 6 exit. Had the police been on the other side of that same exit, they would have seen a black Cadillac making headway through the Sunday morning traffic.

Agent Bowles hasn't seen them either —but he does see something that gets his attention. "McBride, this morning before we landed at the ranch house, we were just due west of that property, right?"

The helicopter pilot confirms Bowles' visual estimates.

Bowles continues, "Well, according to this map, Route 6 curves around Silverton, hitting I-95 right below us."

"Yeah, I think you're right, sir. So what are you getting at?"

"There was a smashed-up van at that ranch house. It hit something or something hit it. But I didn't see another vehicle on site. When we flew over Route 6 this morning, I'm about sure I saw a green tow truck pulling a van, turning off a dirt road onto Route 6. Now here it is again, headed towards Vegas. If you look at this map, that dirt road could come up behind that property, don't you think?"

McBride looks at the map in Bowles' lap, then down at the tow truck Bowles is pointing at. "Yes sir, you could be right – but the map doesn't have that dirt road listed."

They're both peering at the tow truck when Bowles says, "My question is: what was that tow truck doing out there in the middle of nowhere, with a van hooked up to it? And look at that – the front of it has been hit by something! I could be wrong, but let's get one of these sheriff cruisers down there to get a visual on who is in it."

◆————————◈————————◆

Unaware they are the object of the FBI's attention, Nesto and Mann are feeling good about themselves. Las Vegas is less than one hour away, and the four cops they've passed haven't given them as much as a blink. It doesn't even look as if they're going to have to stop for fuel before they reach home.

◆————————◈————————◆

Inside the black Cadillac, Paulie is pushing the Caddy as hard as he dares. They'd managed to make it to the Silverton exit and turn around. Now headed back toward Vegas, Bruiser is in the passenger seat and his head is on a swivel.

"Paulie! Slow down before we get pinched!"

"The hell I will," replies Paulie. "I'm putting as much distance between us and that ranch as possible, and as fast as I can. Besides, they're not doing traffic stops; they're looking for whoever blew up that sheriff's car. We're ok. All the action is in the other direction."

Still not noticing the Cadillac, Agent Bowles and McBride have their complete focus on the tow truck.

"McBride, get me as close to the truck as you can. I need to get a look at that license plate." McBride immediately complies

"Agent Bowles, I have the sheriff on the line. He says he's scrambling a cruiser ASAP. As slow as that thing is traveling, it shouldn't take long to catch up. You think that's your boy down there?"

Bowles squints through his binoculars at the truck's license plate, then relays the number via the copter's radio. "I can't be sure, but in a funny kind of way it fits. But why would they take the time to tow that old van?"

The copter's radio crackles. "This is Deputy Brown, and I'm northbound on I-95. I have a visual on the eye in the sky, but I still don't see a tow truck or van!"

McBride gets Bowles' attention, nodding his head toward the helicopter's police laptop. "Look, sir, at the laptop. The tow truck below us is registered to a C.L. Woods in Silverton, Nevada."

"Well, that doesn't mean much," replies Bowles, "maybe I was wrong. But I still would like to know who's in that truck—Whoa! What is that?" Agent Bowles looks up from the laptop, just in time to see a black Cadillac blow past the tow truck.

"Hey, Maw – don't look now, but that helicopter back there has been hangin' near us for a while. Ju think they're on to us?"

"I don't know....I hope he's watching that Cadillac that just shot by us."

Bowles was dead-set on stopping the tow truck until his pilot pointed out the black Cadillac. He gets another call from the sheriff in the cruiser. "This is Deputy Brown. I can see the tow truck. Do you want me to make a traffic stop? Over."

"That's a negative on the tow truck; he's a local. But I need you to call for back-up – I have a visual on a late model Cadillac SUV, moving at a very high speed. Northbound on I-95. Vehicle fits the description of suspects' car at ranch house. Consider armed and dangerous; approach with extreme caution. You copy?"

"10-4. This is Unit 230. I'm southbound of I-95. I'm coming up on Mile Marker 121. Whoa! I have a visual...yep, he's really moving! I'm turning around!"

"Maw! Oh sheet, there's a sheriff's car behind us, and there's another one on the other side...Fuckin' sheet! He's turning around!"

Mann's looking at the same thing as Nesto. He's getting a sick feeling in his stomach, and his head is killing him. Typical side effect when you know your ass is toast. "I'll be damned! How did they find us?"

"I told ju not to trust that kid and the old man! *Sheet, sheet, sheet!* How much do ju think our bonds will be? I'm outta here the second I make bond. Ju coming, Maw?"

"Bonds? What bonds? We're not going to get any bonds. We got over a ton of cocaine in that van, and did you forget about the bodies at the ranch house? We're screwed, no matter how you cut it!"

While Mann stares off into the distance, Nesto pulls an automatic out of the shoulder bag. Mann can't believe this is happening. All of his life, he's done and acted in a way to *avoid* finding himself in a situation like this one. And yet, here he sits. He's never hurt anyone — at least, not anybody that didn't have it coming - and he's always been fair and straight up, even though most people in this lifestyle can't wait to burn you. It just doesn't make sense.

It must be that guy he shot at the ranch house. His one and only kill, and it's already biting him in the ass. He hates the idea of karma: damn, damn, and *damn!*

Mann is jerked back to the present by the loud clack of an automatic weapon being cocked. He looks over at Nesto, who is in the passenger's seat, looking out the window—with an AR-15 in his lap.

"What the fuck's wrong with you, Nesto? Put that thing away!"

The thought of the rest of their lives being spent in prison is seriously starting to sink in. The look on Nesto's face is pure fear: he looks at the gun, then asks, "Maw, what are we gonna do?"

The hopelessness of the situation grips Mann as Max's face appears in his head. He yells, "Oh, fuck you, Max! We're going down, that's what we're gonna do!"

Mann pulls hard on the wheel. The truck shoots off the highway so fast and suddenly that the sheriff behind him looks to see if he hasn't accidently turned on his police lights.

"Nesto, as soon as they pull up, throw that gun out the truck, ok? We don't need any accidents!"

"Look, Maw, we still have a couple hand grenades…maybe if we—"

Mann hollers at Nesto. "The hell with that, Nesto! Throw that shit outta here!"

Deputy Brown looks at them on the side of the road as he passes them by, thinking to himself, '*what's their problem?'*—and then he gets on his radio.

"This is Deputy Brown. If everybody's ready, I'm hitting my lights as soon as I pass this school bus ahead of me."

Riding in the back seat of the Cadillac, Ike is the first to notice. "Look, Paulie! We've got company behind us!"

"I know…I see…look up there at that!" Paulie points to the helicopter. "What the hell! What's going on? Are they after us?"

"I dunno; so far they're just laying back. Do you see any other cars they might be looking at?"

"Just that school bus. Maybe some nut job's got kids hostage."

Paulie keeps peering up at the helicopter. "I hope so, at least for our sake. I'm gonna slow down, let's see what they do."

Bruiser is riding in the passenger seat, and pulls out a nine-millimeter, fully automatic machine pistol, and tells everyone, "The Feds are still looking for me for that thing in Philly. I got a bogus ID, but if that chopper is onto us that fake ID ain't gonna cut it!" He's waving his gun all over the car, clearly panicky. "I can't go back—you hear me?"

The helicopter swings around in front of the Cadillac. Looking through his binoculars, Bowles sends out a message. "This is Agent Bowles. Be advised – I have a visual of weapons on board. Again, be advised they have weapons on board. It looks to be an automatic of some kind."

Bowles turns to the pilot. "This is definitely our boy, McBride – you ready? I sure hope these local sheriffs are ready because it looks like these guys came prepared for war!"

He gives the final instructions over the radio. "Everyone hold your positions. We're going to try and get them to take the next exit off the freeway. McBride, bring us down as low as you can in front of them. See if they'll cooperate."

After hearing what Bruiser just said, Paulie knows his passenger is on a kamikaze mission.

"Listen, Bruiser – I'm not gonna get all shot up! I haven't done anything, none of us have! That thing in Philly? It was bound to catch up with you. Fuck it – give it up— we ain't kids no more!"

Bruiser replies, "I ain't gonna do life for nobody! I knocked off a made man – how long do you think I'll last before some young punk tries to take me out?"

Paulie looks in the rearview mirror and asks, "Where you at with this one, Ike?"

"Well, I sure as hell ain't trying to get killed!"

With Ike's reply, both he and Paulie stare at Bruiser, then Paulie says, "Ok then, I'm pulling off the freeway up here. I'll turn the car around – you get ready, Bruiser, because when I turn around, I'm stopping and jumping out. You do what you have to – 'cause I'm done!"

Ike adds in, "Shit, Paulie – I'm with you!"

Bruiser's face turns bright red, and he yells, "You fuckin' chicken shits!" Then the Caddy veers off the freeway onto the access road.

Above in the helicopter, McBride says, "Look there, turning right where you wanted them to – what are they up to?"

The Cadillac races about another two hundred yards before sliding to a stop. At the same time, Paulie jams on the brake, and pulls on the steering wheel while Bruiser continues cursing them to hell. As the car slides to a stop, Paulie's door is already open for his escape, but Bruiser lets loose on him with a Tec-9, spitting four bullets in Paulie's upper body. Then he turns on Ike, but it's too late. Ike's already out of the car and tries to roll but hits his head on the pavement, full force.

Full of bullet holes, Paulie's body flops out of the car like a dead fish. Bruiser slides behind the wheel, simultaneously pointing his pistol out of the window and jamming his foot on the gas almost as hard as his finger hits the trigger of the nine-millimeter. The Cadillac rockets forward, while the gun spits bullets at the helicopter.

Bruiser's aim gets lucky and a couple of the bullets reach their mark, just as McBride is trying to settle the chopper down in front of the car. The bullets punch holes in the copter's window. Instinctively, McBride pulls back hard on the controls, putting the aircraft in a serious sideways retreat.

The helicopter is now almost parallel with the ground, and McBride is fighting at the controls to keep the copter from going down. The sheer force and pressure on the helicopter causes a malfunction and it over-corrects, slamming it into the ground in an upright position. The blades flex and snap off.

Special Agent Bowles feels the pain start in his pelvis, then shoot up his back as his spinal column compresses like an accordion, sending a pain so sharp through his body that it knocks him out cold.

McBride tries to compensate for the impact by leaning forward, which causes his head to whip forward into the control stick. Both men are knocked out; one will be grossly disfigured and the other, wheelchair-bound for life.

Bruiser lets out a madman's yell when he sees the copter go down. He envisions his own curtain to freedom begin to re-open. He guns the Caddy's engine, racing back to the highway. Giving a final look back at the site of the destroyed helicopter, Bruiser prepares to turn back onto I-95.

Deputy Brown is on the exit ramp and racing to try and beat the Cadillac to the entrance ramp. Hopefully, he can block the car's path, but the Caddy is moving faster than Sheriff Brown thought, and he realizes he won't be able to beat it to the ramp.

But he can ram it.

Bruiser turns his head to the left, just in time to see the immediate future – but not soon enough to do anything about it. Traveling at over ninety miles an hour, Deputy Sheriff Brown goes headlong into the Cadillac's driver door, introducing Bruiser to the grill of the Ford Crown Victoria police cruiser.

Sitting on the side of the highway less than two hundred yards away, Mann and Nesto watch the whole drama unfold: Paulie's body flopping out of the car; Ike diving out of the back seat, rolling head over heels, his head bouncing off the pavement like a rubber ball; Bruiser sticking his gun out the window and shooting up at the helicopter; the copter's incredible gymnastics as it nearly turns upside down, then almost rights itself before slamming into the ground.

They duck down in the cab of the old tow truck, just as a piece of the helicopter's rotor flips by, missing the truck by inches. Peeking out of the windshield, they manage to catch sight of Sheriff Brown burying the front end of his police cruiser into the driver's side of the Cadillac.

Mann has to fight the urge to run and help the sheriff, as Brown struggles to get out of his cruiser before collapsing to the ground. Nesto grabs Mann's arm to snap his attention away from the collision in front of them. Mann looks at Nesto, then at Sheriff Brown lying half on the ground, with his leg still inside the car. If he isn't actually dead, Brown sure looks like the perfect model for Death itself.

Nesto points down the road at another police car that speeds by, then skids to a stop by the accident. "Maw," yells Nesto, "Maw! Let's get out of here. Let's GO!"

Still in shock, Mann pulls the truck back on the road, and drives slowly by the crash. They both ride in silence. As Mann gazes out the window, he is dimly aware that a road sign has just whizzed by that says that says, '*Las Vegas, Exit 20 miles.* He has no idea how long he has been driving.

"Boss! Boss! You gotta get in here now!"

Cus Barlow comes running into the front room, shot glass in one hand, cell phone in the other hand. Trying to focus, he looks at Lenny's face, then turns his gaze to TV screen. His shot glass hits the floor. He tries to put his cell phone in his pocket, but misses, sending it to the floor as well. Cus and Lenny stand, listening to the reporter on the screen:

> *"Reports are coming in from our On-the-Spot News copter here at News 5. We have yet another incident taking place right outside of Silverton County. As we reported earlier, there have been a series of events taking place in and around the Silverton area."*

The men concentrate on the details coming from the television – none of which are good. The live pictures from the news helicopter gets Lenny's attention.

"Is that Paulie's Cadillac?" asks Lenny, staring at the screen.

"Oh shit, I think it is! Where's my phone?" Cus blurts out.

"I already tried to call them, Boss – no answer! Is this really happening, Boss?"

The announcer continues,

"As we stated earlier, we don't yet have any information on the victims. But with our Tela-5 News SuperLens, we were able to get the license number from the car that's on your screen right now. With that information, we were able to find out that the black Cadillac is registered to a "Paulino Lostro" of Las Vegas. Our sources tell us that Mr. Lostro has a criminal history that appears to link him to the organized crime..."

"Oh no, Boss! It *is* Paulie's car!"

"...Mr. Lostro is a known member of the reputed Barlow crime family---"

"No, no, no!" yells Barlow. "That's all I need! My name back in the press again! What's happening? Is this some kind of set-up? Somebody is behind all this, and we need to find out who!"

"You think it's the Feds, Boss? You know they're pretty pissed that you beat that indictment last year."

"No," says Barlow, "this ain't their style. They don't do things like the shit that's been going on. It's somebody that's trying to horn in on my action!"

Lenny whistles aloud. "Who has the balls to try a stunt like this?"

"I don't know, Lenny. Maybe somebody from back East. One of those crews out of Chicago or Kansas City. We gotta find out who blew up that cop car, and shot up the ranch house. I'll bet they're after my shipment, and probably set up Paulie and his boys!"

Cus' phone rings. "Now who the hell is this?" He looks at the phone display, and the look on his face tells Lenny there's another problem on the other end.

"Who is it, Boss?"

"The damn Santos brothers. Let me see....I can't talk to them right now, and I need to get them off my ass."

Barlow grabs a bottle of scotch, takes a large swig, then tries to get his composure. Clearing his throat, he answers his phone.

"Yeah...Hello. How's it going, Olly? Yeah, I know all about it! I'm trying to find out about my boys now. I think the Feds have a snitch or something...Hell, no – they're not THAT good...the shipment is safe. What? When can you get yours?...Well, uh...it's like this, Olly...I can't move on the shipment until I find out what's going on with my boys...Give me a couple days, so all this can die down. Let's see what happens next....Yeah, it was Bruiser and Ike out there with Paulie...What?...I don't know what they were doing out there! Maybe a vacation…Hey! Watch your mouth – don't talk about my guys like that! Olly, that's real close to disrespect, and I might take offense to that kind of talk."

Hanging up, Barlow is about to throw his phone but stops himself. Lately, he's been destroying about ten phones monthly, and it's really messing up his ability to handle his business.

Lenny sees *That Look* on Barlow's face and asks, "What happened, Boss – everything alright?"

"That piece of shit Olly Santos has a real smart mouth. He might need somebody to close it for him. Paulie and the boys ain't in the ground yet, and they're already talking disrespectfully about them."

"Boss, we don't need that right now!"

"Ok, Lenny – you're right. I'm glad that you weren't with them."

Lenny pauses for a moment. "You really think that they're dead, Boss?"

"Fuck, I don't know Lenny," explodes Barlow. "But look at that shit they're showing on the TV! — Who could live through that?"

They both stare at the TV screen. Lenny breaks the silence.

"I need a drink. How about you, Boss?"

"No. But you need to call Antwan. Tell him to stay put – we'll come to him. We gotta get out of here and lay low until I figure this out."

Trying to get back on track, Mann finally breaks the silence. "You ok over there, Nesto?"

"I don't think so: I can't believe we're alive! This has got to be a dream. We were about to shoot it out with the Feds, and then out of nowhere, BOOM! I'm watching a helicopter being shot out of the sky, people's bodies flying everywhere! Maw – did we cause all of that?"

"Yeah, I think so."

"What? How ju figure that?"

Mann sighs. "I'll tell you later. Right now, we gotta get out of this stolen truck, hide that van full of blow and find you a doc."

They look at each other and say, almost at the same time: "We gotta call Lester!"

Seven hundred and forty-nine miles to the east, and one mile high, Max is staring at the ceiling, lying next to Pat. They're both naked. Pat is sitting up on the side of the bed, playing with the pile of cocaine on the night stand. They've both been hard at it – and each other – for more than three hours.

Max is tired and could really use some rest, but he doesn't know or feel it – another side effect of the constant ingestion of cocaine. As bad as he needs to, he can't sit still. "Hey, Pat – what time is it?"

She's totally preoccupied and doesn't reply. Max gets up, looks out the curtains. The sun's blazing full force. Max can tell that it's already afternoon; he's wasted enough time. Something is bothering him, but he's half high, half tired, and all the way stressed out. The only thing Max is sure of is that Pat's having a blast. He, however, is just numb.

He calls Bill on his cell phone. "Hello, Bill. It's me, Max. I'm coming up."

Pat hears Max on the phone and asks, "You leavin' me, honey?"

"Look, baby – according to my watch, it's 1:30 in the afternoon. I had big fun with you, but I got a lot of catching up to do. I'm going to leave you with something. You gonna be alright?"

"Oh yeah, lover," smiles Pat. She leans over and tries to give Max a big kiss, but he leans away. Max hates this kind of shit. He knows it's all about the dope. Without it, she wouldn't warn him if his hair was on fire.

"Pat, I might need to take care of some business in Anna – uh, and *Nicky's* – room. I don't want a lot of people asking questions if I come and go in and out a few times. You know what I mean? Is there a security guard here?"

Pat nods. "Yeah, but I know him. It's Sunday, so if you're going to be doing a lot of coming and going, it's best to do it after six this evening until about ten tonight. Sunday evenings are slow around here. There's only the front desk clerk and the bellboy until 10. Then the night guard comes on. He's a little nosy, but lazy. He'll be asleep by midnight."

Max pulls on his clothes and heads to the door, stopping long enough to ask Pat another question. "You gonna stay here?"

"If you want me to," she replies. "I'm off until Wednesday, and I don't have a thing to do. You got any ideas?"

She gets off the bed and starts to make her way over to Max. He's looking at her long legs and bright blond hair – upstairs and downstairs. Part of him wants to stay, but he's already screwed up enough to even piss himself off. He's got to get back to business. Somehow, he manages to resist Pat long enough to get out of the room.

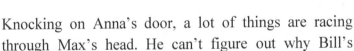

Knocking on Anna's door, a lot of things are racing through Max's head. He can't figure out why Bill's description of Anna – and how Max sees her – are in total opposition. Sometimes she seems to be in control, like Bill said. But at other times, she's totally lost, almost like she's ready to self-destruct for no apparent reason.

Max can't help but feel they're not telling him everything. He really needs to find out what's up with her father, and what her father and Spriggs are up to. From what he knows about Spriggs, it can't be good.

Bill answers the hotel door, and Max walks in.

"Hey, Bill. Where's Anna?"

"She's in the bathroom."

"*Again.* She likes it in there with Nicky, huh? That's good; we need to talk anyway but — *what is she doing in there?*"

"She's trying to clean up."

Max scoffs. "Clean up herself or her…uhm…'mess'? You know what? Never mind, I don't even care at this point. My real concern is what have you two decided to do? I've been trying to figure a way out of this for all of us. Like it or not, Bill, we're in deep shit! I'm not in as deep as you, but we're all still pretty screwed. I hope you guys are ready to call the police and get this over with."

Bill just stands by the bed, rocking back and forth. For the first time since he's come in the room, Max notices Bill's behavior. "What, Bill? How come you won't look at me? Bill! Why won't you answer my questions?"

"Well, Max…it's like this. I think we can make like we haven't been here."

"Bill, what the hell are you talking about? You're not a full-blown criminal, you're a college graduate - now talk to me like one! What do you mean, 'make like you haven't been here?'"

"You know, clean up in here, and go home like we've never been in contact with Nicky."

Max is incredulous. "That wouldn't be a bad idea – *except* for two major problems. This room, and that Pat chick! You can't let them find Nicky's body in this room. Somebody's sure to have seen one of us – probably Anna! Then there's Pat. She's gonna have to say something! She works here, and they're gonna be all over her. You think she's gonna take the heat? Hell, as far as I know, she and Nicky were good friends, and she ain't gonna be happy about her friend being found dead – especially in a room that *she* rented to her! What are you going to do when Pat gets pissed about the whole thing – and really starts to talk?"

Bill has sweat beads on his forehead, and Max can tell he's starting to get through to him. Max tries to position himself so Bill has to make eye contact with him. Bill's eyes aren't darting around the room like they were earlier. They seem to have found a point of focus - Max finds himself following Bill's eyes, turning to see what has his attention.

He should have guessed.

Standing in the doorway to the bathroom, Anna is looking straight at Bill. From the look on her face and the cold stare in her eyes, Max knows she's back. Anna's in charge once again.

Slowly walking in the room, each of Anna's movements seems filled with purpose like she's feeling the room. She walks right in between Max and Bill just like a boxing referee, without being touched by either man. They both take a step back. Anna looks up at Max; they're nearly eye-to-eye.

"Hello, Max. You and Pat have fun?" she asks in a cold voice. "You know, you left here with all my stuff."

Max can't believe it. She's got a dead body in the bathtub, someone she's just killed – and all she's concerned about is her cocaine.

"Oh, thanks for asking, Anna. I'm fine — and yourself?" replies Max sarcastically. "Do any skiing this season? I heard the slopes were the best! Hey, and how's that friend of yours doing? You know – the one in the *bathtub*?"

Bill jumps in. "Max! That's not cool! Why are you trying to screw with her like that?"

Anna waves her hand to signal that she's got this in check, and narrows her eyes at Max. He can feel the pressure from her look, like a hand pressing on his chest. The look alone is enough to put Max in his place. He drops his head.

"I'm sorry," he responds, "but what do you want me to say? I'm not used to this much drama. When it comes to the 'fight or flight' thing, I'm on the first thing smokin' outta town!"

Anna can't take it any longer and screams, "Stop it, Max! You're not in any trouble! I am! If they can't find me or Nicky, you know…if Nicky can't be found, then everybody's safe!"

Max blows up, yelling, "And how do we do that, *Boss*?"

Anna gives Max another look. At this rate, her patience and Max's frustration are going to come to a head, and Max is looking for it. He knows that this is the only way he's going to find out about who she is.

"This is the only way we're going to get away with this," she says quietly.

"What do you mean, 'we' get away with it!"

"Come on, Max, don't try and act stupid now. You know what I mean! It's the only way we're not going to have to deal with the police."

"So. You're not calling the police," replies Max. Anna simply starts to laugh loudly.

Bill finally speaks up. "Max, we're not calling the police. I wouldn't let her, even if she wanted to. We talked about it, and came up with a plan. It's not going to be hard at all. We're going take Nicky's body and put it somewhere nobody will ever find her. Then Anna and I will take off together. Nobody knows about us, except you."

Max scratches his head and says, "Is that the best you can come up with? I wouldn't bet on that plan with counterfeit money!"

"No, Max, listen," argues Bill. "When Nicky and Anna come up missing at the same time, they'll think they are together. Anna's going to leave a note to her father, telling him she's run away and doesn't want to be here. Anna said he'll be glad she's gone; they don't do anything except fight anyway."

Max can't believe their foolhardy plan. "What about Nicky's husband? He's not only a controlling asshole, he's also a cop! If he comes looking for her – and you know he will – it's gonna be hard to hide from a man with his kind of connections. I hear he loves that bitch. Oh – one other little detail: where are you going to hide her body?"

Before Max can say another word, Anna jumps in. "Bill, don't say anything else, baby, you know, just in case….Max, I think l know a good place to take her. But since you're not involved with all this, I don't think we should tell you anything else."

"Finally!" Max cries out. "Somebody here considers poor ol' Max! Thanks a lot!"

With that, Anna blows up. "Fuck you, Max! I didn't call you! *You* put yourself in this one. So you better watch your step, and stay the fuck out of my way!"

"No, Anna! Don't say that," pleads Bill. "Max is the only friend we have!"

Hearing Bill's last statement, Max thinks to himself, *'No, I'm not your only friend. I'm the only one that knows what you're up to…which makes me the only witness. Not a good place to be, especially in light of that head-case, Anna.'*

Walking to the bathroom and opening the door, Max says, "So I guess I shouldn't ask how you're gonna get her out of here?"

He points to the bathtub, and has to do a double-take. Max is no longer looking at Nicky's bone-white, bloodless body. She looks nothing like she did last time Max had seen it.

"I guess you two aren't messing around. This is part of the plan?"

Nicky's body is wrapped from head to toe in black plastic and duct tape, reminding Max of a mummy he'd seen once in a museum. Anna walks over to the bathroom, steps in front of Max, and closes the door.

"You already seen too much. I'm trying to keep you out of trouble – that's what you want, isn't it, Max?" Anna stares directly in Max's face, her voice in a monotone.

Max turns to Bill instead, asking him, "So it looks like you already got this thing planned out. Does that mean you don't need my help anymore?"

Bill replies, "The biggest thing is trying to disappear, once and for all. Like I said, you're the only one that knows about us. So if I pack up and leave, it's no problem. I don't have to make a run for it because as far as anybody knows, I have nothing to run from."

He smiles a little at Anna, then continues. "What we *do* need is a new identity for Anna. Something that says she's over 21. That way we can get married, so not only will she be somebody else, she'll also have my last name. Nobody will be able to follow that trail."

"Never say never, Bill. The only problem I see with your plan is Anna taking off the same time Nicky comes up missing. It's better if you stick around until they start looking for her, then take off. Act like you're so upset about your best friend missing that you took off to look for her. At least that way, nobody will think you could have something to do with her missing. You know, start hinting around that without Nicky, you hate being in this city." Max is pacing a little, getting comfortable with his plan.

"Look at it this way, Bill. If she answers all their questions, then there's no reason for them to look for her. Other than being a runaway, you want them to think you're running *to* something and not *from* something."

Anna has a big smile on her face; Max took that as her approval of his master plan that he'd just hatched. What he didn't know was that Anna already had a master plan. Max just bought the whole thing – and he'd just given Anna the confirmation.

Anna's total demeanor changes, to Max's relief, as she starts to feed Max what he needs: that young, unexperienced kid that Max can control.

"Max, you're right," Anna slyly replies to Max, "I didn't think about that. The only thing I hate about what you said is I have to go home. I hate not being with Bill."

"You don't have to leave Bill alone," Max replies, "but you do have to be careful. You can see him when you need to – but you have to play the role at home and stay patient."

Anna looks at her watch. "Bill, it's going on three o'clock; we need to get started. I'm going to call my friend that I told you about. He can help us with Nicky. Max, can you take Bill to get his car? Oh, Bill – can you ask Max about that favor we talked about?"

Max gets up and heads for the door, trying to predict what Anna's talking about. He reaches in his pocket and pulls out a baggy of coke. He pours some out onto a piece of paper, then lays it on the table. "There - now you don't have to ask. I'll be in the car – but don't take all day! I got shit to do!"

Bill replies, "I'll be down in a minute."

Max leaves out the door, but stops in the hallway. His head is spinning, and for a second he thinks he is about to fall out. He wants out of this situation so badly, but instead, he feels as though he's in quicksand: the harder he struggles to get out, the deeper he feels himself sinking. He contemplates calling Mann. But Mann didn't get Max into this mess; it's not fair to expect Mann to come to the rescue.

Talking to himself, Max heads to the car, wiping the perspiration from his forehead. Looking at his sweaty hand, Max realizes he's shaking - and shaking badly…but it's not from the cocaine. "I need a drink," he muses aloud.

More than 10 minutes pass before Bill appears at the car door, and he seems to be charged up. No surprise there. The stuff Max gave him is high quality.

"Let's go, Max – take me to my car. I gotta get Anna some more clothes, and something to eat."

"What are you two gonna do about Nicky-the-Stiff?" Max pulls out of the parking lot.

"Stop with the jokes, Max! Anna told me not to tell you but I know we can trust you. Anna has a friend that works at a mortuary."

"Come on, Bill! You're gonna sit here and tell me a 16-year old girl has connections to get rid of a body?" Max's face reflects his disbelief at Bill's words.

"Well, kind of," says Bill. "Her friend's dad owns the place. They have a crematorium on the east side of town, over off Smith Road. She said that her friend told her the guy who runs it will cremate anything or anybody for a small fee. All we gotta do is get it there."

"Boy, this is crazy. Kids knocking off people, getting rid of the bodies. What a world! How much money does this guy need to do it?"

"She's calling him now. She said she thinks it's five grand," replies Bill.

"You got that kind of dough?"

"Not really," says Bill, shaking his head. "I've been spending like crazy lately. That's the favor Anna wanted me to bring up with you."

Max starts to laugh, saying, "What *money*? Now I know you're trippin'! If you haven't noticed, I haven't been working in more than a week. Like you, I've been partying like crazy. So I've burned through what little money I had. How much money you talking about anyway?"

"One hundred thousand dollars," Bill promptly replies.

Max's mouth drops open. "Wow! That sure came out of your mouth easy! I don't know who's worse: you or that Nicky chick with blackmail. Seriously, I know you didn't think I had that kind of money. And even if I did, what makes you think I would hand it out to you like Halloween candy? What's with everybody thinking that I'm some kind of rich guy?"

"Don't forget I work at the station with you, Max!" Bill sounds a little argumentative. "I know what kind of contract you have. What is it? One and a half million over five years? You're making at least a quarter-million a year!"

"I wish I was even close to that! It's always greener on the other side. What you don't know is this: I'm always in trouble with the FCC. So the radio station made the most with my contract incentives: as long as I stay out of trouble with the FCC, I get the big paydays. Well, as *you* know, I'm never out of trouble with that Federal agency. I can barely pay my own bills!"

His face reflecting his disappointment, Bill quietly asks, "What about the car?"

"Fuck, Bill! You want me to sell my car and give you the money?"

"Not all of it, Max. This is an emergency! I need your help. Besides, this is the best way to clean up this situation. Do you really want to take a chance on waiting it out? Max, you know as well as I do the best way to fix a problem is with money – and we need cash!"

Max notices a change in the way Bill's handling himself all of the sudden. Almost like he's been coached on what to say. He's no longer talking like he's scared or unsure.

Something's not right here. As Bill continues, a red flag is rising in Max's head.

"Anna's smart, but she's young, Max – she gets in a rush. I'm already doing everything I can to get her to sit down and let me handle things. She's already talking about some crazy plan to blackmail her father. If we keep messing around, she's gonna do something wrong and it's going to blow up in our faces. She's getting desperate, Max!"

"Her father?" asks Max, "What does she have on the head D.A.? Bill, I'm telling you, I *don't* like this!" This latest revelation runs Max's mental red flag to full staff. Bill has a look on his face like he's said too much.

"Nothing, Max. Forget I said it. She's just thinking like a kid."

"I don't know, Bill. Let me think about this."

"What about your friend? He sells dope; I know he has money. Maybe you ---"

"Who? *Mann?* Are you *crazy* as well as stupid? I'm already killing myself trying to keep him out of this shit! That's not an option. Drop that off the table, and get it out of your head."

Hearing Mann's name made Max realize the lack of options he has available. "Let me check on the car thing. If I do this for you, I never want to see or hear from either one of you again!"

Max doesn't know exactly what he's gonna do, but he knows Bill's not being totally upfront with what he knows about Anna and her father. There's something going on, and it's big. Max decides that he's going to find out what it is before he gives up a dime. But the first thing is the body – it's got to go – *tonight.* He turns to his friend.

"Call Anna, and tell her we've got the money. Just for the corpse…I mean, uh, for *Nicky's body*. After that, we talk. But *no more bullshit*. Either come clean or fuck off - you got that? And I mean both of you!"

Nesto's fix-it-all problem-solver, Lester, is adding up in his head how much to charge Nesto and Mann.

Nesto is lying on the hotel room bar, letting an underground doctor work on his foot while Nesto's sister Leta is talking to their brother Lanceo in Colombia.

Telling him a very big lie, per Nesto's request – and she's not happy about it, either.

Mann called Monica, and had her meet them at Caesar's Palace. They are talking in the bathroom, and Monica's telling Mann that she's not overjoyed about it, either.

"Mann, what's your damn problem? Have you totally lost your mind? I've been watching that shit on TV all morning, and you're going to tell me you and that crazy SOB in there are behind all this?"

"I don't think we had anything to do with the helicopter," Mann hurriedly replies, "but the guys in the black Cadillac were friends with the gangster I saved Nesto from. I can't help but feel they're somehow connected with all this."

Monica is as mad as Mann has ever seen her – and she's just getting started. "Drug cartels, Mafia bosses, shootouts with machine guns, blowing up police cars, and 500 kilos of cocaine! You asshole – that motherfucker in there has a bullet hole in him! If this is how you want to go out, please let me know so I can get out of your way. I thought you loved me! Is this how you prove it— by getting yourself killed? And get that stupid look off your face – this shit ain't funny!"

"Listen, baby – it's too complicated for me to go into right now. It's also too late to get out of it."

"No, it's not! We just walk out there and tell them to have a nice day and go home. Please, baby, let's get out of here."

"We are, I promise — but I have to take care of a few things first." Mann tries to reason with the *Very-Pissed* Monica. "If I step off now, it'll be a lot worse than if I ride this out. Do you realize how much money we stand to make off this deal? I'll never have to work again. We can do all the stuff we've always wanted to: travel, buy property, open that scarf boutique that you're always talking about."

Monica starts crying. "I don't care about all that crap if it means getting killed for it. I don't understand you sometimes."

"Ok, Monica, let me finish my shower and get dressed. Go have a drink – there's plenty at the bar." Mann stands up and starts toward the shower.

"The *bar?* Have you seen what they're doing on that bar? You should have said 'operating table'! Yeah, I'll have a drink – I need one! Baby, I have one question: the news said they found four bodies at the ranch house. Did you kill anybody?"

Getting into the shower, the question catches Mann off-guard. He hesitates, deciding whether to reply, then does his best to act like the situation isn't as bad as it is. "Two of those guys got run down by Rico; the other two, they were shooting at us. Nesto was shooting, I was shooting, and who knows who shot who. It doesn't matter – it's over."

Monica holds her head down and says in a low voice, "I hope so. At least you're alright. Finish your shower. I'll be in the other room." She walks out, closing the door behind her.

Mann hadn't had time to think about the whole thing at the ranch house. His internal know-it-all, the Little Voice speaks up inside his head for the first time in a long while. *'Yes, we popped that guy right in the head. One shot, one kill. It was either him or us!'*

Mann replies silently. "Haven't heard from you in some time. Where have you been?"

'Had your hands full,' jeers the Voice. *'Didn't need me bugging you. You did a good job, too. Now finish this shit so I can start in on you again. Until then, I'll stay out of your way!'*

Finishing the back-and-forth chat with himself, Mann stands in the shower under the hot water, enjoying the peace and quiet, thinking maybe he'll just stay there.

The sound of his cell phone ringing breaks the silence. Maybe if he puts his head right under the showerhead, the ringing will stop. It doesn't work. Even though his head isn't cooperating, his body already knows what to do: His hand is already reaching for a dry towel so he can answer the phone. He knows who it is. It's Max's ring tone. Mann hates special ring tones.

"Hello?"

The twin-engine Corsair is headed due north from Las Vegas.

It's only been in the air for ten minutes, headed for a small private air strip just south of Reno. Cus Barlow's entire empire is riding on the success of this flight.

Lenny finishes up on his cell phone. "Boss, that was the lawyer on the phone. He said Bruiser's dead, Paulie's dead, and Ike is in a coma in the hospital. He probably won't make it – he's busted up pretty bad. If he lives, they're charging him with aiding and abetting a fugitive, with more charges coming."

"*'More charges?'* What charges, Lenny? They didn't do anything!"

"I know that, Boss, but get this – the lawyer said the police got after them because some witness at the ranch house said some gangsters in a black Cadillac shot up the place, killing everybody they could find!"

Barlow slams his fist down on the arm rest and explodes. "Like hell, they did! Paulie never made it to the ranch house! They're lying!"

"Well, if the police are lying, how did they know Paulie and the boys were in that car?" Lenny peers at Barlow. "And who is the witness who said there were gangsters in a black Cadillac?"

Barlow has to think a while about Lenny's questions; he's really baffled. Finally, he tells Lenny, "Get that lawyer back on the phone. Tell him to find out who this witness is and to call us the second he finds out. Somebody went out there and took my shipment, and set my boys up. Who else did that piece of shit Singleton try and sell that stuff to?"

"Boss," muses Lenny, "I was just thinking. After we met that guy Singleton up there at his house, with all his fancy books, and his butler –"

"Yeah, Lenny – so what? The fucking guy is rich…or *was* rich."

"Yeah, I know that – but he's not the type, you know what I mean? He's not like us. He ain't the type of guy who sells dope; he belongs on Wall Street or somewhere like that. He don't know the first thing about dealing that stuff, or how to handle people like us."

"So what's your point, Lenny?" asks Cus, running his hand over his head, clearly frustrated.

"Where did a guy like Singleton get that much cocaine in the first place?"

Barlow stops and stares at Lenny. "That's a good question, Lenny…You think it wasn't his?"

"He said that you guys agreed to fifteen million dollars – but when you told him *ten* million, it didn't take Singleton five minutes to agree to a five million-dollar cut! If he paid for that stuff himself, a five million-dollar discount is gonna kill his profit."

Barlow's mouth is open. "Yeah! Unless he didn't pay for it to begin with, then who cares about four or five million?

He's getting ten million just for showing up! Lenny, you got something there!"

Barlow falls silent again for a moment, then says, "We need to find out who he got the stuff from! Even if they don't have my shipment, we might be able to work out a deal. I still got five million dollars, if that brother-in-law of yours ain't fallen off the face of the earth with my money. I just might be able to pull this off yet! Tell the pilot he gotta speed this thing up. I need to be on the ground, ASAP."

Barlow leans back in the seat of his private plane, a self-satisfied smile on his face. "So...they think they're smarter than Cus Barlow! Well, them idiots got another think coming!"

Lenny doesn't remind Barlow who really figured it out.

Mann and Max are going back and forth on the phone while Mann tries to get dressed. Actually, Mann still doesn't know what Max is talking about: it's obvious that he's high.

"Max, you're talking too fast —Slow the fuck down! Now, what did you say about Nicky?...Ok, so if you can't talk about it on the phone, why are you calling me? ...I know what I said about if you need anything... stop bullshitting and tell me what you need!...I hope it's important, bugging me out here, especially with that bitch's name —*How* much did you say?...Max, if you need some stuff, look in the car under the dash---"

Mann pauses for a moment, listening to Max's response on the phone, then continues the conversation. "Oh. You found that already...Do you owe somebody for some shit?...Ok, ok, we'll talk!...Find a pay phone in one hour to call me back, then we'll talk....Yes, if it's an emergency, I'll send the dough, but I'm getting my money back if even I have to pimp your ass out, you hear me?....Ok. Call me in one hour. You'll get the money tonight."

Walking out of the bathroom, the first thing that Mann sees is that Nesto is off the bar and laid out on the couch. Monica and Leta are talking, and Lester and the doctor are gone.

"Who was that on the phone, Maw," asks Nesto.

"A major pain in the ass!" Mann looks annoyed.

Hearing that, Monica jumps in. "Must be Max. What did he do this time?"

"I'm not sure," responds Mann, "but I'm going to need you to take this money to him, ASAP. What time did you say that flight is leaving for Denver?"

Monica smiles at the thought of leaving Las Vegas, answering back, "We leave at 8:00 o'clock tonight. And I do mean '*we*'. "

Mann feels the pressures of the day closing in on him. He does his best to control himself, but his tone of voice changes, getting everybody's attention — especially Monica.

"Monica, I need to you to take this cash to Max *tonight!* He's in a jam, a bad one. I don't care if you turn around and return on the next flight, but right now I need you to stop with the questions and comments. Do *exactly* as I ask, and get your butt on that flight. Me and Nesto are about to hit the highway ourselves."

Nesto looks at Mann with a puzzled look on his face, then says, "Where are we going? I didn't know we had to go anywhere."

"Well, you can stay if you want to, but I'm taking my cut of that shit in the van and going home. Ever since I got here, it's been guns, gangsters, police, cartels, and killings. If this is a vacation, I'll take the drama back home. I need a vacation from my vacation!"

Monica jumps out of her seat and salutes Mann, saying, "Yes sir, I'll call the airline and confirm my seat, sir! What about the other ticket, sir?"

Mann looks over at Leta, then asks her, "You ever been to Denver? You want to meet us there?"

Leta points at Mann and Nesto. "I wouldn't cross the street to meet ju two *loco pendejos* – but somebody's got to watch Monica's back."

Lying in a hospital bed, Special Agent Bowles is talking on the phone to the FBI's head office in Washington, D.C. He's giving an assessment of the situation. It hasn't been 24 hours since the helicopter crashed; Bowles is in pain but refuses to let it get the best of him.

Junior Agent Taylor enters the hospital room; Bowles glances at Taylor and continues talking on the phone with the D.C. office.

"Yes sir, it's important that we find out what the shooting at the ranch house was about. I'm sure that it had something to do with the truck stop blowing up...I'm sorry, sir — I'll have to call you back. My junior officer just walked in with the latest report... No sir, I'm a little banged up, but I hope to be on my feet soon...Yes, sir...Thank you, sir...Goodbye."

Without expressing any concern about Bowles' condition, Agent Taylor jumps right into his report. "Sir, the property does belong to Mr. Singleton, just like you thought. The crime scene guys at Mr. Singleton's Reno house report that it seems as if there was three to five million dollars in that limo when it went up. There's still no ID on the victim in the limo, but it's believed he was the butler. Regarding the men in the Cadillac: Mr. Ikeovoni Gellino, or 'Ike the Spike' – is still in a coma. What's interesting is Mr. Paulino Lostro – 'Big Paulie' – seems to have been shot by Mr. Bruvel Carvolli – 'the Bruiser' – who was wanted out of the Philly office for the –"

Bowles waves his hand. "Ok, ok, Taylor. That's good enough for now. Anything else?"

"No sir, just the report from the local sheriff's office."

"Good job, young man; that's all for now. Go get yourself some rest – I know you need it. And leave those reports with me – I need something to take my mind off this pain."

Taylor places the reports on Bowles' lap and departs for a well-deserved sleep.

Bowles stares at the ceiling. He can't feel anything below his waist. He wants to cry, but fights it off: he is an agent, an FBI Special Agent. Bowles pulls himself together as his training kicks in.

There still is a job to do, even if he's not the one to complete it, his fellow agents can use his help. He picks up the local report, more to give himself something to keep his mind occupied than anything else.

Bowles knows there's nothing to gain from the notes. As he scans over the pages, it's just like he thought: everything is just like he already knew…*except:*

> *'A Mr. C.J. Woods reports at 16:30 hours, his 1986 Ford F150 pickup missing from his backyard. Vehicle description: faded dark green, with tow truck package on the back.'*

The agent closes his eyes, going through every step right before the crash. He can't figure out why it's so hard to recall something that just happened hours ago. It must be a result of the trauma of the crash: the fear and intense pain, with the brain doing its best, trying to wipe it away.

Bowles closes his eyes: he can see himself, talking on the radio…he's telling the sheriff that he's getting close to the --------.

He can't remember, but he knows it's not the Caddy. He squeezes his eyes shut, trying hard to bring it back…it's got to be -----. But the images continue to slip by his mind's eye, just beyond his grasp.

Taking a deep breath, Bowles fights his frustration, trying to keep his mind clear. His memory puts him back in the helicopter and sees the Cadillac turning off the highway. Two people are falling out of the car…the chopper getting too close to the Cadillac as it races toward them. Now he sees a weapon being pointed at the helicopter from the car's window…suddenly, holes are being punched in the chopper's window, right in front of him.

Bowles is breathing heavily, sweating and grabbing the side rail of his hospital bed; mentally, he's about to crash in the helicopter all over again. Telling himself to *Calm Down,* he leans back in his bed, willing his heart rate to slow down, taking it out of high gear. He's here. It's over. They didn't die.

Ready to let the memory fade out of his mind, Bowles' brain provides a little flash of something: as the helicopter danced from side to side, he remembers spotting a green truck on the side of the road. At first, he thought the copter might even hit it.

The picture in his mind becomes clearer. They were about to pull the tow truck over, something to do with the van hooked up in the back. Bowles felt a dull, throbbing headache starting: it was still difficult bringing all the details back.

Looking at the report, it says the owner of the truck lives at 40 West Titan Road – just down the road from the sheriff's car bombing. Bowles would bet his life that the tow truck has something to do with this case. He doesn't realize it, but he had already made the bet…and very nearly lost his life.

With each passing second, the whole thing starts to come back to him…Yes – that was it! There was something in that van. Bowles had seen that truck pull off a dirt road onto Route 6, just west of the ranch house.

Realizing he'd had it all along, Bowles starts yelling. "Damn it, damn it – it was right there in my sight. Taylor! Somebody!! Shit! *Where's my phone?"*

Sitting in Mann's car parked a few feet from the pay phone in front of the King Soopers store on Colfax and Speer Boulevard, Max is trying to end a too-long conversation with Bill on his cell phone.

"Bill, you have to call me back; I'm waiting on an important call. It's about the money you need."

"We got the body moved," responds Bill. "You know, I mean Nicky."

"How'd you get it done so fast?"

"We gave the maid a few dollars to use her laundry cart. I put Nicky in it and covered her up. I used the radio station van to take her away. Nobody saw a thing, and we rolled her right out the back door. We're on our way to the crematorium now."

Max took a deep breath. "That's cool, I guess. I'll call you as soon as I'm done with this business."

Hanging up, Max shakes his head. He's really involved in covering up a murder. He'd never have thought in a million years that his life would take this kind of turn. Now he knows that he'd better make this work.

Pondering Bill and Anna's off-again/on-again behavior, Max is still troubled and a bit uneasy. Why did they seem so helpless when Max was around, but on top of things the second he was gone?

They came to his house that morning, seeming to be lost and turned out, then managed to talk him out of some blow and practically ran him out of his own place.

Now here they are again, in the hotel room, talking craziness – and in the short time that Max is out of the room, they have Nicky wrapped up like a Christmas present. To Max, they really don't need his help, and he is racking his brain, trying to put a finger on what is missing in this equation. "*I gotta find out more about that father of hers*," he says to himself.

His thoughts are interrupted by his ringing phone: it's Mann.

"Max. Dial this number right now!" Mann gives Max a Las Vegas phone number, then hangs up.

Max jumps out of the car, runs over to a payphone, and dials the number faster than he's ever dialed in his life.

Mann answers on the first ring. Max is waiting with his story, like a racehorse waiting to get out the gates.

"Max, what have you done now?" Mann asks.

"Uh, Mann? Nicky's dead!" Max said it so loudly, he had to look around to see if anybody had taken notice. There is a pause on the other end of the phone connection, then Mann replies.

"How the ---? Wait. First off, you don't expect me to shed a tear, do you? That's no surprise, unless it was you that put her in the grave — ha!"

There's silence on the other end of the phone.

"Max?...Max? Oh shit! — *Max ?* You didn't somehow manage to kill her, did you?

"I didn't do shit! It's Bill – Bill and that Anna chick." Max's voice is getting increasingly panicky. "Mann, they're out of control! Anna cut Nicky's throat from ear to ear! I didn't want to call you with more problems, but I can't get a handle on anything!"

"Ok, Max, ok. Calm down – don't say anything else on the phone. I don't know what the fuck you've been doing, and I really don't *want* to know. All I know is that my friend is asking me for some money – is that clear? I can guess what the money's for. No more talking, Max – Monica's coming in tonight with the dough; she's on a Southwest flight coming in at 10:30, my time."

Listening to his friend's voice over the phone, Max doesn't even want to guess at the stress that Mann is feeling.

Mann starts barking instructions to Max. "Pick her up at Denver International Airport. She's got what you need. Don't tell her shit about any of this, I don't care what she asks you. *Don't say shit!* I don't want her in any of this. Take her straight home. I'll be there tomorrow evening. I've got a lot on my plate right now — I don't need this extra BS. Take care of this," Mann warns. "You understand that if I have to get involved, you are going to hate your life!" With that, Mann hangs up.

Max stood there with the phone at his ear, then finally realizes the call has been disconnected. He knows he fucked up calling Mann. He can't remember the last time Mann sounded that pissed at him. His hands are shaking as he gets back in the car. He dials Bill.

"It's Max. I have to go to the airport. I'll have the money before midnight. Where's the crematorium? ....At 39th and Oneida? Ok, got it. ...I'll call you when I am on my way."

He glances at his watch: two hours before Monica will get into Denver. Time to take a long ride.

Max wishes he could just keep going.

Cus and Lenny walk into a small airplane hangar in Brooksville, Nevada, 60 miles south of Reno. Antwan Rose is standing, with the help of a cane, in front of a large flight bag.

Cus Barlow walks up with a smile on his face. Looking at the bag, he says, "Mr. Rose, I don't know whether to kiss you or blow your head off! How could you let five million dollars go up in smoke?"

"Believe me, Mr. Barlow, it ain't what I had planned! I almost went up in smoke with it. My crew's in pretty bad shape. I had to burn down my own garage to explain what happened to us."

"They buying your story?"

"Yeah," replied Rose, "so far, so good. It's cool."

"Yeah, for your sake it better stay cool!" Barlow nods his head at the flight bag. "Lenny, check the cash. Rose, you know I shouldn't pay you shit, right?"

"Mr. Barlow, I'm sure you're pissed."

"Pissed? You just fucked off *five million dollars* – but at least you got half of it back."

Antwan nodded. "Only because that dude didn't take both bags out of the house at the same time. Otherwise, he would have been long gone by the time we got there."

Lenny looks inside the bag, then zips it closed. "It looks ok, Boss."

"Ok, Lenny – give him the envelope. It's just like my money, Mr. Rose: it's half of what we agreed on. You got a problem with that?"

Rose shakes his head. "No, Mr. Barlow."

"So, Mr. Rose – I take it that you're out of business for a while?"

Antwan sees Barlow and Lenny as they check out his neck brace, the leg cast and his walking cane, then replies, "Yes, Mr. Barlow – I'm down for a while. At least, as far as field work goes. But if you need equipment, I can fix you up with anything you like."

Barlow looks hard at Antwan. "That's good to know, because when I find out who has my shipment, I want the same thing to happen to them that happened to that limo. *Capiesce?*"

"No problem, sir – no problem at all."

Barlow has already received word from his lawyer that the police report said that a local resident from the Silverton area told the sheriff about a black Cadillac with gangsters in it.

Lenny is immediately on the phone, getting some of his men together so they can pay the old man and his retarded grandson a small visit. Barlow isn't too worried. Between money and muscle, people can't seem to keep their mouths shut.

Mann is near the departure gate at Las Vegas' McCarran International Airport, helping Monica and Leta get their bags out of the car. As Mann hands Monica an envelope full of money, she quietly says, "I love you, baby. But please — no more drama — I can't take it!"

Mann squeezes Monica's hand. "Don't worry. All I'm gonna do is load up the stuff in a U-Haul. Me and Nesto are gonna try and get some rest, then hit the freeway first thing in the morning. Max will be at the Denver airport, waiting for you and Leta. Just give him this envelope. Don't worry about whatever it is he's into. The less we know, the better – ok, baby?"

Monica takes the envelope from Mann and stuffs it securely in her handbag. "All I know is this: he better not be getting you into any of his shit!" Mann looks nervously at the seriousness on Monica's face. She gives a wan smile and says, "I love you. It's almost 8:00 — time for us to get out of here." Kissing him once, she follows Leta inside the airport.

Watching the women walk away, Mann says aloud what he has been thinking all day. "It's too late to stay out of Max's shit. If it wasn't for him, we wouldn't be in Vegas in this mess." He sighs, and gets back into his car.

Driving back to Caesar's Palace, Mann's focus is on taking care of the loose ends in Vegas. He reviews the list in his head, mentally checking off the various items. Thanks to Lester, the van and the tow truck are history; the U-Haul is also loaded up. The last thing on Mann's list is getting cash to Rico, the old man and his grandson Donnie. Nesto was so happy to be alive back in his hotel room; he said he'd pay the money they asked for.

Mann likes the way things have finally come together. How he managed to get himself so deep in less than a week still has him baffled. He's also not sure about Nesto's plan, but he knows getting that shipment back to Denver will bring him a bigger payday than he's ever dreamed of.

The only thing that's really worrying him now is Nicky and what happened with her. The kind of chick Nicky is...*was* – there's no telling. It will be a relief to have her gone…but then, having Max involved makes it a little too close to home.

Spriggs is gonna be on the rampage, and Mann hopes this whole drama will drive Spriggs over the edge, making the cop do something stupid…something that he can't get out of. Turning onto Las Vegas Boulevard, Mann calls Nesto.

"Hello, Nesto? It's me, Mann. Have you talked to Lester? Is he gonna take the money to Silverton for Gramps, Donnie and Rico?...Good! I'll call the grandfather; you call Rico. I'll be back in a couple of hours. I'm headed to the casino – I feel lucky!"

Nesto gives Lester the address in Silverton where Rico stays. On the other side of the paper is the address for Gramps and Donnie. Nesto gives Lester final instructions.

"Lester, there's two hundred grand in that bag by the door. They each get a hundred grand. Call me when ju get there. Rico is waiting at his cousin's place; he has two broken wrists, so ju can't mistake him."

Heading out the door, Lester asks, "Where's the brain at?"

"Who ju talking about? Maw? He needed a break; he's somewhere playing blackjock."

Two hours into his game, Las Vegas is rearing its ugly head and is sinking its teeth into Mann. "Nobody leaves with more than they came with', as the saying goes, and Mann loses two thousand dollars at the blackjack table as easily as if he came to pay a utility bill.

But that's ok. Mann's focus isn't on winning – he's taking some time out to figure out what is really going on.

Mann had a talk with Lester, who told him that the word on the street is that Cus Barlow has a major shipment coming in any day – and Barlow has everybody on hold waiting for it. The way Lester and Mann figured it, Singleton must have sold the shipment to Barlow …which means it was Barlow's people loading the van when Mann's group showed up at the ranch house and took it. Barlow must have figured Singleton had double-crossed him and sent somebody to get his money back.

Both Lester and Mann know that Vegas isn't the best place to try and sell this shipment, even if it is Nesto's. Whether Barlow bought the shipment from Singleton or somebody else, they're going to be looking for it. The way Lester put it, anybody in Vegas with a bag of cocaine worth more than a thousand dollars better watch their back.

Mann is so lost in thought, he doesn't even realize that he's finally won a hand his first in a while. He looks up at the dealer and puts up his palm. "Keep it, it's your tip. We gotta go. *Tonight!*" Mann gets up from the blackjack table and walks away, leaving the dealer with a puzzled look on his face.

When Mann walks into the hotel room, it's dark and the only sound is the TV. Nesto's out cold on the couch; Mann kicks at the cushions. With all the madness he's been through the last couple of days, the peacefulness of the hotel room is foreign to him. "Nesto, wake up! Where's Lester?"

"He's taking the money to Rico. What time is it?"

"It's 11:30. He should be there by now. I told him to call me." Mann quickly paces from one side of the room to the other. He fires another question at Nesto, "Is the truck loaded and ready to roll?"

"Yeah, Maw – it's ready! Lester parked it in the VIP lot before he left."

"You gotta be kidding me! Rolls Royces, Ferraris, Lamborghinis – and a big ass U-Haul truck loaded down with cocaine, sitting in the VIP parking lot! Could we be any more obvious? Come on - it's time to get the hell out of here. We're on the road tonight!"

They made a quick exit from the hotel. Once they hit the freeway, Mann feels a sense of relief he hasn't felt in a while.

But it's short-lived.

"Nesto, you fall asleep again? Wake up – it's your phone."

Nesto's eyes crack a little. "Oh, jeah...ok." He answers the phone. "Hello? ...Who? How did it go...What? Nesto sits straight up in his seat and right away, Mann knows something's wrong.

"What the problem, Nesto?" Mann hisses at his partner.

Nesto doesn't answer, but keeps talking on the phone. "Ok, ok, ju guys stay low! Call me when ju get back to Vegas. We're already on the road." He hangs up, and before he can get it out, Mann already knows.

"It's Donnie and the old man, uh?"

Looking at Mann, Nesto says, "How'd ju know? Lester said he took Rico his money first. Then Rico rode with Lester to show him where the old man's house is. When they got there, the door had been kicked in, and the old man was dead! Lester said he was shot in the head said it looked like he was pretty beat up before he was killed. The place was a wreck, and--"

Mann cuts him off. "The kid. What about the kid?"

"No sign of him, Mann. Who do ju-"

"Goddamn it, Nesto – who do *you* think? Whose fucking name keeps popping up?"

Nesto thinks for a minute, then said in an unsure voice, "Jour not talking about Cus Barlow, are ju?"

"There you go! Think about it: that was probably Barlow's people at the ranch house, loading the van. It was *definitely* his guys on the freeway yesterday. And who else would try and blow up Singleton?"

The surprise on Nesto's face was clear. "Ju think Singleton sold my stuff to Barlow?"

"Yep. Barlow went back to Singleton to get his money when we took the dope. Something must have gone wrong, because that limo blew up with a load of cash in it. Maybe Singleton was trying to leave the country for real this time, but didn't make it…What are you smiling about?"

"I got them – well, *we* got them – both of them! In one move, we got Singleton and that big mouth gangster Barlow. I hope that the both of them wind up in Hell together!"

"Yeah," agreed Mann, "I guess we're sitting pretty right now, but what about Gramps and that kid? We wouldn't have gotten away if it weren't for them."

The smile instantly disappears off Nesto's face. "How did they know to go after Gramps and Donnie?"

"That news report said that witnesses stated that there were gangsters in a black Cadillac. Remember the old man made up that story for the cops? How in the hell did Barlow's boy wind up in a black Caddy?" Mann frowns, trying to put the pieces together.

"Ju remember what the old man said? The gangsters, they always ride in black Cadillacs. That's why the sheriff bought his story and sure enough, the real gangsters show up in a black Caddy! How crazy is that?"

"I don't know, Nesto, but we gotta find that kid! Call Rico and Lester – and tell them to be real careful. Anybody that has anything to do with us is on Barlow's shit list."

"Ju figure Barlow knows we have the coke," asks Nesto.

"Yeah, I'm sure of it. The old man probably gave us up. You said Rico told you that Gramps was pretty beaten up, right? They probably also threatened to hurt the kid, so the old man had no choice. Then they up and kill the guy anyway." Mann's jaw tightens up. "Damn! I hate that."

Nesto dials Rico's number to check on him and Lester – and the news goes from bad to worse. "Hello, Rico? It's Nesto – where are ju?"

"Hey Nesto, we got another big problem. Me and Lester just went back by my cousin's place. There are two cars in front that I've never seen before, and there's somebody standing on the porch. He's wearing a suit, and he's not from around here."

His blood pressure racing, Nesto tells Rico, "Don't stop, whatever ju do!"

"Don't worry about that, Nesto! My cousin's at his girlfriend's house, waiting for me. I got the money you sent. I think I'll take a long vacation. Maybe Texas – I got *la familia* down there, *la familia grande*. I think I might need them. Lester said to tell you this: he's headed back to Vegas – to see what he can find out for you. He's going to hold the other hundred grand – but he said if the heat comes his way, he's out of there with the money. You guys forfeit the cash for getting him caught up in this shit."

"Tell him to keep it," replies Nesto. "He earned it. Hey, Rico, has anybody heard anything about the old man's grandson, Donnie? Ju haven't heard anything?…Ok, that's cool. Let me know if ju do. …Alright, I'll talk to ju later. Stay safe and take care of those wrists, ok? Bye."

Nesto disconnects from Rico and turns to Mann. "So what's the plan? We going back to Vegas?"

"No, Nesto, I don't think so. I need to be on *my* turf before we do this."

"Do *what?*"

"Call Cus Barlow."

Chapter 6

It's 3:30 a.m. in Las Vegas, Nevada. There's been more action in the surrounding area recently than in the last three years put together. And it hasn't stopped yet.

Barlow's contracted some 'outside help' to go into Silverton to try to find out who's causing him so many problems. By asking questions in Silverton and Las Vegas, they've found out – to Barlow's surprise – that the people who took the shipment from the ranch house didn't steal it. They repossessed it. Between what the old man said before they killed him and what the contractors found out, Barlow knows who has his shipment.

"Damn, Lenny – all this time I forgot about those two fucks in the alley that night. The one we beat up, even when said he was Lanceo Quintana's brother! I should have put it together. What else would he be doing in Vegas? In Quintana's eyes, all he was doing is taking back what belongs to him."

"Where do you think they took it?" asks Lenny.

"Can't be too far – that's not something you ride around with. We gotta get in contact with them before they find another buyer…if they don't already have one. This sure has turned into a great big fuckin' mess!"

Lenny shakes his head. "When we do find them, how are we gonna come at them?"

"I'm not sure," says Barlow, thinking. "I've called around, trying to find someone that's got connections to Lanceo in Colombia...so I can tell him how Singleton tried to screw both of us, and see if we can work something out. The problem is that my guy in Arizona tells me Lanceo is real paranoid. He doesn't deal with people. He thinks everybody's a Fed, trying to bust him. So he sends everybody to that little shit brother of his – the one we beat the crap out of in the alley the other night. To make matter worse, nobody knows where the brother is! I had Slim check with his people. They said he was at Caesar's Palace, but he checked out a few hours ago."

"Boss, what about that black guy he was with? You remember him?"

"Oh yeah! What was his name? 'Mr. Mann' or something like that. How hard can it be to find a black guy and a Colombian running around Vegas with over a ton of cocaine?"

"You got that right, Boss! They're bound to make a mistake sooner or later!"

"It better be *sooner*; we don't have time to wait this one out. If they're smart, they're headed to the West Coast, or at least to Reno. It's way too hot around here to try and sell that shit right now."

"Yeah, Boss – either they're real smart, or the luckiest bastards in Vegas. I don't even think the Feds know what's going on. They're still talking about possible terrorist plots on the news."

"I know what you mean, Lenny – they *have* to be lucky. If we'd killed them that night in the alley, I'd still have my shipment. Slim said the old man told the cops about a black Caddy, just to throw them off their trail – and it was pure dumb luck it worked out perfectly."

"Damn! I wish I had that much dumb luck!"

"No, you don't, Lenny. The problem with dumb luck is it always runs out on you at the worst possible time."

Barlow closes his eyes, thinking about his next move. He and Lenny may not be the smartest men — but they have formidable, cut-throat reputations. He knows it's a powerful equalizer.

He snaps his finger and tells Lenny, "Get Slim to bring that kid up here, the one they got at the old man's house. See if he knows anything. And get the word out on the street. If anyone can tell me where those two are with my shipment, I'll personally hand $10,000."

"Ten large? I might even do some snooping around for that kind of money. Boss, you think those two even know what they're into?"

Lenny's boss paused for a minute. "I don't know. But that 'Mann' character has paid his dues. He's got balls, and he uses his head. We'd better not underestimate him. And that Colombian – he's *cartel*: those sons of bitches are nuts. Slim said the old man told him it was just the two of them that came and took the shipment. If they're on one of those 'Do or Die' missions, this ain't gonna be easy!"

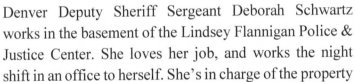

Denver Deputy Sheriff Sergeant Deborah Schwartz works in the basement of the Lindsey Flannigan Police & Justice Center. She loves her job, and works the night shift in an office to herself. She's in charge of the property room. A very important job, and she's paid good money to keep a close eye on the items in this area.

About 4:00 a.m. every Monday morning, she reviews the list of items that are scheduled for disposal. They're no longer needed as evidence, as the cases that they are being held for have been resolved. The items include everything you can imagine. And many of them — including items such as rings, watches, televisions and tools – are sold at police auction.

But some items, such as knives, guns, and —Sergeant Schwartz's favorite — narcotics, are held back and set to be destroyed.

She goes through the list and marks the ones that are to be pulled. Then she enters the storage area, and puts red tags on the marked items. The Denver Police Department has a protocol in place that restricts admission into the room that stores the narcotics. Simply stated, it says that *"No one officer can enter, inspect or remove any item[s] in the narcotics area without the presence of another officer."*

This regulation is meant to insure that having narcotics at hand doesn't get the better of one lone officer, as it had in the past.

But Sergeant Schwartz has been in charge of the Evidence Room for so long, the rules have been relaxed for her. That's one of the reasons why she loves her job —and why she's turned down promotions to cushier jobs more than once.

This morning, there will be a large amount of narcotics tagged for disposal. She keeps a special shoulder bag in her locker for days like this. The bag contains an assortment of fake drugs. When Sergeant Schwartz takes the real stuff off the shelves, she uses her homemade placebos to replace them.

The sergeant doesn't use the drugs to support her drug habit: she doesn't have one. She uses the narcotics to supplement her income.

Schwartz walks through the aisles this morning, doing her "grocery shopping." She picks up a few hundred Percocets, and a large baggie of crystal meth, all of which are big money nowadays. As the sergeant reaches for the meth, she tells herself, *this is my new Lexus truck!* It's the shiny, all-red one, down the street at the local auto dealer: she's had her eyes on it for a couple of weeks now.

And then there's her favorite items on the shopping list: a key and a half of cocaine. That's not easy to find these days because now, when large amounts of coke get picked up by the D.A.'s office, they are sent on to the Feds for their cases. Schwartz had been hoping that they wouldn't come get this load before its disposal time came up.

Seems like every week the police would confiscate a large quantity of coke, then the D.A.'s office would send a courier to pick it up. Sergeant Schwartz *knows* that this is high-grade stuff: this batch is from some Mexicans busted coming through Denver via I-70.

The sergeant takes her goodies to the locker room, and deposits the meth, the Percosets and the single kilo of coke into her locker. No need to rush, since she's in charge.

Putting the remaining half-key of coke in her shoulder bag, Schwartz replaces the confiscated baggie of real coke with her homemade mixture of baking soda, cake mix, and crushed-up salt rock (to give it that special sparkle.) She heads to the ladies' room, locks the door behind her, and pulls out the cocaine. With her pocket knife, she cuts a small hole in the bag, and puts a little coke on the card that she's retrieved from inside of her bra.

Using her manicured pinky, she scoops up an appropriately large nail-full (*after all, she doesn't have a habit*), and pulls it right up her nose.

Waiting for the sting that tells her that she's got the goods, her wait is longer than normal. As a matter of fact, it's been a good thirty seconds and there's no sting, no kick. It burns, but not in the right way. She looks at the powder on the card. It's white, but it's hard to tell the quality just by looking at it.

The sergeant does another pinky nail-full: same result.

Wetting her finger, Schwartz dabs it in the powder, then sticks it back in her mouth. Instantly, she spits it out. "This ain't blow!" She's *pissed.*

She heads out of the bathroom, going straight to her locker and yanking it open. Giving a good look around despite knowing she's the only one down there – she pulls out the larger bag of coke, and sticks her knife in the baggie (like she's stabbing her ex-husband and that bitch he ran off with.)

She cuts a good five-inch gash in the bag, and she pulls out a large amount on the end of her knife. Using her lighter, she puts flame to it; she knows the smell it should give off when the flame melts the powder. Instead of melting, this shit catches on fire and smells like burning paper.

Whatever it is, *it isn't cocaine*! Pushing her hair back off her face, Schwartz thinks things through. She had seen the laboratory test report on this batch. This should be the best stuff they've had down here in a while.

Putting everything back in her locker, Schwartz tries desperately to figure it out. The only other person with access to this stuff is Baker, on the day shift. And she knows he's not up to anything; there are too many people on the day shift to try something slick.

Punching up the file on her desk computer, it shows the stuff came in from the lab on December 18 - it was inventoried by Baker. That's all in order. She continues to read, and almost overlooks it.

Reading the report for a second time, she catches the clue: it was checked out by head D.A. Simons on January 15 for evidence in a trial, then brought back on February 7.

Sergeant Schwartz feels a big lump in her throat. She knows this is…well, she doesn't know *what* it is -- but it isn't right. Why is the head D. A. picking up evidence? And why was it out for so long? Nobody's allowed to keep evidence out of this room for seven days, especially *drugs.* The third problem she's having with this report: How could the D.A. have presented it as evidence in trial? *Nobody* in the modern justice system goes to trial just thirty days after their arrest.

Her heart is pounding, she wishes they had come and gotten this counterfeit stuff for the Feds.

Is the head D.A. dipping in the drug evidence? It sure looks that way to her, but that doesn't make any sense: he's zero tolerance on drugs.

Schwartz swipes at the sweat that's forming on her forehead. She doesn't want to be the one to discover this. How long before something else is out of line? Then sooner or later, the crap starts rolling down from the top — and it won't stop until the people at the bottom get screwed!

◆────────────────◇────────────────◆

Meeting Bill and Anna at the crematorium, Max is in bad shape – and his attitude is worse. He has just came from dropping off Mann's girlfriend, Monica. She lit into him and didn't stop from the time he picked her up until he dropped off her with that pretty Latina who accompanied Monica on the flight.

Monica chewed on him about everything – *Why do you need money from my man? Why are you driving Mann's car? Why can't you drive your own —that is, if you still have one?*

Max had wanted to try and get to know Monica's friend from Vegas, but thanks to Monica's mouthing off, he can't even remember the friend's name.

"What the fuck," Max figures aloud, "at least I got the money."

Pulling up to the address that Bill gave him for the crematorium, Max doesn't see the radio station van. A couple of cars are parked on the side of what looks like a warehouse, but it's dark and deserted. If Anna wanted to jump out of the dark and shoot him, this is the perfect place to do it. "Stop freaking yourself out! Everything's gonna be cool," Max bravely says aloud.

He slowly dials Bill's phone number. It takes a couple of tries to get it right because he's so busy looking for an unpleasant surprise to leap out of the shadows. Finally he hears Bill's voice on the other end.

"Max is that you? Where are you at?"

"I'm at the address you gave me, on 39th and Newport Street," replies Max.

"Good - don't move; I'll be right there."

Max is still looking around. He's not feeling this at all, and he fights down a small panic attack. Reaching for the key, Max tells himself, *to hell with all this, I'm outta here!* Right as he's about to start the car, he jumps at the sound of a loud bang. He whips his head around, looking for the source of the noise.

The garage door right in front of him starts to rise. Inside, standing to one side is Bill, waving his arm. Max gets out of the car and runs in the doorway.

Looking at Max, Bill calls out, "Hey, Max! You ok? You look…I don't know… not yourself."

"Don't let it bother you, Bill; it's my crematorium look. You know, something about this place brings out this look on me."

Bill shakes his head at Max's sarcasm. "Yeah, you're alright."

Max looks around. There's a big open area where trucks can pull in, but Max still doesn't see the radio station van. For some reason, that fact really bothers him. "Bill, where's the van? I thought you said that you used it to move, uh, You-Know-Who."

"Oh, yeah. Well, it took you so long to get from the airport, we took it back so no one would miss it."

"So what are you driving now," asked Max pointedly.

"I – uh, took a cab. We didn't have time to get my car."

Max is tired and half-high, as usual – but it's still not enough to keep him from feeling that something's not quite right. Bill is acting really strange, and Max can tell that Bill is lying about the van. But why?

"Do you have the money," Bill asks.

"That's the *only* reason I'd be at a place like this, Bill!" Max pulls a large envelope out of his shirt, handing it to Bill. "Where's Nicky's body? And where do they, you know, burn people up?"

"Come on, Max," replies Bill. "It's back here. We already put her in; the guy's waiting for his money before he starts it up."

Max follows Bill to the back of the building; it's dark. Very dark.

Bill disappears through a doorway. Max stops; he can't see a thing. A dim light comes on from the other room. Walking through the door, Max sees a long hallway, leading down a ramp — which leads down into more darkness. Bill looks back and sees Max is hesitant to follow him.

"Sorry, Max — I forgot you don't know the way. They're right down here by the ovens."

"Oh boy! Ovens. My great-grandmother was Jewish. That's not a good word for me, you know!"

Bill looks back at Max and smiles.

As they walk down the ramp, Max feels the heat building up around him. He can hear the sound of machinery, like a rushing sound, and then realizes that it's the sound of the exhaust vents for the oven.

At the bottom of the ramp, they walk through a doorway into a larger room. Two other people are standing by what looks like (to Max, anyway) an oversized pizza oven. They're talking, laughing, and having a great time.

Seeing this sight gives Max a sense of relief; he didn't know what to expect at the bottom of that ramp. He's not as trusting of Bill and Anna as he was when this first started.

Anna sees Bill, and the first thing out of her mouth is, "Yeah, Max! Bill, you got the money?" Bill nods his head with a smile on his face.

Anna looks back at Max, saying, "Max, I love you!" She runs over and hugs him. He doesn't hug her back.

A tall man in a black smock walks in from some unknown place. Bill approaches him; they turn their backs and start to talk business. Max sees Bill hand the man some money out of the envelope. Max is doing his best to pay attention to what's going on between Bill and the Smock Man.

Anna, seeing Max pay too much attention to Bill's business, grabs Max's hand and pulls him over by the giant pizza ovens. There's a part-Asian kid standing there. He looks to be about Anna's age. Seeing them standing together, Anna looks all-kid now; their talk, the way they dress, they have a lot in common.

Max hopes that's *all* they have in common.

"Max," says Anna, "this is my friend T.W. His hero is Tiger Woods."

Max looks at the fuzzy-headed kid and says, "Oh. 'T.W' Tiger Woods, Asian, I get it."

Anna continues to talk. "His father owns this place; that's his brother-in-law over there talking with Bill. Max – it's almost over! All we have to do is turn this knob and 30 minutes later, Poof! Nothing but dust."

Max is having a hard time with this scene. Everyone seems to act like they're at the park or something. Max pulls on Anna's hand, leading her away from her friend T.W. Talking in a low voice, Max says, "Anna, why the fuck do you have your school friend here? What if he tells somebody else?"

"Who—T.W.? He's not going to tell anybody. His father owns the place. If he did that, that could get his father in all kinds of trouble. Besides, this isn't the first time they've done this, you know."

The heat is starting to get to Max; he's blinking, trying to keep the sweat out of his eyes. "So —where's Nicky's body," asks Max, clearly suspicious.

"In there." She points at the giant oven

That's not good enough for Max. "I want to see it. I want to see her right now!"

The man in the smock hears Max, and walks over by the oven. He opens a small port hole in the oven door, then looks at Max and points to the hole.

Max steps up to the hole; he can feel the heat rushing out the small opening.

"In there?" he asks Smock Man. The man nods his head. Max turns and looks inside. He sees a long slab with a row of small fires burning on either side of the slab. On top of the slab is the mummy-looking body that Max had seen in the hotel bathtub.

Smock Man turns a knob, and the fire on both sides jump to life. The mummy disappears in the fire. Heat from the fire jumps out of the hole. Max snaps his head back, just as Smock Man slams the port-hole door closed.

The heat is becoming too much for Max. He takes a large step away from the oven, trying to wipe the heat from his face. Max looks at Smock Man, making eye contact, but the man doesn't say a word. He turns away, puts his hands in his pockets, and plays with whatever it is in there.

Max knows what it is; it's his five grand.

Before Max can gather himself, T.W. puts his hand on Max's shoulder. Looking up at him, the kid shoves a card in Max's face.

"Hey! Anytime you need to clean up a little mess - if you know what I mean - just call me. I got your back, ok? And when are you going to be back on the radio? That other guy, DJ Tone? – He sucks!"

They follow Anna and Bill up the ramp, through the building and out of the garage door. T.W. lets them out. As the door is closing, Max looks back at T.W.; he's smiling and waving. Max can't help but think about the way that "The Beverly Hillbillies" used to wave at the end of each weekly show: *'Y'all come back now, y'hear?'*

Bill and Anna are standing by the car, waiting for Max to unlock the doors. Max looks around; the sun is rising. It's gonna be a hot day.

Looking at his watch, it's already ten minutes to six in the morning. He should be taking his seat at the radio station, getting Metro Denver off to work or wherever they have to go.

"This is Mad Max, and you're on KBPO, the only Rock and Rap station in the nation!" That's how he started every morning, when life was simple: No Anna. No Nicky. Bill was still a square, running around the station with his pop bottle-bottom glasses, and ill-fitting polyester pants.

What wouldn't Max do to find out that this is all a long, complicated nightmare. He'd just wake up, and Mann would be at his front door, handing him a baggie of blow, and that friend of Monica's would be waiting for him in his bedroom.

His fantasy goes down in flames at the sound of a familiar voice. "Max! Let's go. Bill, I'm tired and hungry."

Halfway across Utah, Mann pulls the U-Haul off the road at a rest stop.

"Nesto. Nesto! Wake up!"

Nesto is clearly not quite awake. "Wha...What? We here jet?"

"Not yet," replies Mann, "we're past Salt Lake City. That's more than halfway. I had to stop. That sun is in the eastern sky. It's blinding, and my eyes are killing me. You think you can drive for a while? We're gonna have to stop for gas soon anyway. I don't know about you, but I'm starving."

"Ok, Maw, let me take over." Nesto stretches and yawns, then peers down at his foot. "I gotta take the medication the doctor gave me. He said that it's gonna be a while before this hole in my foot closes, so I can't let it get infected or they'll cut it off."

Mann rolls his eyes. "Hell, cutting off your foot should been the least of your worries! I was there – you're lucky to be breathing! I was sure you were dead. That bullet hit you so hard, you did a complete flip!"

"It felt like a hammer hit me, too! I don't ever want to go through that again. Maw, ju ever been shot?"

"No, but I've come pretty damn close. I'll get out and walk around the truck; you slide over behind the wheel. And by the way, it's early in the morning. If we keep pushing, we'll be in Denver by this afternoon. The only problem is this U-Haul ain't gonna like going over the Continental Divide. It's over ten thousand feet, all uphill."

"What ju got planned when we do get there?"

Mann walks around, jumps in the truck's passenger seat, and leans his head back. It's the first time in a while that he's be able to relax. Closing his eyes, Mann answers Nesto's question.

"I've been thinking about that. First, we need to talk to Lester and find out if he's learned anything. Depending on what he says, we need to make that call to Cus Barlow."

Nesto's not happy to hear that name, and it shows on his face. "What do ju think he wants to do? And before ju answer that question, I'll want ju to know this: I don't give a sheet if Singleton burned him on their deal. I didn't get any money out of the deal. All I did was come to take my property back!"

Mann nods. "What if he wants to deal – you know, work something out?"

"Maybe before. But now, I don't know. He sheeted me at poker, beat my ass, and took jour money. Said if he ever seen us again, he'd kill us. Then the son of a bitch killed the old man, and there's no telling what happen to the kid! I say, fuck him! He can't be trusted."

Mann's voice goes cold. "I agree. As a matter of fact, that's what I wanted to hear, but know this: if that was his money that blew up in the limo, then he really did pay Singleton for that coke. The only way to get rid of him is to either deal with him, or kill him!"

"This is getting like, how ju say it? *'A broken record?'* As soon as we get over one hump, here comes another one, just like the last one."

Mann sits straight up in his seat and hits the dashboard with his fist. "Well, I'm about to put an end to this party. I got word that there's some other shit going on back home. I don't have the time or patience to deal with anybody else's shit! If it'll make him happy, I'll sell Barlow my half of the shipment, but he better come correct, because he'll be on my turf now. If he starts that 'big-shot gangster' shit in the Mile High City, I got a trick for his ass!"

Nesto watches as his friend's demeanor becomes fierce. "Maw, I'm glad ju do, because jour gonna need it. I know guys like him; I deal with them all the time. First they tell ju what they think ju want to hear. Ju know, talk nice to ju, make ju feel real comfortable. Then if they don't get what they want, they blow up on ju. Tell ju jour a piece of sheet for not trusting them and honoring their deal. Jour gonna wind up dead if ju don't play 'fair'."

Nesto's eyes are glazed over, seeing all his past deals with snakes like Barlow. "By now, ju either give in, or watch jour back, 'cause he's gonna cross ju out! And if ju do give in, he still might cross ju out. He'll tell ju some bull about, *it's nothing personal, just business*, ju know – then blow jour fucking brains out. Either way, jour screwed. The guy can't help himself – he's got to do ju dirty. It's *in* him. I grew up watching my older brother jump from 'nice guy' to 'killer' in a blink of an eye...Until he got fat, rich and lazy."

"What's up with you and your brother," asks Mann, "and why did you have Leta tell him that bullshit story over the phone before we left Vegas?"

"'Cause like I said, he's only got one thing on his mind. Money! He don't give a sheet about nobody or nothing else. That bag of money I showed ju? He wants Leta to bring it back to Colombia!"

"For what? That was only a few hundred thousand. Doesn't he have millions?"

"Yes," Nesto replies, "he's got millions on top of millions! He wants to keep the money so we have to run back to him every time we need anything. It helps him feels like he's in control. Well Maw, after this one here, I'm on my own. I'm tired of coming over here, playing 'fetch dog' for him! Everybody around him, they kiss his ass all day long. He's so far out of the loop, all he knows to do is say 'Bring me my money.' I say this to him – 'Ju want jour money, *ju* go get it from the guy ju gave that shipment to. And good luck with that one, because he's dead!'"

Trying to be half-funny, Mann says, "So I take it you're not happy about the way things are going?"

"Hell, no," fumes his friend. "He tell me, 'Nesto, ju handle everything.' Then when Mr. Big Shot Singleton asks for a shipment of coke, I say, 'OK, money upfront – ju get what ju pay for.' Singleton gets mad and calls my brother, tells him I'm not 'being fair'. So my brother tells me to '*Go ahead and give it to him; he's good friend, he'll pay up.*' The next thing ju know, he *can't* pay, and my brother is going loco, telling *me* to go get his money or his property! Maw, if he listened to me in the first place, I wouldn't have hole in my foot!"

Mann doesn't quite know what to think about the news Nesto just told him. He looks at the expression on his face; it's really obvious that Nesto's had about all he can take. Doing his best to analyze Nesto, Mann asks, "So we won't have any problems from your brother if we don't come up with this shipment?"

"No. He already knows I'm done playing his game. Leta told me he said that he was surprised that I haven't already took a shipment and told him to fuck off!"

"Sounds to me like he wants you to," replies Mann.

"That's good, because he's about to get his wish."

"Hold on, Nesto – don't burn that bridge yet! We might need him to fix this thing with Barlow. Keep him as an ace in your hat – or to use your words, an 'ace in jour chew.' "

Nesto thinks about what Mann has just said. He doesn't like it, but has to admit that it makes good sense. "Ok, Maw, if ju think he can help us. But the first time he starts giving orders, I'M DONE!"

It's eight in the morning. Barlow has been up all night trying to save his empire, along with his ass. One of Barlow's up-and-coming protégés, a hot-headed street thug named Slim, brings the kid Donnie to Barlow.

Barlow's attitude is bad, as usual, and Donnie doesn't give a fuck. The perfect mix. Barlow sees the kid, and pats the couch next to him. "Hey kid – come sit by your Uncle Cus. So you're the guy who's gonna save the day, huh? You know, I'd be real happy if you'd help me out. I could get you anything you want."

Donnie, knowing a phony line when he hears one, jumps all over Barlow. "How about my grandfather? Can you get him back?"

Barlow's surprised at the fire in Donnie's answer, and takes a moment to respond. "Well, we both know that's not possible. Look, kid —you're young, but you're not a baby. There's something very important I need to know, and I think you know what it is."

Donnie gives Barlow the meanest look he can manage. "What's that?"

"Tell your Uncle Cus where that fuc-- uhm, where are the two guys that took that stuff from the ranch house?"

"Who? What guys?"

"You know – the Mexican and the black guy."

"Oh! You mean Nesto and Mann. I don't know where they are. Besides, I don't think Nesto's a Mexi –"

Barlow's "nice Uncle Cus" immediately drops off the map. "I don't give a fuck *what* you think he is, kid! But you better think real hard on what they talked about!"

"I heard them say, the guy who owns the ranch house didn't pay for that stuff. So they're taking their shit back, and— *fuck you!*"

Cus almost socks the kid. "Listen, you little shit! Nobody talks to me like that, you hear me? I'll kill your little black ass so fast!"

"What are you waiting for? A permission slip from your mother?"

Infuriated, Barlow hits the roof. "Why, you little son of a bitch!" Cus pulls out his pistol, Donnie jumps over the couch, and Lenny grabs the kid and pulls him to the side.

"No, Boss! He's just a kid!"

"And that's as far as he's gonna get in life if he don't watch that smart-ass mouth of his!"

"Let me talk to him, Boss," answers Lenny, trying to placate Barlow. "You're a little pissed right now."

Cus looks at Lenny, then at the kid. He take a deep breath and realizes that Lenny is taking a breath, too, almost coaching Cus to calm down.

Cus turns and leaves the room. Lenny looks Donnie straight in the eyes.

With just the look, Donnie gets the message: *If you want to live, don't ever do that again.* Donnie nods his head.

Lenny has been by Cus' side forever. He's saved so many people from Barlow's flashes of anger, he's lost count.

Lenny seems to be the only one who can talk Barlow back to earth. Cus has killed a lot of people over the years, and had it not been for Lenny, that count would be twice as high.

Lenny takes the kid into the kitchen.

"Hey kid, you hungry? And what's your name anyway?"

Without Cus' presence, Donnie opens right up to Lenny. "I'm Donnie, and I haven't eaten anything since yesterday."

"Look in the fridge over there, there's some pizza. Grab yourself a piece. On second thought, bring the whole box. I'm kinda hungry too."

From the other room, they both hear Barlow. "I know if that kid don't speak up, and soon – that pizza gonna be his last meal!"

"It's ok, Boss; give us a minute. He's cool." Lenny gives Donnie another look of warning, and again Donnie nods his head to say, *I get the message.*

Grabbing a slice of pizza from the box that Donnie had put on the table, Lenny asks, "Where you from, kid? You don't look like no country boy to me."

"Don't call me 'kid'! My name is Donnie. I'm from Chicago, and I've been dealing with tough fucks like you two all my life."

Lenny can't help but laugh; this kid is tough. Right away, Lenny knows why he likes him. Lenny and Cus grew up in Chicago. Lenny yells to Barlow in the other room. "Boss! Guess where the kid's from."

"Yeah, Lenny – I heard, I heard!"

Lenny turns his attention back to Donnie. "If you know as much as you act like you do, then you know that this ain't no game, kid—uh, *Donnie*! Those two guys you're trying to help. We're not going to hurt them. We just want to talk with them. That's all."

Donnie is playing with his pizza at the same time he's eating it. "I don't know where they went. They said something about Vegas. If all you want to do is talk to them, why don't you call them?"

Lenny stares at this skinny kid, chewing on a slice of pizza. "Call them. Of course – why didn't I think of that? Real funny, kid…and I guess you have their number?"

"Duh. Yeah, I know their phone number! Why else would I say that?"

Lenny can't believe how ballsy this kid is. "If you keep being a smart ass, I'm going to let the boss in there kick your little ass. Why didn't you tell me that you had the phone number a long time ago?"

Donnie looks at Lenny with a shit-eating grin on his face, saying, "Well, nobody asked me."

Cus Barlow, having overheard Donnie, made a beeline into the kitchen. Mouthing the words, "*I'm gonna kill this kid*" to Lenny, Cus turns to Donnie. "You got their number. Give it to me, kid!"

"The name's not 'Kid', and ain't you forgetting something?" Donnie gives a sly look at Barlow.

Cus looks at Donnie and scratches his head. "Forget something? What are you talking about, ki--, uh, Donnie?"

"I'm talking about my money! On the way over here, I heard that Slim guy tell his friend that you would give up ten grand to whoever knew where they were. The way I see it, I got 10 big ones coming. No money, no number! Period."

"What kind of shit is this? Do you know who I am?"

Donnie shakes his head from side to side, and says, "I don't know who you are, but I know *what* you are – and that's a big, fat, full of shit liar." Lenny flinches on that note; Cus is about to pop his cork.

Barlow knows he could beat it out of the kid, but Lenny loves kids. And beating this young punk wouldn't sit well with Lenny.

Lenny looks at Cus. "Well, Boss? A deal's a deal."

Barlow shakes his head at the both of them. "Ok, kid – here's the deal. I said anyone who knows where they are. All you have is a phone number. So you give me the number, I'll buy you an X-Box, or whatever they call it."

The kid bursts out laughing. "An X-Box? Ha! I don't even play games. I guess you didn't hear Lenny tell you I'm from Chicago? I know this number is the key to millions. You give me the loot, I give you the number." With that, Donnie crosses his arms, looking Barlow directly in the eye.

Barlow balls up his fist, saying "Loot! I'd like to give you the loot, alright! I'll tell you what: I'll give you half the money. It's only a number. And I'm gonna hold the dough until I get an answer. That, my friend, is my final offer. If you don't agree to that, I'll just have Slim here take you out back and shoot you. I don't care if I ever get that number!"

Cus turns and winks at Lenny. Lenny is more into these negotiations than when Cus and Singleton were going at it over the price of the actual shipment.

Donnie lets out a sigh just like a kid, and answers Barlow. "Ok, you got a deal – but I want to see the money first. And you have to let Lenny hold the cash."

Cus looks at Lenny, then at Donnie.

Lenny holds up his hands. "What can you say, Boss? He's from Chicago!"

Sitting at a stoplight in Mann's Mercedes-Benz, the three of them look like any group of friends talking about anything from what movie to see tonight to what baseball team just won the big game.

But images are deceiving. If anyone happened to hear the topic of discussion in the Mercedes' closed windows, they would have been shocked: whether or not the passenger in the back seat should leave town before or after the police start looking for her now-murdered friend.

Max is doing most of the talking, and his patience is running on fumes.

"I told both of you I'd help. And unless I'm missing something here, I think I've gone above and beyond 'help'. If the bottom falls out and we get caught, I'll go to prison for at least twenty years for helping a so-called friend!"

In the back seat Anna is tired of hearing Max complain, and doesn't say a word. Bill is staring out the window at some kids standing on the corner, waiting for the streetlight to change.

"Max," Bill says, "for one moment, would you please stop talking about getting caught? All we need now is for you to do the car thing, give us a little of what you make off the sale, and we're out of your hair!"

"Just like that," scoffs Max, "I give you what? Seventy-five? One hundred thousand dollars? And what do I get?"

"Max, we'll be gone for good," says Bill, trying to reason with his friend. "If we do get caught, we'd never tell them that you had anything to do with this. The longer we're around, the more chance there is of you getting caught up with us, if something goes wrong…"

They've sat at the traffic light for so long, the light has turned green and back to red again. No one in the car notices.

Max is furious. "You two sure are asking a lot! I'm in a position where I can't win, no matter what happens. With friends like you two, I might as well go to my enemies! At least I know they're out to screw me – none of this, 'Hi, how are you doing Max, you're looking good these days – so good I think I'll fuck you over!'"

The light changes to green. Again. "That's right! I said it – that's how I feel. You two are fucking me over so bad, I hope you live long enough to enjoy it!"

He's on a roll, and there's no stopping Max now. "You want something from me? Well, my good friends, I'm not giving you shit until I get something from you! I've thought long and hard about this. Anna, you said *your father isn't going to do shit to Bill,* because you have something on him! I hope you're smart enough to know where I'm going with this. If you don't, let me spell it out for you: I need that same insurance policy. You tell me the dirt on your dad, or forget the deal we have."

Bill and Anna clearly weren't expecting this, and the look on their faces gives Max all the fuel he needs. "And until you make up your minds, you're on your own. Now go fuck yourselves, and get out of my car. NOW!"

Max hurls the craziest look he can muster at them. They sit for a second, then Anna flips Max the bird, and gets out of the back seat. Kicking the door closed, she storms off. She's not used to someone else having the last word. Cars behind Max are honking, as the traffic light has changed to red, once again.

"Bill, get the fuck out!" Max turns up the radio and starts to sing. Bill takes the hint, and slowly climbs out the Benz. Before he can shut the door, the wheels are spinning and Max is gone.

After stashing the U-Haul, Mann and Nesto go to Mann's house, entering through the back door. Walking through the kitchen, Mann calls Monica's name. No answer.

It is obvious that no one's there, and Mann tells Nesto to make himself at home. Get a couple of beers out of the fridge, they try to relax. A car door slams in front of the house. Surprised, he gets up to see who it is. Something doesn't feel right, but he can't put his finger on it.

Looking out the window, he sees his car in the driveway. Monica and Leta have just pulled up. Mann turns to walk to the front door when he hears a familiar voice coming from outside. Someone is calling Monica. As Mann turns back to the window to see who it is, a sense of urgency runs through his body, but he does his best to ignore it.

There's a noise behind him. Mann looks back in time to see Nesto cursing because he spilled his beer. Mann tells Nesto where the paper towels are; he reaches back and opens the blinds to see outside.

A large, black limousine parked across the street from his house. Standing next to the open back door is someone who looks like they're handing Max a wad of cash. Leta and Monica are pulling their luggage out of the trunk of the car. Mann freezes in place for a moment. He turns to look at Nesto — and sees the back door is open. Nesto is gone.

The Little Voice in Mann's head has returned and is screaming, *"Somebody's gonna die!"*

Mann turns back to the window and sees Max pointing at Monica and Leta. He's laughing, and there's money in his hand. The other man starts to turn around; before he can see the stranger's face, Mann already knows who it is. Only one man wears a suit like that.

It's Cus Barlow.

Suddenly somebody jumps out of the back seat and runs toward Monica. It's Donnie, and he's telling them to *run!* Cus snaps his fingers, and then points at Monica and Leta. The front door of the limo swings open and Mann sees one of the thugs from the alley that night in Vegas. He's getting out of the limo - with a machine gun in his hand.

Mann tries to run to the front door, but it's as if his feet fastened to the floor with panic. The Voice in his head is filled with laughter: *'You blew it, smart guy!'*

Donnie is only a couple steps from Monica when the machine gun starts to spit. Mann is frozen in place, looking on as Donnie is hit in the back of the head. Max is across the street, jumping up and down, clapping and laughing uncontrollably. There is a girl next to him, doing the same.

Donnie skids into the ground, head first, landing at Monica's feet, and she's spattered with his blood and brain matter. She's trying to wipe it away when she's hit in the chest by at least three slugs. She falls back into the car, as the front of her shirt is instantly red.

The gunman turns on Leta. One shot and Leta's beautiful face explodes.

Mann hears a female voice he recognizes: it's Nicky. She and Max are dancing around, laughing and throwing money in the air. Mann doesn't understand what he's seeing.

Cus Barlow, however, is looking straight at Mann through the window...

"Maw! Maw! Wake up, Maw!" Nesto is standing outside the U-Haul reaching through the window, trying to wake up Mann. *"Hey, amigo! Ju awake?* Looks like jour dream not so good, huh?"

Covered with sweat, Mann looks around. The sun is beating down on him. They're sitting by a gas pump at a truck stop, right outside of Grand Junction, Colorado.

Disoriented, Mann sits up and looks at Nesto, who is leaning in the passenger window of the U-Haul. Mann wipes his eyes to refocus: the gas nozzle is in the tank, and Nesto has a pistol sticking out of the top of his pants.

"Nesto, where are we? And why are you standing in plain sight with that pistol showing?"

"We're in Grand Junction," replies Nesto, "and I have the pistol because somehow, ju found it under the seat!"

Mann is confused. "I found it under the seat? What are you talking about? I've been asleep!"

"I know ju were asleep, Maw. I had to stop to get some gas and something to eat. I was gonna let ju sleep, but ju were having a bad dream." Nesto's eyes are scanning Mann's face, concerned about his friend. "Ju reached under the seat and pulled out the gun. I had to grab it out of jour hand, 'cause ju had it pointed out the window!"

Mann shakes his head, trying to get the sleep out; he hadn't slept for days, and was still foggy. He couldn't remember the last time he had a nightmare – or at least, a nightmare while he was actually asleep. "Damn, Nesto," he mumbles, "that was a bitch!"

"Who was it in jour dream? Let me guess: was it Cus Barlow, or was it the Feds?"

"I don't want to talk about it." Mann frowns for a minute. "But now I'm sure that Barlow has the kid."

Nesto nods his head in agreement. "If he does, then he's got his hands full. That kid's a gamer. But no worries about it right now. Let's get some gas and food, and then get back on the road. I'm tired of this truck. Hey —ju think they sell tequila in there?"

Smiling a little to himself, Mann nixes his friend's question. "No, Nesto – this is Colorado, not Vegas…but a drink right about now doesn't sound like a bad idea."

After topping off the gas tank and grabbing some food, Mann and Nesto find a bar. Sitting and nursing their drinks Nesto asks, "Maw, so tell me: what was that dream ju had? Where I'm from, they use dreams to help ju. Ju know, like a warning or a clue. Especially when jour in danger. I mean, come on Maw, ju were dead asleep, and ju found a gun under the seat! If I hadn't been there to grab it, ju would have shot somebody for sure!"

Mann takes a large swig of his drink. "I dreamt that Barlow was waiting for us in Denver. He was at my house when we got there. He killed Monica, Leta and the kid. I couldn't do anything to stop it. What do you think, Nesto? Is that some kind of warning?"

Nesto didn't like what Mann just told him. "Aw, sheet! I wish I knew. One thing's for sure – whatever it is, it's not a good dream to be having right now! Is there anyway Barlow could figure out where we're headed, or where jour from?"

"I don't think so, but you know how hard it is to keep a secret — especially when people start asking questions with money in their hands."

Nesto smiles a little. "I know what ju mean. Money is the best mouth laxative they ever invented; that - and guns."

"Let's finish these drinks and get back on the road," says Mann, throwing some money on the bar. "We need to get to Denver as soon as possible. I gotta call Barlow pretty soon, but I want to be home when I do it."

They get back on I-70 heading east; Nesto is at the wheel while Mann makes a few phone calls.

"Hello? Monica, it's me...Hey baby, what are you doing?...You're still in bed? That figures. Where's Leta? ...Asleep, too, huh? It must be nice. I'm calling to tell you something very important. I ain't sure about this guy Barlow. You know, he thinks this stuff is his. Nesto and me are still a half-day away. I'd feel better if the two of you weren't at the house. ...I want both of you to stay away from the house until we get there. ...It's nothing for sure, but he's desperate and dangerous. Why don't you and Leta go shopping or get a hotel room, 'cause right now, you're a couple of sitting ducks."

Mann listens to Monica for a minute. "So if you need me to put it in plain English: Get your asses out of bed, get dressed, and get the hell out of that house! Don't come back until I say that it's safe!" He takes a breath and calms down. "We'll be there in three, maybe four hours. This U-Haul is slow, and we still have to drive over Vail Pass...Ok, baby - now get going, and don't drag your asses. And if you see something strange, like an unfamiliar car in front of the house, call me right away!...Love you too. Bye!"

Mann hangs up, and Nesto shoots him a quick look. "Wow! That dream is really messing with ju, huh?"

"You can say that again! I need to make another call."

The intensity as he talks on the phone speaks volumes to Nesto.

They're a long way from Vegas, and a long way from being done with Barlow. Mann has the phone to his ear, and he dials a second number. Staring out the window, finally there's a voice on the other end. "Hey, Max – what's happening?"

Mann is trying to sound less anxious than he feels at the moment. "Did you take care of that thing we talked about? ... Ok! Is everybody happy now? ...You say what!? They need money? ...For what now? ...Sounds to me like they're trying to work you for as much as they can. So what are you gonna do? ...Ok, but be careful! I'll get with you when I get to Denver. I should be there before nightfall."

The dream pops into Mann's head again. He can't get the image of Barlow handing money to Max out of his brain, and a question suddenly occurs to Mann.

"Hey, Max? How much would it take?"

Max is puzzled. "How much would it take for *what*?"

It's very clear to Mann now. "I want to know: how much would it cost a person to buy all your problems? You know, if I didn't know you and walked up to you on the street, and said 'I could make all your problems go away, and all your dreams come true.' How much would it cost?"

There is a long pause over the phone. Max still doesn't know what to make of Mann's question. Mann is the first to break the silence.

"Max, I'm asking you this, because if somebody approaches you in the near future with a deal that sounds something like this – they're *lying*. Don't buy into it – as a matter of fact, you'd be smart to run for your life! I'll talk to you later. Bye."

The conversation has Nesto's full attention. "Sounds like ju don't trust ol' Max! What did he do?"

Mann sighs. "He didn't do anything! It's that damn dream!"

Max hangs up from Mann's call, looking at the cell in his hand for a while — as if the phone could better explain that conversation to him. What was Mann talking about?

Who's trying to fix his problems? Was that phone call some kind of warning, or was it a threat? Max is wired, worried, and burned out.

After leaving Anna and Bill on the side of the road, he went back to the hotel and picked up Pat, his new six-foot tall blonde plaything. They went back to his place and have been all over each other since.

He wants to ask Pat about Nicky, but knows he might start something he can't stop if he does. He tries to let it go, but now this last phone call from Mann is eating away at him.

He needs some rest – but he also wants another hit of dope.

"Pat, load up that pipe and come over here. I need you."

"Anything you want, Superman," calls Pat.

Back at his house, Bill is sitting on his couch and is frantic. "What are we gonna do, baby? Max is acting like he doesn't care if we get away with this or not! I think he *wants* to get caught!"

"I don't care what Max wants," replies Anna. "If he doesn't give us the money, we will just *take* it!"

"To hell with that, Anna! We already have enough money to get out of here. We don't need a lot. I'll get a job as soon as we find a place to settle down."

Anna thinks about Bill's suggestion for a moment. "What about our partner? She needs the money more than we do. I just can't tell her to fuck off!"

Bill is really pissed, and feeling trapped. "Damn! If I had to do it all over again, I'd never agree to that deal! Now we're really starting to get in over our heads. And now you guys are talking about your dad too. Baby, it's too much! Let's just walk away right now. Leave the rest of this shit for them. They're all too greedy, and we're going to get caught up in it!"

Anna's tone says she's not budging. "Bill, I told you that my dad's gonna pay. That's not an opinion, that's a *fact*. We're not going anywhere until he gets his, ok?"

"Fine, Anna – but are you gonna tell Max about your dad?"

"I don't know, Bill, and I don't care right now! Beside, we have some cash, so let's go have some fun." She grabs Bill between his legs and starts to kiss him. Bill knows right now is *no* time to even think about getting loaded and messing around. But when his Anna acts like this, he's hopeless. He smiles, reaches in his pocket and pulls out some of the money Max gave them.

"Ok, baby – let's go!"

With Lenny's help, Barlow has managed to come to a peaceful agreement with Donnie. He is even talking to Donnie in a civil tone.

"OK, kid – I mean, 'Mr. Donnie' – if there's no answer, there's no cash, *capiesce?*"

"Whatever, Al Capone," replies Donnie.

Lenny smacks Donnie in the back of the head for that crack. "What did I tell you? Show respect!"

Lenny loves this kid – he has heart. He's never seen anybody give it to Cus like this – and live to tell it, anyway. He also knows he better watch this kid. Donnie doesn't realize how dangerous Barlow is. The only reason Donnie's still alive is because of Lenny.

Donnie peers at Cus for a second, then writes the number on a piece of paper and hands it to Barlow.

Nesto is still driving; he likes the scenery. Mann has fallen asleep again. They're passing through Glenwood Canyon, one of the more beautiful sections of the Rocky Mountains along I-70.

It's late afternoon, the sun is to their backs, and Nesto's ears are starting to pop from the elevation. With the latest ear pop, Nesto clearly hears Mann's phone ringing. Mann is sleeping so soundly, the phone doesn't stir him. Nesto tries to ignore it, but for some reason, it seems to get louder with each ring.

Exasperated, Nesto gives up. "Fuck it!' He grabs Mann's phone. "Hello?"

"Uh, yes. Is there a Mr. Mann there?"

The voice on the other end sounds familiar, but Nesto can't put a face to it. The fact that he is answering Mann's phone has Nesto off of his game.

"Well, no it's not. Who's calling?"

"Is this the right number to reach Mr. Mann?"

Again Nesto knows the voice, but is unsure who it is. The mystery voice has gotten on his nerves that quick.

"If ju tell me who ju are, I might be able to tell ju what ju want to know," snaps Nesto, still not recognizing the voice on the other end of the phone.

Cus Barlow instantly realizes who he's speaking with, and pulls the curtain wide open for Nesto to find out. "Well, well, well, Mr. Quintana! Good afternoon! We really need to talk."

Nesto's heart jumps. "Maw? Maw! It's him, it's Barlow!"

Mann hears that name and is instantly awake. He sits up in the car seat and starts looking around, expecting to see Barlow in a car behind them.

Nesto sees Mann's reaction. "No, Maw! On the phone! It's Barlow!"

Mann looks at the phone in Nesto's hand. He really wants to talk to Barlow, but the dream has seriously messed him up. He's not ready to talk. Mann's still haunted by the thought of Barlow at his house. He looks at Nesto, frozen. Nesto looks back at him with a questioning look on his face.

"Ask him where he's at," whispers Mann to Nesto.

"What?"

"I said, ask him where he's at. Is he still in Vegas?"

Nesto looks at the phone then slowly asks the question.

Barlow's voice sounds pissed off now. "Yeah, I'm in Vegas! Where the fuck are you two?"

"Good," says Mann quietly, "Ask him where Donnie is."

Nesto relays the question to Barlow.

"I got him. Yeah, he's right here," snarls Cus.

Without instruction, Nesto jumps in. "Let me talk to him!"

Barlow instantly replies. "Oh, no, no, I don't think so! Not until we talk about my shipment. The kid's fine…but I don't know how long that's gonna last."

"Well, if ju hurt him," replies Nesto, already angry, "ju can kiss that shipment goodbye!"

Mann's whispers frantically to his friend. "Give me that phone, Nesto! As long as Donnie's alright and we have the shipment, we're cool!"

Mann takes the phone from Nesto and hangs up on Barlow. Turning the phone off, he throws the cell on the seat between them, and promptly goes back to sleep. Nesto tries to say something, but he is at a total loss for words.

Then he realizes: they are on Mann's turf now.

The Denver County Courthouse Building. The city's head district attorney Chris Simons, looks up when his secretary pokes her head in his office door and says, "Mr. Simons, Officer Richard Spriggs is here to see you."

"Please send him in."

He greets the officer as Spriggs walks in. "Hey there, Rich! And to what do I owe this visit?"

Spriggs flops down in a seat, his face looking strained, and it's obvious he is not happy. "Where's that daughter of yours?" The stress in his voice is also very obvious.

"She called me this morning: said she was at a rock concert with friends this weekend. I don't even ask anymore." Simons shakes his head wearily. "Why do you want to know?"

"I can't find my wife," replies Spriggs. "Seems lately that every time I can't find Nicky, she tells me she's been with Anna."

"When was the last time you saw her?"

"Last week, Thursday. She said she needed some money, so I met her at the bank. I gave her six hundred dollars; I haven't seen or talked to her since then."

Simons averts his eyes from Spriggs' face, asking quietly, "You think she's on one of her binges?"

Spriggs doesn't like the question, but the idea has crossed his mind. The vision of Nicky high as a kite, doing whatever to whomever, really eats at his gut. He answers Simons in a defeated tone. "I hope not. But if she is, she normally runs out of energy and money by now. I thought she'd be home last night."

"Rich, how much longer are you going to put up with her?"

"I don't know! One minute, everything is fine. Then just like that," Spriggs says, snapping his fingers, "she's out of control. Ever since she took Anna to that concert, she's been a fucking mess!"

"What are you trying to say, Spriggs? That my Anna is the reason Nicky's acting stupid again? And what was the excuse before they met? When Nicky was working Colfax Avenue, sucking off anybody with a five-dollar bill sticking out of his fly?"

"It wasn't like that, and watch your mouth!" Spriggs has jumped out of the chair, wild-eyed.

Simons knows that he has to say what needs to be said, whether Spriggs wants to hear it or not. "Don't blame the messenger, Rich! I'm just stating the facts. Hell, man – she was doing *you* just to stay out of jail years ago – and you told me that yourself! Get a grip, and dump the whore!"

Dejected, Spriggs flops back down, shaking his head. "I can't…I just can't!"

"Stop with the love thing, Spriggs. You're an asshole; you don't give a fuck about anybody except yourself. Why can't you dump her? What's she got on you?" Simons stops talking for a minute, and sizes up the officer. "Does she know anything about our business arrangement?"

"No, she doesn't know a thing. That stuff I caught her dipping into, I hid in the closet. When she asked me why I had coke in the house, I told her it was used to set up dealers, so I could bust them."

Simons looks dumbfounded. "And you think she bought that line? She's a street girl – she knows better! A vice cop with nine ounces in his house – even the little old lady on the corner wouldn't fall for that bullshit line, Rich!"

The cop's wild-eyed look returns. "I'm telling you: she doesn't know anything! All I know is I have to find her!"

The district attorney can see that the vice cop hasn't heard a word he's said, and Simons needs to move Spriggs out of his office — at least for the time being.

"Well, when Anna gets in tonight, I'll ask her if she's seen Nicky. But I'm glad you stopped by. It'll save me a trip." Simons reaches in his desk drawer and pulls out a box about the size of a loaf of bread. He shoves it across the desk to Spriggs. "Here. This is what I was able to get out of the evidence room. It's supposed to be real high-grade stuff. Take it to those low-lifes on the West Side. Tell 'em it's fifteen thousand, upfront. No more credit: they take too long to pay. If they don't have the money, take it to our friend at the bookstore on Capitol Hill. He's always on time."

Spriggs picks up the box and feels it for weight. "Is this all you have? I got the East Side punks bugging me for more. They like the prices."

"I know they like the prices. Last I heard, we're undercutting the Mexicans' prices. But what are you doing, dealing with those Eastsiders? I thought you cut them off after, well you know: your wife and that gangbanger thing we had to fix." Simons starts laughing.

Spriggs snatches the box off the table. He's really growing tired of Simons making jokes about his wife's past. He tells himself that one day this stiff-shirted phony is going to go too far. But for now…

"Let me know what Anna says, ok? It's important; I'm a little worried."

Simons watches the cop's face. "Spriggs, I'm sure she's alright. In a way, that's too bad. If she does come up missing for a while, you might start getting out from under her spell – if that's all she's got on you."

Spriggs sees the look of doubt on Simons' face as he says it. Walking out of the D.A.'s office, Spriggs is unable to admit that he's also worried about how much Nicky really knows about his little side activity with Simons.

"Ok, Bill. This is the last time we'll have any time together for a while. I told my dad that I was at a weekend concert with some friends, and that I'd be home tonight. He didn't ask about Nicky, but if and when he does, I'm ready."

Bill is tired and looks it. He's trying to keep up with Anna, but she seems to be on some kind of autopilot and he's worried. He's also concerned about his DJ friend, asking "Have you thought about what you're gonna tell Max?"

"Yes, I have," replies Anna, annoyed at having to say the same thing to Bill, once again. "I'm gonna tell him to pay up all the money from selling his car, or I'm going to find his friend Mann, and tell him the police know they're both involved in Nicky's disappearance."

Bill's on his feet like he's been hit by a bolt of lightning. "No, Anna! *No!* What's wrong with you? That'll never work. We don't know anything about Max's friend. I've seen him before: he's not someone we want to piss off!"

"Don't worry, Bill," replies Anna, trying to placate her lover. "Max is as scared of Mann as you are. He'll give us anything we want to keep that friend of his out of this. Don't forget the plan, baby! By the time we leave Denver, everybody we know in this city is gonna pay! This is only the beginning."

Bill is trying to hide his fear. He knows it's showing, but he has to try and talk some kind of sense into Anna's head. "You said this is only the beginning. I guess you're going to go ahead with that crazy blackmail plan Nicky came up with, aren't you?"

As young as Anna is, she's already figured Bill out. She can tell by the tone of his voice he's starting to have doubts about their plan, and she knows just how to get him back on track.

"No, we're going to take 'her' idea and 'our' plan, and get enough money to disappear. We're going to get high and see the world, and do whatever we want!"

Anna's talking crazy, and Bill knows it. But she wraps her arms around him and buries her face in his chest. No matter how crazy she talks, when she's this close to him, in his arms —it's useless. He's signed on for the duration. Whether they land on top of the world, or the graveyard: Bill couldn't get off if he wanted to.

In all his years as a boss, Cus Barlow demands, gets, and takes his respect. Between this smart-mouth kid Donnie, and that wise-ass black son of a bitch Mann, Cus is feeling like an underpaid busboy at the local greasy spoon. He's having a temper tantrum that Lenny could do without right now.

"Has that fuck answered yet? I can't believe he's trying to play games with me! Who does he think he is?"

Lenny, tiring of Barlow's mouth, snaps. "Boss! Take it easy and calm the hell down! You know what he's doing to you, and yet you still let it get to you! Try and calm down and stop talking so much shit!"

Barlow looks at his good friend Lenny. He's about to go off on him, but knows Lenny's right. Mann's playing him, and he's only making it easier, running around the house, pulling his hair out and yelling at nobody. Sitting down at the table, Cus pours himself a stiff drink.

"You're right – but I have so much riding on this deal, if I don't have something to give to the Santos brothers – and soon – I'll have to give them that five million! And if *that* happens, we're broke! I've been thinking. You know what? They sure seem to be worried about that kid in there. Whatever you do, don't let Donnie out of your sight. He's the only ace up our sleeve we have left. Now get back on that phone and keep calling until you get an answer!"

Cus is looking, acting and talking like a desperate man. Something Lenny's not used to seeing out of Cus; he knows when you get desperate, you make mistakes. And in this game, there's *no* room for mistakes.

Lenny walks back into the kitchen not only to get away from Cus, but right now he prefers Donnie's company over Barlow's. Going straight through the kitchen, Lenny doesn't see Donnie at the kitchen table. Looking in the back room, there's still no Donnie. With concern leaking into his voice, Lenny calls out. "Hey, Donnie! You want some more pizza?"

He waits, but there's still no answer. He looks around the room. In the closets. Under the couch. He double-checks the bathroom and everywhere else he could think the kid could possibly go.

Finally Lenny has to tell Cus. It's the last thing Barlow wants to hear, and Lenny knows it.

Barlow explodes. "What the fuck do you mean you can't find him? Didn't I just tell you to keep a close eye on him?"

"I left him the kitchen. The door has a dead bolt on it, and the windows have bars. He couldn't have gotten out!"

Barlow looks crazy. "I don't know, but I'm killing the next person that comes back in here and tells me they can't find him!"

Slim runs in the room from downstairs. "He's not down there; I checked everywhere, Boss!"

"He's small," snarls Barlow, "maybe he slipped in between the bars on the kitchen window!"

They all run into the kitchen, unlock the back door and spread out, looking under cars and behind bushes. Slim takes off down the alley, looking in trash dumpsters.

Looking in the trash was the right idea, but just the wrong place.

When Donnie doesn't hear them anymore, he pops the lid off of the kitchen trash can next to the back door and peeks out. He doesn't see anybody, but he knows that they're close. He's about to run out the door when he takes a look back in the house. Sitting right in the middle of the bar is the black flight bag with five million dollars in it.

Donnie runs in the room and grabs the bag. It weighs more than he thought it would, almost as much as his own body weight. He heads to the back door, straining to handle the bag, down the back porch steps, and tips to the back gate. Looking around the gate Donnie sees Slim, way down the alley. Donnie runs across the alleyway, ducking in a hole in the neighbor's fence – just as Lenny spots Slim down the alley, and asks if he sees anything.

Slim puts up his hands and shrugs his shoulders while shaking his head saying, "the kid simply disappeared."

Talking more to himself than Slim, Lenny mutters, "I hope you've cleared out, kid – if Cus finds you, you're history!"

Less than ten feet away, his body rolled in a ball around the bag of money, Donnie crouches stone-still and terrified under a trash dumpster. Hearing every word that Lenny has said, and the tone of Lenny's voice puts a cold chill of fear through Donnie's body. The smell of the garbage is almost more than he can take, and there's something crawling on his neck; Donnie wills himself not to move an inch.

Then he hears Cus Barlow let out a scream, followed by a long stream of cursing that puts a smile on Donnie's face.

"HE'S GOT THE GODDAMN MONEY!"

Monday June 10th; it's 5:30 in the evening in Denver, Colorado. Mann and Nesto are just pulling off I-70 onto Quebec Street. They're less than a mile away from Mann's house.

As close as he is to his home, Mann's still having visions of Barlow from his dream.

He makes a quick right off Quebec Street and stops at the Cosmo Bar. Walking into the lounge, Mann finds a couple of seats near a few people who are nursing their drinks.

Ordering a couple drinks himself, Mann looks at Nesto, who has his foot propped up on a chair next to him. It's obvious that he's in pain.

Mann points to his friend's foot and raises his eyebrows.

"Jeah, it's the foot – and my head is killing me, too."

"The foot I can't help you with," replies Mann, "but your head is hurting because we are at a mile-high elevation and there's not as much oxygen to breathe. It's called 'altitude sickness,' happens to a lot of people when they come up here. You'll get used to it."

Mann turns on his phone and checks his missed calls.

"Hey, look, Nesto! Barlow's been blowing up my phone ever since we hung up on him!"

"What do ju mean 'we'? Ju got a lot of balls, hanging up on that nut. Why'd ju do that, anyway?"

Mann sits back in his seat with a smile on his face. "I told you it's all about the upper hand. In Vegas, we're out-manned, out-gunned, and out-muscled. We don't even have a safe place to go. We're like a big green bug running around in the open, waiting to get stepped on, and Barlow knows it. It was just a matter of time before we walked right into one of his bottomless pits. Vegas is *his* town. We had to get somewhere that he's not so sure of himself – you know, outside of his comfort zone!"

Mann's eyes narrow as his mind works on his strategy. "I don't know what kind of connections he has up here, but I'm willing to bet everything that I've got him beat on that. Up here, he's on thin ice –he's playing in my back yard!"

Nesto's face reflects the doubt that running through his mind. Mann smiles again, and shakes his head.

"Don't worry, Nesto – he's not going to do anything to Donnie as long as there's a chance at making a deal with us for that shipment." Grabbing his phone, Mann calls Monica.

"Hello, baby – I take it you and Leta didn't buy up the whole mall. We're at the Cosmo Bar. I'm gonna put the truck in a safe place, so I need you to come pick us up at the storage on Colorado Boulevard in about thirty minutes, ok? Good! Bye, baby."

Nesto's about to say something, but Mann puts up his hand to stop him. "I got one more call to make." Mann punches in another number on his cell. "Hello, Max? Meet me at my house in one hour. Don't be late."

No sooner than Mann puts his phone down, it starts to ring. Looking at the number, he smiles and nudges Nesto. "Look – it's a Vegas number. I'll give you ten-to-one odds that it's Barlow."

"I wouldn't take that bet with house money. Ju gonna answer it?"

"Not yet," smirks Mann. "I'm gonna let him sweat a little longer."

Finally away from Vegas, both Mann and Nesto start to decompress and they have a good laugh, looking at Mann's phone as it continues to ring.

At the same time back in Vegas, Donnie slams the pay phone down in its cradle. He's got five million dollars; he can't find Mann; Barlow is tearing up the city looking for him. He can't get a room: he's too young. Can't take a chance going to the bus station. The money has done nothing for Donnie, except turn him into a sitting duck.

He walks out of the laundromat and heads around to the back of the strip mall. Climbing on top of a dumpster, he uses a drainpipe to get access to the top of the building.

With the heavy bag on his back, the relatively simple climb up is long and exhausting. Taking a wad of hundreds out of the bag, he stuffs them into his pocket. Then he pries the cover off a rooftop air conditioning unit, places the bag inside and replaces the unit's cover. He needs to go buy a cell phone, but he's worn out. Planning to close his eyes for a quick minute, the boy is sound asleep in no time.

◆———————◇———————◆

Having put the truck in a safe place, Nesto and Mann are sitting on Mann's porch, enjoying a drink as they wait for Max's call.

"Hey Maw," says Nesto, "Ju think it's time to call the godfather?" They both laugh Monica and Leta fail to see the humor in it, but play along. Pulling out his cell phone, Mann hits the speed dial.

"Well, here goes nothing!"

After only one ring, Barlow's on the phone and he's not wasting any time.

"Well, Mr. Mann! Please, don't hang up before you hear me out. It's important that we talk; no more games – I'm ready to deal! If you give a fuck about the kid, you won't hang up, you hear me?"

Mann wants to disconnect Barlow's call in the worst way, but Cus knew what he was doing when he started in on Donnie. That put the brakes on any sarcasm or smart-ass moves that Mann was thinking about. He needs to buy a little time to figure out Cus' next move.

"Ok, Barlow – what's up? You sound a little – how should I say it? – a little 'unstable' out there."

Barlow is trying to negotiate. "Listen here, Mann – I paid for that stuff, fair and square. It's not my fault or yours – but that no-good son of a bitch Singleton was trying to burn the both of us. So — on everybody's behalf, I took care of that."

"And you're telling me this to say what, exactly?"

Cus the Diplomat continues his ploy. "Well, if you think about it, Mr. Mann, we need each other. It's a matter of doing good business. I can move the shipment, and move it fast. I know for a fact that it's not easy getting rid of that much coke without some kind of problem. That was my five million dollars in that limo, so you see, I know how to generate cash!"

Mann has to admit that Barlow has a good point. Still, Mann's instincts are on full alert: Barlow is not the man to trust, ever. It's time to test him, and see where Barlow goes with it.

"Now we're talking, Barlow – so, how much cash do we have available right now?"

It doesn't go over Barlow's head that Mann just said, "how much cash do WE have." Barlow hopes it's a good sign, but figures that it's only the beginning of the game. He clears his throat, and puts his best offer on the table.

"How about this, my friend," starts Barlow, "You give me the shipment - the *whole* shipment I paid for, and I can get you a couple of million in, let's say, a month. Then we'll work out the rest over time."

"You said that you paid for the whole shipment, and you lost five million in the limo blast. What I'm trying to figure out is, the whole shipment cost well over ten million dollars. Where is the rest of the money? You're a good eight million short!"

Mann did the right thing by questioning Barlow. Try as he might, Barlow just couldn't keep his cool.

"Listen, you fuck, you gonna try and play me, or are you gonna do this in good faith? I said I'll get you the rest of the cash!"

In a calm voice, Mann answers Barlow. "You give me a couple million – and a couple million's worth is all you're gonna get."

"I got investors," Barlow responds, "and if I tell them you're not playing ball, they're gonna come looking for you. And I don't think you want that."

Mann laughs, realizing how desperate Barlow is. "They're going to come looking for *you*, Barlow, not me! Try that line on somebody that doesn't know any better."

Barlow snorts out a sarcastic laugh. "I didn't want to go there, but I see we're not on the same page. How about this one, smart guy: If I don't get my shipment, I'm gonna send you that kid – ground up and stuffed in about a dozen dog food cans!"

Caught off-guard, Mann stays silent longer that he wants. He hopes Barlow didn't pick up on his hesitation.

Trying to regroup, Mann answers back. "Mr. Barlow, you have to understand that I have investors as well, and there's not two or three kids that hold much value over these negotiations. How about we do this, what would make your investors happy? I mean, what would it take to get them off your back?"

Barlow grits his teeth. "I don't have anybody on my back! Don't forget who you're talking to!"

"Well, why are you holding children hostage and pulling your hair out? Mr. Barlow, I don't have to remember who I'm dealing with. It might serve you better if *you* find out who you're trying to bullshit!"

Mann looks at everybody on the porch, then holds the phone up so they can hear Barlow cursing up a storm. After about 15 seconds, Mann hangs up.

The shock registers in Monica's eyes. Both Leta's and Monica's faces reflect a look of total horror.

"What are you doing," gasps Monica. "That nut is going to hurt that kid!"

"He's not going to do shit to Donnie. Barlow's ass is in a vice; he's in too much of a rush," Mann says coolly. "Either he used somebody else's money and they want their stuff, or he's broke and can't deliver to his customers – and they're going to his competition. He's starting to sweat, and that means pressure from somebody else. If it was just him, he'd probably just give up the kid and take whatever we offered. That way he can keep his customers happy, and keep the business running. It only make sense."

Nesto nods his head in agreement. "I know what ju mean. He did that to me the night we played poker. He kept giving me markers so he could set me up for the big payoff. He knows not to try and get it all at once. He's in too much of a rush; ju got him right where ju want him!"

"Not just yet. He's a hot-head and he's still got Donnie." Mann stares at nothing on the wall, his mind works out the next move against Barlow. "He won't hurt Donnie as long as he thinks there's a chance we'll give up that shipment to keep the kid safe. But the longer we go on with this, the less time we have to get Donnie back in one piece. Next time I talk to Barlow, I'm asking to speak with Donnie. We'll go from there."

While everybody else sits around watching Mann handle business like the boss they believe he is, Mann does his best not to let his doubts show. Everyone has put so much faith in his actions, he wonders what they would do if they realize how uncertain he really is.

He knows he's playing a very dangerous game with an equally dangerous foe, and the wrong move will cost lives, no second chances.

If matters weren't tough enough, Mann's Little Voice is back and it's not happy or helpful. Mann doesn't want or need to hear it, but he listens nonetheless.

"Well, what do you know? We made it back home in one piece, and what have we accomplished? Let's see, where should I start? One old man shot in the head: game over for him; his grandson a hostage; a Las Vegas mob boss hot on your ass; a Colombian drug cartel family member sitting in your front room with a bullet hole in him.

"And the best I can tell is, you're no closer to fixing the problem in Denver with your good old buddy Max than you were when you first went to Las Vegas. Oh, should I remind you about the truckload of cocaine that will earn you a life sentence if you're caught with it?

"And all this because you don't listen to me. If I recall correctly, didn't I say -- didn't I plead with you not to go back in the Happy Snake Eyes that first night? You know something, you would do a lot better if you listen to your first mind - that would be ME, if you're wondering. Without you there's no me, so believe me I'm not going to tell you anything wrong."

Mann shakes his head, trying to put a stop to the ass-chewing he's managing to give himself. Without speaking to anyone in general, but directing his comment at his inner voice, Mann says aloud, "Well, we made it another day, what's the chance of that? All I can think to say is, '*We're all in.*'

The Little Voice gave Mann the answer he didn't want to hear.

"*I thought you knew:* **there's one way in, but there's no way out.**"

END

He found away in – But will Mann be able to find a way OUT?

GET THE ANSWER IN THE NEXT MANN WALKER ADVENTURE:

"MANN IN THE MIDDLE"

The preview starts on the next page!

MANN IN THE MIDDLE

PREVIEW

Walking into his house at 6:30PM on the dot, just like every day of the week, Denver's head district attorney Chris Simons prides himself on his self-disciplined control over all his actions. Nothing is left to chance; everything is thought out, pre-planned, no loose ends.

That's why his daughter - whom he hasn't seen in days and is presently standing in the middle of the kitchen - is his living, breathing nightmare.

Trying to keep his composure, he is careful of his tone of voice as he speaks to her. "I'm glad you're home for a change. How long do I have the honor of Your Majesty's presence this time?"

Anna gives her father a look that tells him that he's already started their conversation the wrong way. "I'm home because I have to go to school tomorrow."

Simons stares at his daughter. "School? Since when did we start attending school in the month of June?"

"I didn't say high school," replies Anna, "I'm taking music lessons. I met a guy downtown, and he plays the guitar. He says that I have long fingers, and that I should play."

"And how do I know that you're actually going to music school, and not to some boy's house?"

"Because I said so!" Anna snaps back at her father. "If I was going to some boy's house, I would tell you! Besides, I don't like boys!"

"*What?*"

Anna knew that her statement would get under her father's skin - and she couldn't wait to answer him. "That's right! I don't like boys - I like *men!*" She walks out of the kitchen, knowing her father is burning up - and she is loving every minute of it.

Losing his precious self-control, Simons yells, "If your mother were here—"

Anna cuts him off. "If my mother were here, you wouldn't be—" She stops short of what was about to come out of her mouth.

Simons starts after her. "If your mother were here, I wouldn't be WHAT? I wouldn't be what, Anna? What were you going to say?"

Anna runs into her room and slams the door, leaning against it. In between sobs she whispers, "If my mother were here, you wouldn't be a murderer."

Mann was back in town, and Max needed to give his car back. He also had to explain what was happening with Bill and Anna. Max needed Mann to help him get his Ferrari out of the car pound so he could sell it, and hopefully, get Bill and Anna out of his life once and for all. Max was hoping Mann would just lend the money and Max would pay him back later.

He just didn't know how to ask Mann.

Pulling up in front of Mann's house, Max sees him and Monica sitting on the porch, along with the beauty who came with Monica from Las Vegas. And next to the beauty was an evil-looking Latino guy that Max had never seen before.

Max took one last look at himself in the rearview mirror: he felt like shit – and didn't look much better. Getting out of the car, Max puts on his bet *Glad-To-See-You* routine with a big smile. "So, how was Vegas? Looks like you had a ball!"

Without saying a single word, Mann heads to his car and gets behind the wheel. In a straight-forward voice he tells Monica, "I'll be right back." Glaring in his direction, Mann spits out, "Max – get in."

Max jumps into the passenger seat. "Mann, you OK?"

"Don't start with the phone shit! I'm not mad. Yet. So let's try and keep it that way. Now – what's the deal? Did you take care of the crap, or is the CIA out looking for us now?"

Max tells Mann everything he could remember: the tattoos on Anna's leg, the way Anna's leading Bill around by the nose, the way she said her father ain't gonna do shit to Bill, how Nicky and Anna were gonna try and blackmail them for that night in the Adams Mark Hotel, but Anna fell in love with Bill and didn't want to do it anymore. Then Anna and Nicky had a fight, with Anna cutting Nicky's throat. And how Max wants to sell his Ferrari, give the money to Bill so Bill can take Anna and get lost. Forever.

"...and you know the rest, Mann, about the crematorium and burning Nicky's body. Mann, I'm sorry! I didn't know what else to do. You said to call you if I needed help. This type of shit ain't my thing! Mann, I wished you'd never left town."

Mann is more frustrated than anything else; he closes his eyes, truly wishing he really was somewhere else. "I thought you could do this! How hard is it to grease some pockets and powder a couple of noses? Run around town throwing cash and blow at everybody and act like you're pissed and ready to kick ass if they don't do what you want? I do it all the time, and you've been there and seen me do it. *Max, how could you fuck it up this bad!*?"

Lenny picks up the phone, looks at Barlow and says, "Boss, guess who's on the phone!"

"Please - don't tell me: the Santos brothers?"

"Nope - it's that Mann guy."

Cus almost leaps out of his chair and snatches the cell from Lenny. "Hello? --*Hello?*"

"Hello, my fucking *friend-in-need.*" Mann's voice comes through the phone smooth - and dead serious. "You still unsure as to who you're dealing with?"

"No, no, I'm not!" Barlow catches his own desperate tone of voice, and takes a deep breath to get his game together. "I'm clear on that. I see you're a lot like me when it comes to business, Mr. Mann. You know what you want and how you're going to get it. Not much compromise in you. I wish I could have dealt with you before all this bullshit happened. We could have made a lot of money together."

Mann thinks about reminding Barlow what his last name is, but thinks better of it. Right now the less Barlow knows, the better.

"I could almost agree with you on us doing business together. But our styles are so different, sooner or later we would conflict on something. But the good news is - *because I still have what you need, and you still have control over a certain friend of mind –* I'm willing to do you a favor to help you get out of the hole: *I'll send you one hundred keys - and you send me the kid and one million dollars."*

And this is just the beginning for...

'Mann In The Middle'
The next thriller from
Malcolm Boyd